HEIST IN PARADISE

The Crowmarked Series

Elliot Ray

AF250209

Copyright © 2026 Elliot Ray

All rights reserved. No part of this publication may be reproduced, distributed or transmitted in any form or by any means, including photocopying, recording, or other electronic or mechanical methods, without the prior written permission of the publisher, except in the case of brief quotations embodied in critical reviews and certain other noncommercial uses permitted by copyright law.

Publisher's note: This is a work of fiction. Names, characters, places, and incidents are a product of the author's imagination. Any resemblance to actual persons, living or dead, or to businesses, companies, events, institutions, or locales is entirely coincidental.

Author's Note

Heist in Paradise is a fast-paced dark romance thriller featuring strong profanity, explicit sexual content, kidnapping, torture, murder, violence, drugging, implications of sexual assault, and scenes involving dubious consent. This story explores dark themes and morally gray characters that may be disturbing to some readers. Proceed with caution, buckle up, and get ready for a wild ride!

1

JAX

"Jax? You in here?"

It was too late to run. For a second, I considered crawling into the engine bay like a grumpy weasel, but I knew that wouldn't work. For one thing, I was six foot two and built like a fucking tank. For another, I valued my Jag way too much to risk damaging it.

The door opened behind me, the slant of sunlight instantly warming my back. I shot my baby a regretful look as I dropped the hood. We had a good run, almost a full hour of uninterrupted peace. I couldn't smell smoke, so the Compound was still standing, and the lack of gunshots meant nobody was dead or dying. Still, I didn't trust it. My crew were a pack of assholes that thrived in chaos.

"There you are." Ryle gave me a beaming grin as he strolled in. "You shouldn't work in the dark. It's bad for your eyes."

Said the kid who liked to play fast and loose with his ADHD medication. "You need something?"

"Nope."

"Piss off, then."

"Actually," he said, and I groaned. "It's nothing bad," he assured me, hefting himself up onto my workbench. His foot immediately started bouncing. No meds today, then. "Just wanted to see if you're okay."

"I'm fine," I said with an even tone. Practiced.

"Sure you are," Ryle agreed easily, his eyes clearly stating otherwise. "On an unrelated note, I convinced Zola to buy some of that valerian root tea that tastes like wet dog."

I grimaced. "Over my dead body."

"You *will* be a dead body if you don't start sleeping." He looked me over meaningfully. "You look like warmed-up shit."

I picked up a nearby wrench and tossed it at his head. He ducked it easily, my aim off-center. The little shit gave me a smug look. "A well-rested Jax would've made that shot."

"Yeah, well, *this* Jax is about to knock you out with a mallet."

Ryle laughed and held up his hands in surrender. "Okay, okay," he said. "I take it back. You're clearly very fine. The finest. You wouldn't do anything to put us in danger."

Kill shot.

Ryle knew what he was doing. I was the leader of the crew, and that made them my responsibility. That meant I couldn't get sloppy. I couldn't make mistakes. I couldn't strangle Ryle with my jumper cables, no matter how much I wanted to.

I sneered at him, but it was more posturing than real anger. He was impossible to stay mad at. With his big brown eyes, auburn curls, and freckles. He was only nineteen, our youngest, and not as damaged as he should be, considering his past. It made me protective of him.

"We all set to go?" I asked him.

He nodded eagerly. "Callum has mapped the perimeter and floor plan. He's worried about the isolation. Not that he'll admit it."

No, Callum wouldn't. His pride was like the rest of him—huge, commanding, and stubborn as hell.

"It *is* risky," Ryle added, the first to rush to Callum's defense. The two of them were thick as thieves, all pun intended.

"It always is," I grumbled. Every job had its risks. Every job had the potential to blow up in our faces. The last one certainly had.

And now you'll pay for it.

My fists tightened at my sides. Our employer, Dr. Z, was like the goddamn boogeyman. Everywhere but nowhere.

Always watching, always listening. Even though I'd never met him (and definitely had no burning desire to), his reputation alone could make a goldfish paranoid.

For six years, I'd been under his thumb. His recruiter had found me at a low point—barely twenty, with a record, and no family worth keeping. He'd offered me an easy score, a gateway drug into bigger hits.

That first job had snowballed into long-term employment. Then the others had started showing up, bruised and battered and hungry. Working alone had always suited me just fine, but I adapted. The crew became my family. And, like family, I gave myself a gold star every time I didn't run them fuckers down with my car.

I supposed it could be worse. The job came with perks, like the Compound: a four-building estate on the outskirts of Washington. There was also the protection—the fake identities, the untraceable bank accounts, the access to weapons and military-grade tech.

All I'd ever wanted was a safe place to put my head at night. No knives buried under the pillows. No screaming. No flashing lights. Now I had a king memory foam mattress with Egyptian cotton sheets. Now I washed my balls with French soap, all fancy and shit.

Eau de testicles.

"Anything else?" I asked Ryle, who, among his cheeky habit of playing peacekeeper, was also a massive snoop. He could give the tabloids a run for their money.

"Ah, you know, the usual." Ryle shrugged, picking up my wrench and fiddling with it. "Zola is fighting with Nate again. Something about finding an earring that wasn't hers."

"Jesus."

"Yeah. He's trying to save face, the poor numpty."

My brow ticked up. "Numpty? You've been spending too much time with Callum."

As expected, Ryle blushed to the tips of his ears. "Madoc is up in the trees again," he plowed on before I could tease him. "He keeps hurling pinecones at me when I try to talk to him."

A weird, fluttery feeling unfurled in my gut. "Give him space. He'll come down when he's ready."

"I don't know. Madoc could probably live up there. He's basically a raccoon."

I chuckled, unable to stop the image from forming—Madoc, our resident brood, with twigs in his hair and a little pair of fuzzy black ears, armed with pinecones to protect his hollow. Affection and something hotter flared in my chest.

Jesus, I was getting sappy.

I needed a beer. Or a hard fuck. Preferably both. I settled for a cigarette as I loaded up the cars and took stock of our supplies. Most of our weapons were already shipped ahead to our next job. It saved us from being ass-probed at the airport, though it'd probably happen anyway. I was just hot like that.

Patting my pockets uselessly, Ryle came to my aid with his trusty Zippo. He didn't even smoke, but he liked to keep them on hand. That, or he was a secret pyro. One problem at a time.

Quietly, I mouthed around the cigarette: "You think he's alright?"

Ryle shrugged again. "Madoc is Madoc. He'll keep going. That's all we can do, you know. Take it day by day. Find the good in the bad. Ride the waves to calmer seas."

I huffed in amusement. "We need to cut down on the fortune cookies."

"Can't. I'm addicted. Cookies are my crack."

Basking in the soothing hit of nicotine, we fell into an easy silence. The metaphorical calmer seas. On habit, I glanced over at the two motorbike-shaped sheets in the corner. It had been months since Madoc and I hit the road, no expectations, no set locations. Just us and the open air and the zinging danger that came with every hard corner.

I missed him, not that I'd admit that to him. We didn't do things like that—confess shit, open old wounds, *talk*. It was my fault that things had changed between us. I'd overstepped and then withdrawn too quickly, and instead of being mature and talking about it, we both shut down.

Feelings weren't my strong suit. I almost wished he'd punch me out, so at least we'd have an excuse to engage.

My jaw clenched. "Tell the numptys to get packing. We leave at four on the dot."

Ryle slipped off my workbench. He threw the wrench at me, hitting my chest dead center. "Aye, aye." *Cheeky fucker.*

I rubbed my new bruise and flipped him off. "Blood-thirsty twat."

"Be nice to me. I'm about to get a pinecone to the head."

"Duck."

"You know that won't work. Madoc doesn't miss."

With that, Ryle slipped out the door, leaving it open so the message was clear: my solitude was over. Either I joined him, or he would set up camp in the workshop.

I couldn't blame him. Ryle acted like a needy fuck when he was rattled. Our last job had been a spectacular fail. We'd lost half our loot in an ambush by a lowly street gang. Nate had nearly been shot for it. Our success rate was high—higher than any other crew this side of the

Pacific—but one bad hit could ruin us. Dr. Z didn't keep dead weight.

It didn't help that he'd already sent us a new job. A dangerous one, far outside our usual territory. I knew it was a test...one we couldn't fail.

All our lives depended on it.

2

JAX

A bumpy plane and a humid car ride later, we arrived at our first destination: *Puerto Morelos. Mexico.*

Already, the job felt like a punishment. It was scorchingly hot, the locals were bitterly distrustful of tourists, and a dodgy sandwich at the airport was wreaking havoc on my guts. All in all, not the best start.

And that didn't even factor in my crew of unhinged hellraisers.

"Why are you walking like you sat on a garden rake?" Nate asked Ryle as we headed to our boat. The sun had barely risen, but already the locals were crowding the boardwalk. The smart ones kept clear of us.

Ryle stumbled up ahead, his eyes bruised with exhaustion. "Funny you mention it," he snapped back at Nate. "Guess who was stuck in the room next to yours?"

Beside me, Callum snorted. "Poor kid."

Our cash-in-hand motel had paper-thin walls. Twice I'd woken up in a cold sweat to wailing moans and ramming headboards. Normally, I'd be into that sort of thing. It had a been dry fucking month, and porn was porn. But I antsy about the new job, and just *tired.* It took everything I had not to punch straight through the drywall and kill them both.

The loud fucking I could handle. It was the screeching arguments in between that tested my patience. Nate and Zola fought like it was foreplay. The more they hurt each other, the harder they tried to make up for it.

"Don't be a downer, dude," Nate chirped back. "It's my pregame ritual. I got to keep it up." He slung an arm around Zola. "We took one for the team, right, baby?"

Zola shrugged him off. "Idiot."

Ryle glared at them, looking like he was two seconds away from kicking them both off the boardwalk. I debated letting him right as my gut twinged.

Never trust airport tuna.

Thankfully, we made it to the boat and took off without a hitch. I separated the morons and tried to catch some much-needed shut-eye by curling up on some fishing crates. That brilliant idea lasted until my tuna-baby kicked through my large intestines. Groaning, I took up an irritable pace on the bow.

"At least it's not a rowboat this time," Callum remarked cheerily when he joined me.

"Barely," I muttered. The trawler was made for fishing, not transporting six thieves and a cargo full of weapons and tech. Discretion was necessary, albeit often unpleasant. The deck was oily with fish guts, the smell an unwelcome prod at my uneasy digestive track.

"You look like shit," Callum said without preamble. "More than usual."

I rubbed the grit from my eyes and flipped him off with my other hand.

Then the wind changed, and with it came snatches of fresh foreplay from Nate and Zola. *Give me a fucking break.*

Callum cracked his knuckles. "Them two are doin' my head in. They're like siblings who fight and then fuck."

I grimaced. "Piss off with the incest talk. I'm already feeling woozy."

"Seasick or sandwich?"

"Still sandwich. It's putting up a fight." I pressed my hand to my navel and felt the growing rumbles. "Pretty sure I'm losing."

"Here." Callum fished the box of camels from his pocket and revived the severely squashed soldiers within. We smoked in silence for a bit. My eyes grew heavy, lulled by the gentle rocking.

"I got a bad feeling," I muttered. Part of me hoped he hadn't heard me.

Callum took a long drag, then exhaled. "Me too."

I wasn't expecting that.

Any semblance of calm was instantly wiped out at his admission. Callum wasn't superstitious. He was my strategy guy. He liked puzzles and riddles and won every single board game, a sore winner that was never humbled. Scottish-born and stubborn as a mule, Callum would sooner stick pins in his eyes than admit defeat.

My gut cramped hard, adding insult to injury. "You haven't said anything."

Callum shrugged one massive shoulder. His ginger-blond hair glared white under the sun. "You know I don't put much stock in feelings. I'm just a paranoid old fuck."

We were the same age.

"Forget I said anythin'," he said.

"Fat fucking chance."

We were headed to an island thirty miles off the coast. The island reportedly had only one resident—our mark, Theodore Salvadore. An eighty-two-year-old art dealer. Our intel on his residence was extremely limited—no images of the property itself, no satellite feed, no sale history or land titles, not even an address. For all we knew, we were headed to a barren outcrop of rock and dunes. The perfect place for a long, messy execution by our vengeful employer.

Callum's large hand settled on my shoulder. "Seriously, Jax. Forget I said it. I'm just tired and grumpy."

At my dubious squint, he grinned, then jostled me hard. "Look at us. We could be sweethearts right now. Jack and Rose on another charming voyage."

I fought my smile and lost. "Which one of us is Rose?"

"Aye, me, obviously. Us redheads got to stick together."

I finished my cigarette and made to flick it overboard when I caught myself. Ignoring Callum's amused rumbles, I shoved the dead butt into my back pocket. Callum followed, his grin just on the side of shit-eating.

Then someone retched over the side of the boat. Callum and I exchanged a startled look—and then he was gone, the large man prowling like a cheetah across the trawler. I was slower to react, my own throat convulsing reflexively.

Ryle groaned where he was purging his demons over the side of the stern. "Kill me... *please...*"

"Deep breaths, lad," Callum said, stroking his back. "You just got sea legs."

Zola appeared on my right, already digging through one of our many packs. She pulled out a travel-sized packet of ginger cubes that I recognized from the plane. "Here, Ry. These will help."

Ryle reached back with his hand and accepted the lifeline. Zola stood and gave me a sheepish look, which quickly shifted into concern. "You need some as well?"

"I'm fine."

"Bullshit. You're greener than a sea monster." She forced a packet into my palm. Under her hawkish glare, I shoved a handful of sugary cubes into my mouth.

"Where is your worst half?" I chewed, the silence and general peace suspicious.

Zola turned up her nose. "I exiled him to the cabin. He can annoy the old fisherman instead."

Great. Our watery deaths were now imminent.

Zola turned furious eyes on me. "You should've heard what he said, Jax. He called me controlling. Me? Controlling? Just because I found out about his secret online—"

Ryle's next retch was damn near music to my ears.

I swallowed and gripped the railing behind me. Nausea bubbled in my stomach. I closed my eyes and rode it out.

I felt the shadow before I saw him. A hand ghosted my side, there and gone.

I pried open one eye and croaked, "Hey."

Madoc raised one brow derisively. "Hey."

Madoc in the shade was beautiful. Madoc *in the sun* was breathtaking. Tall, with windswept ink-black hair, unfairly sharp cheekbones, and a defined, silver-pierced brow. Sea green eyes and a mouth that would've been considered soft without the cutting jawline. The faintest spatter of pale freckles across his nose. He wasn't perfect—his stubble was patchy, and he got the occasional spell of acne when he overindulged on sugar. He had a killer sweet tooth. Not that his body reflected his poor eating habits. He was lean and cut, muscled without the bulk that I had. I was unconventionally attractive, the roguish guy you'd fuck to get it out of your system. But Madoc—man, he was divine.

I only ever fucked women, but Madoc made me question things. I didn't like questioning things. It was what drove me to that threesome a few years ago—Madoc, me, and a beautiful redhead. Naturally, it'd been a disaster. Just having Madoc in the room threw me off my game. And to top it off, the poor girl between us had patted my head and cooed: "Next time you'll do better, stud."

No next time. Never again.

Pain seared through my stomach. I grunted, wincing.

Madoc hovered without touching, a concerned dent forming between his brows. He wasn't naturally expressive—his apathy was borderline certifiable—but I knew him well enough to read the tells.

I straightened with another wince. "Old man still happy?"

"He hasn't killed Scooby Doo yet."

"There's still time."

Madoc's gaze slid over to Ryle and Callum. It felt like a blessing, a momentary reprieve from his needling attention. I took a breath. Forced my ribs to open and expand.

When I was confident I wasn't going to blow chunks, I called for a debrief. It was probably overkill—we'd already discussed the plan at length on the plane, and again over breakfast—but I couldn't shake my dread. Madoc went to fetch Nate while Ryle took measured breaths under Callum's heavy-handed swats. Zola munched on whatever other snacks she'd thrifted from the plane. Few people could maintain an appetite while standing ankle-deep in fish guts and seasickness, but Zola was special. She was nearly my height, with warm brown skin and thick black hair, braided in a way that made her striking and intimidating. She was iron-willed and cunningly clever, even if she was prone to bouts of self-sabotage, notably her on-again, off-again relationship with Nate, our resident narcissist.

Speaking of the devil...

"Why so glum, chums?" Nate hollered as he pranced across the deck. His ability to read a room was, as always, spectacularly terrible.

Zola straightened, her hackles rising like a scorned black cat. "Are you high?"

"High on life, baby."

A headache tugged at my temples. Nate and his fickle sobriety were an issue I'd set aside for another day. That day kept jumping away from me. Interventions were always a disaster—none of us had any leg to stand on when it came to healthy coping mechanisms—but I knew something had to be done soon. Nate was naturally hyper, sliding into mania when doped up.

"You're such an idiot," Zola snapped. "How could you think—wait, you never think. You are so selfish—"

"Not this again," Nate groaned, raising his hand to shield against the sun. It was a futile effort. He was already burnt, his face red and shiny where he'd tucked his chestnut hair behind his ears. He was classically good-looking, an All-American boy from a fine pedigree. His longer-than-usual hair was adorably rebellious, like a frat boy going through a punk phase and falling short.

His eyes were dilated and bloodshot. His grin was downright sharky.

I grabbed his collar and dragged him toward me like an errant puppy. "You better not be."

His lip dropped in a playful pout. "Naw, don't be mad, Dad. I promise I won't get caught."

Don't strangle him. Don't strangle him.

"How the fuck did you smuggle drugs through airport security?"

Nate shrugged awkwardly, still pinned by my fist. "I didn't shelf them if that's what you're asking. I found a guy at the motel."

My fist tightened, and for a sweet moment, I allowed my imagination to run wild. Seeing murder on my face, Nate started to wilt and shuffle nervously. "I was antsy, alright? The last job nearly killed me. It's just to take the edge off, nothing else."

I released him with a shove. "You're scrubbing every fucking toilet when we get back."

He groaned. "Come on."

"Keep it up, and I'll make you use your fucking toothbrush."

Nate nodded dejectedly, knowing better than to push it. My control was shaky on a good day, and I hadn't had one of those in a while.

Zola looked as murderous as I felt. "Let me drown him, Jax. No one will miss him."

"Aw, babe."

"Don't touch me."

"You liked it last night."

"Well, I hoped you liked it too. Because it's *never* happening again—"

Ryle retched so loudly, it was a wonder he didn't pop an organ. "Please," he begged them. "Please, god, just stop. I can't listen to you anymore."

Both Zola and Nate opened their mouths, but I cut them off before they could devolve into another pointless argument. "Enough. One more word and I'll throw you both overboard."

Zola scoffed in outrage but remained blissfully silent.

"The plan," I said firmly, rubbing my eyes where they burned and burned. "Let's go through it again. Scooby, you start."

Nate smirked at the nickname. "Rest assured, little crows, I am the logistics wizard. Old man will drop us ashore and return at zero five hundred tomorrow. A light plane will be waiting for us at the International. I've even accounted for extra cargo." He gave himself a pat on the back for a job well done.

"Ugh," Zola said with a shudder. "I hate light planes. It's like flying in a tin can at fourteen thousand feet."

"As long as we all fit this time," I said, giving Nate a meaningful glare. We all remembered the squashy hybrid we'd been forced to commandeer a few months ago. Ryle had to curl up in the trunk.

Nate nodded cheerfully. "Got us an eight seater this time. Had to account for Big Foot over there."

Callum flipped him off. "Just because I'm not a wee thing like you."

"Oi. You haven't seen my wee thing."

"We've *all* seen your wee thing," Ryle muttered thickly.

I snapped my fingers. "Focus. Zola, go."

Zola stopped glaring long enough to run us through her tech speak—isolate, wipe, loop—the usual. "Network is through a satellite, so once I get past the encryption, it should be easy to hack in and shut down his surveillance."

"Easy, she says," Nate chortled.

Zola glanced at him, her mouth pursing. "Our mark is practically ancient, which means he's either ridiculously tech savvy or thinks Bluetooth is a dental problem."

"We consider both," I said.

Ryle went next, between heaving gags. "We're looking for a painting. Not sure of the exact dimensions, but considering it's worth a hundred million smackers, I'm thinking it's big. Like, stuffy-royal-portrait big."

"I don't get art," Nate said with a shake of his head.

"That's because you, boyo, are an uncultured swine." Callum flashed his teeth at Nate's affronted scoff. Taking his cue, Callum straightened, one hand still plastered on Ryle's back. "Right. If the architectural drawings are accurate—and that's a big *if*—then we're lookin' at five floors, the bottom ones reserved for the cellar and staff quarters. Master suite on the top floor. Guest rooms in the middle." He paused, then added with a quick look in my direction: "We got nothin' on the outside. Could be simple, could be bloody Fort Knox."

"Madoc," I said, feeling queasy again. Madoc ghosted to my side. I swallowed thickly and nudged him hard with my elbow.

Madoc rolled his eyes. "I'll find a way in."

Simple, confident. No hint of doubt in his ability to infiltrate any fortress. It would be arrogant if he weren't so bloody good at it.

Ryle snapped upright. "There it is."

The island was a mere bump on the horizon, a jagged shark fin, equally foreboding. Predatory. There was nothing else around it, just open water. We'd left civilization behind and were entering primitive territory. My gut clenched hot.

It felt like a final warning.

We're so dead.

We sailed on.

3

·—

JAX

The old man dumped us onto the private dock and sailed away without looking back. Ryle collapsed onto his knees and kissed the sand reverently. "Never again," he pledged. None of us had the heart to remind him of the repeat journey tomorrow morning.

The island wasn't what I expected. No swirling rain clouds and violent winds; no crossbones or unmarked graves of long-dead sailors. Instead, it was downright picturesque. An oasis of palm trees, bright white sand, and rolling green mountains. The air was sweet and exotic. A manmade track split through the treeline, like it was welcoming us to the island.

"Damn," Nate said with a whistle. "I'm about to find me some Cabana girls—ow!"

A smug Zola dumped the packs onto the sand. "I'm not carrying all the tech," she said, and delegated the heavier packs to Nate. We each took one while Zola unzipped a small silver suitcase and began unloading the gear.

It was standard protocol to use a drone to scope out the property. But not a minute later, Zola groaned and jabbed angrily at the drone. "It's dead," she said. "Someone forgot to pack the power bank."

I frowned at her. "Check again."

She came up empty. "How did we forget this?" she asked incredulously. "That's, like, one oh one."

Because we are off our game. Because it is a trap. Because this whole thing is fucking doomed.

A deep, uncomfortable tightness settled in my chest. "Fuck it. Leave it," I said. "We'll just have to go in blind."

"Ew," Ryle said. He squinted up at me, shading his eyes. "You don't look so hot, Jax."

"Says you, puke monkey."

He laughed, and just like that, the tightness eased.

I scanned the beach for Madoc. A moment later, he stepped out from the shadows of the palm trees, his face lowered, a gun held loosely in his left hand. No threats found.

I watched him without watching him. He'd removed his oversized sweatshirt and knotted it around his waist. His inked arms were on display; a majestic crow on his left elbow, wings embracing his impressive bicep. His other arm was a network of barbed wire and stemmed roses, ending at his shooting hand where a skull grinned rose petals. It was morbid as hell and pure him. Dark, deadly, and bitterly romantic.

My own ink told a similar story. I had each of their names on my skin. Callum on my bicep. *Strength*. Zola on my hand. *Intelligence*. Ryle on my ribs. *Compassion*. Nate on my collarbone. *Charisma*. Madoc on my shoulder blade. *Protection*. I had a crow behind my right ear that I scratched at like a nervous tic. It already felt raw as hell.

"Wait," Zola said as we shouldered our packs. Already the sun was hotter, bleaching the world around us. She tapped away on a portable device. "Alright. Our mark is officially in the sky. His plane boarded twelve minutes ago."

"We got eyes on him?" Callum asked.

Zola confirmed: "Private Jet chartered to a Mr. Theodore Salvadore, destination Cancun International. Arrival time is six am, Sunday."

"Twenty hours, give or take," I said. Plenty of time to get in and out. The isolation continued to bother me. If everything went to shit, we'd be trapped. No quick getaway, no clean escape.

Shaking my head, we headed into the island. A fork appeared ten minutes into the rainforest. I considered both, staring hard left and right. Without the drone, all I had was guesswork.

"Left," Madoc said. He took the lead without question.

The heat intensified. The air became thick and soup-like. Nate kept up a constant stream of babble—"I've heard the spider monkeys here can give you herpes" and "...say what you want, herpes or not, it would still be cool to keep one"—as we bashed our way through the foliage.

Then we were climbing. My thighs burned, and sweat ran in rivulets down my back. Madoc lost his shit and swung a branch directly into Nate's motormouth. The resulting scuffle was short-lived, a victorious Madoc falling into step beside me. The silence was brief.

"Soldier Island!" Callum crowed suddenly, like he'd been struggling for some time to find the words. At our questioning looks, the large man wiped his brow and said: "It's been buggin' me for hours, what this all reminds me of. It's Agatha Christie."

"Who?" Nate asked, still petulant as he rubbed his jaw.

"Who? Who!" Callum made an aggrieved sound. "Aye, the American education system triumphs once again. You, lad, need to visit the shelves once in a blue moon. It'd do wonders for ya' wooden head."

"I'll have you know, ginger, that I attended some of the finest institutions in the country."

"For all the good it did ya'."

Zola wisely stepped in between them before Nate decided to throw himself at the larger man. "I think I read that one in juvie," she said thoughtfully. "From memory, ten strangers are called to a mysterious island by some rich white dude who picks them off one by one."

"Hey. Spoiler," Ryle protested from the rear.

"It is kinda spooky," Zola remarked. "Salvadore has properties all over the world, but he chooses this place as his main residence. Nobody needs *this* much privacy unless they're up to no good."

"Maybe he's running secret lab experiments," Nate said excitedly.

"For the hundredth time, *Jurassic Park* isn't going to happen."

"Bite your tongue, Muggle."

Nate started loudly humming the *Jurassic Park* soundtrack.

My right eye twitched in annoyance. Madoc grabbed another branch, but Nate dodged his next swing. It was around his fourth verse that we struck gold. The path ahead cleared, paved steps built in. There was a notable glimmer above, like sun glare on a windscreen. We were close.

Madoc stayed at my back as we climbed. Nate went behind him, still humming obnoxiously. I kept an ear out for Ryle at the tail.

Between one blink and the next, the house appeared.

It was definitely no humble cabin. Five stories tall, half-embedded in the mountain like the rock had eroded around it over time. Large panoramic windows and a long, wraparound porch. Big stone pillars and arches. Ugly as fuck decorative statues that looked like lumps of granite.

In other words, it was a goldmine. Pretentious, isolated, and full of priceless junk. A younger me would've raided every nook and pissed on his silk pillows.

"Damn," Nate said between blustering pants. "Call me Goldilocks. I'm trying out the beds."

"Yo' baby bear." I grabbed Nate's arm and hoisted him up the remaining steps. "What's that look like over there?" I pointed to the left side of the property.

Nate squinted through his sweat-stiff locks. "That...is a helicopter pad, boss."

A groan traveled through the group.

Nate held out his hands in exasperation. "How the fuck was I supposed to know? We had limited intel, remember?"

"Logistics wizard, my freckled ass." Callum helped Ryle up the last few steps. "We're revoking your wand. It's back to maintenance for you, boyo."

My eyes tracked Ryle intently. He was too pale, and he kept blinking like he'd been flashed. *Brain auras.* I knew them well, usually after a concussion or a bad hangover. I walked over and gripped his chin, forcing him to look up. He winced. "Hey, you with me, Sunbeam?"

"Stomach still hurts," he admitted, clutching his middle. "I'll be good in a minute."

A chrome water bottle was thrust between us. "Drink," Madoc said. I hadn't heard him move.

Ryle shook his head. "Nah, really, I'm fine."

"Drink."

"But I have barf mouth."

Madoc's eyes narrowed. "Drink or I'll waterboard you. Choose quickly."

Ryle snapped up the bottle and chugged it.

As we moved back to the front of the group, I smirked at Madoc. "Waterboarding, huh?"

Madoc's own mouth ticked up faintly. "Junior needs a firm hand."

"It's just zero to all-out torture with you."

Madoc shrugged. He faced the mansion and began silently mapping the access points. I left him to it, knowing his mind had already disengaged from me. Meanwhile, Zola was merrily ripping Nate a new one for his careless oversight.

"The guy is, like, a hundred years old, Nate! Did you really think he was going on a four-mile hike every time he came home?"

Nate glared at her. "A chopper isn't exactly conspicuous, is it?"

"The less time we're here, the better, dingus. We could've planned a backup."

I rubbed my face tiredly. "Jesus, morons. Enough."

Not for the first time, I considered knocking their heads together and banning them from fucking. If I were smart, I'd enforce the no-relationship rule like some of the other crews under Dr. Z's syndicate. I'd bet my left nut the Japanese Vipers didn't tolerate shit like this.

Because you're soft, my father's words jabbed at me inside my head. *Soft and weak, boy.*

Inwardly wincing, I turned my back on them. At least I had Madoc. He looked at me with nothing but bored determination. My dependable soldier.

"Remember," Zola said as we each slipped in our covert earpieces. "These are only short-range because we're in the middle of nowhere. Don't stray too far or we'll lose you." She gave Nate a pointed look.

He grinned and plastered himself to her side. "Don't worry, beautiful. I'm sticking to you like wet on bread."

"That's not even a thing."

I raised my hand toward Madoc, then paused. After a short nod, I gave his bare shoulder a squeeze. His skin was hot beneath my palm. "You got this?"

Madoc removed his trademark face bandana from his back pocket, black with white roses. "Don't ask stupid questions."

I grinned at him.

Once Zola disabled the alarm system, Madoc ducked beneath the canopy and disappeared into the thick brush surrounding the mansion. I listened to his careful breathing in my ear, matching it to my own. Heartbeat to heartbeat.

What felt like an eternity later, he confirmed: *I'm in.*

I checked my watch. "Six minutes, Sparrow. Not bad."

"Shut up."

I did, biting back another grin.

Showtime.

4

OLIVIA

“Ow. Crap.”

Wriggling through an air vent wasn't as easy as the movies made it seem. *John McClane lied to me.* The vent was dusty and tight, and the only way I managed to move at all was by thrusting upwards like a worm, my arms trapped uselessly by my sides. Every inch gained was a punishment to my sinuses. I sneezed so hard that I saw Jesus.

Note to self: clean air vents at home.

Not that I planned to do this ever again. I wasn't someone who broke into houses. I was a nice, normal, preppy cheerleader with a stable boyfriend and a trust fund. Or at least, I used to be.

I hadn't picked up the pom-poms in a few months, hadn't tumbled or cheered for anything other than reruns of The Bachelor. That stable boyfriend was being a total dick, which was usually my type except that he'd doubled down on the dickery lately. I'd drained my bank account to fund this crusade, and the prevailing hope that I'd finally escape my parents' toxic scrutiny was becoming a distant dream.

Still, I had no regrets yet. In fact, I couldn't believe I'd even made it this far. I kept expecting the universe to screw me over. But that skeevy fisherman I'd bribed this morning hadn't chopped me up like white girl sushi. That dingy boat he owned hadn't sailed into a random storm and sunk. Not even the alarm system around the mansion had tripped yet.

It was probably temporary, the calm before the storm.

Thank god Salvadore had been in London for that art show. Every second counted, and I needed all the time I could to search his house.

Everything about the old guy was suspicious. A billion-aire who lived on a remote island. Never married, never had kids. The public dubbed him a recluse, one of those artsy types who actively snubbed interviews and shirked away from politics. He didn't do charity work, didn't rub shoulders with the elite, or mingle with high society. Not that I blamed him for that—I hated the circles more than anything—but it made tracking him down way more difficult.

It seemed impossible that someone like him could have ever crossed paths with Molly, a diligent twenty-two-year-old college student. It wasn't like Molly ever took an interest in art. She never painted or took up photography, and never mentioned Salvadore as a potential patron to showcase her pieces. Molly was a law student. She was dry, boring, and practical, just the way my parents liked it. It wasn't in her nature to rebel. And yet, somehow, she was convinced to travel five thousand miles away from home to a remote island without telling a single soul. Molly, the same person who couldn't swallow a single mouthful of yogurt without scrutinizing the fat content.

How did they meet? How did she get here?

What did he do to her?

My head smacked into metal. I froze, the sound reverberating like a gunshot all around me. I'd reached the end. Drawing on my superior flexibility, I freed one arm and used my body's momentum to punch through the grille. It popped out with surprising ease, clattering loudly to the ground below.

My backpack went next. Once it dropped, I wriggled through the opening and tucked-flipped to the ground. My fists shot up like muscle memory, a perfect high V.

Goooooo me!

Huffing at my own ridiculousness, I smoothed down my hair and tugged on my shirt to remove the creases. I was covered in dust and grime from the boat, but it didn't matter. I'd actually done it. I'd broken in.

Unable to shake my pessimism, I looked around warily. I expected to end up somewhere terrifying, like a torture room. Instead, I found myself in the pantry. High shelves stacked with canned goods and pickled condiments, giant sacks of flour, salt, and sugar in the corners. It made sense; he couldn't exactly make a quick pit stop at his local Walmart.

I still eyed the jars suspiciously, half expecting to find pickled organs or a perfectly preserved fetus. My hands were shaking when I reached the door. I opened it slowly. But no bodies fell out. No human meat locker or table full of bloody surgical instruments. Just a normal, windowless service corridor. I exhaled in relief. So far, so good.

I crept soundlessly down the corridor until I came to a pretty spiral staircase made of solid wood with ornate iron banisters. I peered upwards through the cavity and counted three floors. Then I looked down at the basement below.

Big fat nope.

I didn't like horror movies, and I was secure enough in myself to admit that I wouldn't last very long. I wasn't the Final Girl. I was the girl who got killed in the first ten minutes, probably wearing a skimpy bikini and forgetting how to run without tripping over every possible obstacle.

Shuddering, I climbed up to the next landing and found myself in a bright atrium connecting the two main living areas. No doubt the architect wanted to maximize the ocean's views and natural light—instead, I felt like I was caught in a petri dish.

A pretty foreign invader.

Unnerved, I took out the switchblade I'd bought from the gas station. There was still a plastic film on the blade, which I removed with a loud rip. Then I continued up the stairs. The top floor was bright and airy, with natural wood paneling and large skylights that created incriminating spotlights. For an art dealer, he had a surprisingly rudimentary collection: a few portraits of beautiful landscapes, some abstract pieces with natural undertones like clays and browns. I was no art critic, but I could appreciate the consistency of theme.

The master bedroom gave me an itchy feeling. It was perfectly innocuous, tidy, and clean. But it still felt like the ultimate violation.

I thought of my own bedroom—the gentle pink and white hues, the mantle of cheer trophies and ribbons, the dozens of scented candles that had become like a vigil to

Molly. I had a beloved soft teddy collection that Heath, my dickish ex-boyfriend, liked to pin down and hump because he had the emotional maturity of a sock.

I was glad I'd dumped him. It was a bit pathetic that I'd cried over it. Heath had accused me of milking my depression. I'd retaliated by throwing my favorite lamp at his head. A blistering argument later, I'd called it off. Part of me still dwelled on what he said, the scrap of truth in it.

I *had* been stuck on Molly for two years. Trapped by the unknown, held hostage to the grizzly possibilities that ran rampant in my head. That was why I'd finally decided to do something about it.

I was going to put my demons to rest, even if it meant uncovering them first.

Starting with Salvadore.

Fighting off the icks, I raided his nightstands. They were completely empty, which was strange. Just dust and lint balls. I did a cursory check under the bed—nothing. Not even a stray sock.

It was like a hotel room. Cold, impersonal. The wardrobe proved just as disheartening—shirts ironed and sorted by color, shoes polished on the racks, a mono-grammed bathrobe on the back of the door, slippers slotted neatly beneath it. By pure luck, I found the secret compartment with his expensive watches and accessories. I stared at the collection pensively.

Was I petty enough to steal from him? I knew my morals had become wonky lately. I'd done some pretty sketchy things to get where I needed.

Groaning, I pushed the compartment shut. Not even a full second later, I yanked it back open and stuffed a watch and two diamond cufflinks into my backpack. Molly's judgmental face hovered in my mind. *Thief*, she said. *Karma*, I snapped back.

With the main bedroom yielding no results, I moved on to the ensuite. The shower was enormous, all exposed rock and two hanging showerheads. The countertops were lined with expensive colognes and lotions, a solitary toothbrush, a ceramic plate with folded towels, and hand soaps.

"This guy screams American Psycho," I murmured aloud, catching myself in the reflection. As predicted, my skin had bronzed under the sun, my honey-blonde hair frizzy where it swung in my high ponytail. My lips were chapped from the salty sea air. I shopped the lotions consideringly, then quickly dismissed putting anything on my body that had touched *his*. On habit, I found Molly in the gray-blue of my eyes, the roundness of my face. We'd been mistaken as twins when we were younger, but her late teens had been kind to her. She'd grown a foot taller, her face had become sharper, and her lips fuller. She'd been offered modeling jobs by small labels, who described her look as "girl-next-door with an edge". I was still waiting for my own glow up—I desperately wanted to lose the baby fat that clung to my face—but I feared the grief had stunted me. My eyes were a bit too sunken, the lines a bit too deep. I was still a ruthless gymnast, and I kept it tight, but the late nights and caffeine addiction were catching up to me. I drank guilt smoothies, so I wouldn't die from scurvy or malnutrition, but looking after myself had become an afterthought.

Mouth twisting in disdain, I continued my search of the top landing. A sitting room that looked like it belonged in a showroom. A small study nook with personalized letter-heads: *Theodore Salvadore*. Black pens only. A collection of limited-edition encyclopedias.

A shiver of unease traveled up my spine. Everything was too perfect. Too pristine. The feeling lingered, an uncomfortable knot twisting in my stomach. Scratching the back of my neck, I glanced nervously over my shoulder. Shafts of green-tinged sunlight siphoned through the skylights, the trapped dust swirling at my intrusion.

I felt like prey. Exposed, out in the open plains.

Observed.

Gripping my knife harder, I returned to the main bedroom so I could peek through the window that overlooked the front of the mansion. So focused on my destination, I didn't clock the shadow until it was too late.

A force barreled into me, toppling me onto the bed. My mouth went dry as bone, my body lashing out instinctively in terror. A hand caught my flailing fist, pinning it next to my head. My knife was plucked from my fingers in one seamless motion. Then the weight shifted, trapping my insurgent legs and my hips to the mattress.

The air was punched out of my lungs.

"Stop," a voice commanded drily in my ear.

Mindless with panic, I obeyed. A man hovered over me. To my fear-sharpened eyes, he appeared in stark definition: dark hair and pale skin, vivid green eyes above a black face bandana with white roses. A glint of silver on his eyebrow. A very faint spatter of freckles across his nose, just above the cloth.

I had a funny suspicion he wasn't the handyman.

His grip tightened on my wrists, my fingers pulsing at the lack of blood. "Who are you?"

"I…" God, my mind was blank. I couldn't form the words, couldn't think beyond the white rush of fear.

He lifted up onto his knees, straddling my hips. What I could see of his expression was disturbing. Blank, empty. We could've been discussing the weather.

"Nobody," I gasped out. "I'm—nobody."

His pierced brow twitched up in vague interest. "You don't look like a maid. No cute uniform."

I said nothing, just floundered like a fish.

His head cocked, eyes still cold and pitiless. I wondered if he was smiling beneath the cloth, and that disturbed me even more. "I see. Just a pest then."

Alarm bells rang in my head. He sounded bored, like I was something easily removed. Exterminated.

I bucked my hips violently. The tightness of my shorts was painful, cutting into my thighs. His own thighs were like steel bands, trapping me between them. The way he moved was purposeful, anticipating each wild thrust of my hips so we wouldn't make unnecessary contact. Relying on pure muscle memory, I hooked my leg around his waist and flipped us. Then I was on top, straddling him, and his eyes flashed dangerously before he snapped upright and tackled me off the bed. My head thudded hard against the floor, carpet burning against my bare skin. His weight was suddenly overwhelming, crushing me to the floor.

"Get off me!" I hissed.

To my surprise, he instantly obeyed. He snapped upright, keeping his leather-gloved hands locked on my wrists so I had no choice but to move with him. Facing each other, I realized he had at least an extra foot on me. But that wasn't the disturbing part.

The disturbing part was how *ridiculously* fit he was.

I still aimed my shoe at his balls.

He shifted back, easily avoiding it without releasing me. In one swift motion, he flipped me around, my back to his chest, my backpack squashed in between us. Leather-gloved fingers wrapped around my throat.

"Upstairs," he said.

My throat convulsed around his cruel fingers. "We're already upstairs."

Fabric brushed my temple. "I wasn't talking to you."

My breath caught. There were more of them. I was outnumbered. Trapped. Alone.

A terrible, terrible thought burrowed into my brain. *Was this how Molly felt?* I wanted to scream. As if sensing it, the hand on my throat squeezed.

Blood pounded in my ears. It wasn't enough to drown out the unmistakable sound of approaching footsteps.

And then he walked in.

5

OLIVIA

The leader.

It was obvious from the way he walked—confident, commanding. Dirty blond hair tumbled around a black face bandana with a grinning skull. The eyes above it were Nordic blue and utterly terrifying. He looked at me without surprise, flat and furious like his comrade behind me.

The rest of them piled in. An enormous guy with red hair took up post by the door, his face obscured by a tartan green-and-black bandana. He was joined by a slimmer bandit with wind-tousled auburn curls and big, searching brown eyes above his own mask, which had bright yellow sunflowers on it. Fear clawed at my chest. My only exit was blocked. The four of them surrounded me, the one at my back with his hand like a vice on my throat.

The leader stopped and looked down at me. He was far more expressive than his counterparts, his brow furrowing, his eyes narrowing like he was trying to beam the answers directly from my head. He was huge, his chest wide and defined like a quarterback, his black t-shirt highlighting every muscular dip and crevice. I could feel the heat radiating from his sun-soaked skin.

"You shouldn't be here," he said. His voice had a hoarse quality that made me shiver. "Who the fuck are you?"

"Nobody," I wheezed out. The fingers on my throat squeezed.

He stared me down. I refused to look away, even as tears burned my eyes. Then his penetrating gaze flicked up to the man behind me in question.

"She was armed," he said, his voice rumbling through my squashed backpack and into my spine. "We've already established she's not here for the turn-down service."

Furious blue eyes returned to me. "How did you get here?"

"A boat," I said slowly.

"What kind?"

"Um, the ocean kind?"

His eyes closed, and he took a deep breath. It was obvious he had no patience for bullshit. That didn't bode well for me.

His eyes snapped open. "Either you cooperate, or I'll make you."

The lie formed quickly in my head. It was the performance needed to sell it that worried me. "I'm supposed to be here," I said, gagging a little on the chokehold. "I work for Mr. Salvadore. I'm h-his assistant."

"Assisting in what?" There was a sarcastic lilt to his voice. His gaze dipped, leering at me in a way that made me flush hot all over.

"General duties," I hissed out sharply. "It's not like *that*. I'm just here to water his plants."

There. That sounded convincing. Not that I'd noticed any house plants.

Blue eyes continued to stare me down, then he stepped around us and out of my immediate sight. I fidgeted, my skin prickling with awareness. The fingers spasmed on my throat in warning. The leader returned a moment later with my switchblade in his hand, and my heart sank.

"And what was this for? Hedge trimming?"

My chin lifted. "Maybe."

"Bit young, aren't you? For such a big responsibility." Okay, he was definitely mocking me. I needed to up my game. Whip out the big guns.

Forcing myself to go slack, I let my head drop forward despondently. I didn't like playing the victim, but I was desperate. *Manipulative*, Heath would've said. Fuck that guy. I pushed out a tiny sob, making myself look small and pathetic. The tears came easier than they usually did—blinding terror was excellent source material.

The pitiful performance had the desired effect. The hand on my throat loosened just slightly. Hot tears streaked silently down my face.

"Let her go."

My first captor released me and stepped back. I swayed a bit at the unexpected freedom. Cool air brushed the sweat on the back of my neck and knees. I hugged myself, really amping it up.

Fingers locked suddenly on my chin, wrenching my face up. A gasp punched out of me. I blinked hard, trying to read his expression through my tears.

"Real convincing." I sensed his smile behind his freaky skull bandana. It was not kind. "Too bad I don't buy it for a second."

"Please—"

"Don't do that." His own gloved fingers were bruising, tilting my face this way and that, searching for fissures in my façade. "I know a grifter when I see one."

Grifter? How *old* was he? "I'm not," I blubbered. "I swear on my life."

"Doubling down." He nodded like I'd only confirmed his theory. "Either you don't hold much value in your life, or you're just as morally crooked as the rest of us. Which is it?"

I swallowed, my tongue thick and my words starting to clog. "I choose C," I choked out. "Please. People will notice if I go missing."

My heart twinged in grief. It wasn't a lie, necessarily, but I'd been deliberately vague on my whereabouts and when I'd return. The only person who knew what I was up to was Preacher, and I wasn't sure I trusted him entirely. My parents weren't bothered unless I didn't show up for our weekly dinner—*god forbid* they missed a chance to unload their grocery list of grievances against me. But I wasn't due for another two days. A lot could happen in that time.

With a small grunt, the leader released me and nodded to my shadow. Suddenly, hands were on me again, tearing at my clothes, ripping the backpack off my torso.

"No. Wait—stop!" I reached out but was smacked away. Hands stinging, I cupped them to my chest and watched in outrage. My backpack was tossed carelessly across the room to the leader, and then just as carelessly ripped open.

He removed my spare clothes first, tossing them onto the floor, lacy panties and all. Next, it was my assortment of snacks, mostly gas station loot like chocolate bars and pretzels. Then he froze, elbow-deep, and fresh apprehension needled at my soul. His eyes found mine, one brow arching knowingly. He extracted his arm and held out his prize—the stolen watch.

How's that for karma? Molly sang smugly in my head.

"Stealing from your employer gets you a bad reference," the blue-eyed cretin said, tossing the watch to the large redhead behind him. "How much?"

The redhead examined it with deft fingers. "About twenty grand," he said, with a slight twang.

That made the leader scoff. "He probably has pillows worth more than that." His eyes found mine again, darkening. "I notice you've stopped crying."

"He told me to get that," I said defiantly, feeling caught. "It's a gift."

"You don't lie as good as you cry."

I crossed my arms. "I'm not lying."

"Who's the gift for? You?"

"Yes."

"That's generous." Even though I couldn't see his mouth, I felt his grin, the way it mocked me. "You fuck him first, or is it a down payment?"

Anger flashed hot through my veins. "Fuck you."

That amused him. His eyes roamed over me from head to toe, calculating my scuffed sneakers and cut-off shorts, my salt-wrinkled linen shirt. His lack of comment said nothing and everything.

The violation continued. Next, he found my passport and travel documents. "Olivia Wood. Born June eleventh. Twenty years old." His eyes crinkled slightly. "You're far away from home."

I clung to my story and said nothing. From the corner of my eye, I saw a gloved hand snake around me and snatch up a chocolate bar from the floor pile. Before I could splutter in disbelief, the leader reached in one last time and hit the motherload. He froze again, eyes narrowing as he felt the smooth plastic cover of my binder. A war drum pounded in my skull as he pulled it out. Shit, shit, shit.

"Stop," I said, but he was already flipping open the cover, my backpack dropping empty and gutted at his boots. Emotion clogged up my windpipe as he dived into my obsession. The newspaper articles, Molly's diary entries, coroner's reports, police reports, and Salvadore's business travels. I watched in real time as his shoulders tightened, tension bleeding into his frame.

Then he snapped it shut like he couldn't stand to look at it anymore. He hadn't even made it halfway.

When his eyes met mine again, a new danger lurked there. I straightened like prey caught in a trap. My stomach gave a sickening lurch, a missed step.

"You better start talking."

His words promised violence.

"Okay," I said, holding out my hands placatingly. I wasn't dealing with a potential burglar anymore—I was dealing with a killer. I could see it in the coiled tension of his body, the restless twitch of his fingers, the unwavering hardness in his eyes. I'd lost control of the situation and was spinning out, heading toward a fatal collision.

"I'll tell you," I said, swiping absently at my face to remove the last residue of tears. "Just—please. It's not easy. You have to be patient with me."

"Start. Talking."

But I barely got a word out before he tensed up, and the two masked men behind him exchanged a quick look. He pressed a finger to his ear and barked: "Not now."

Whatever reply came made him inhale sharply. A bated breath later, he exhaled and said, "War room."

The meaning of that was lost on me, except that I was once again manhandled into the same hard chest from before. Without my backpack, his warmth bled through my shirt and into my skin. My already raw nerves zinged at the contact.

The faint scent of chocolate wafted over my face.

With a jolt, I glanced up and realized he'd removed his mask. The dark fabric was bunched under his jaw, and, god, what a jaw it was. So sharp it could cut ice. Green eyes watched me in amusement. The rest of his face was absurdly striking, the kind of face you wouldn't easily forget.

I knew that was a bad sign.

6

JAX

"*Found the painting.*"

What should've been good news fell flat in the wake of our unwelcome discovery. It had taken Nate less than ten minutes to locate the painting. He was still nattering in our ears like the obnoxious prick he was, uncaring of our resounding silence.

Nate's shocking lack of awareness lasted until we reached the dining room on the second floor. A long stone table beneath a deer antler chandelier seemed oddly fitting for the occasion.

"*Is this thing on? Hello?*" Nate's voice pitched in annoyance. "*Come on. This has to be some kind of record. I bet Big Foot is seething right now—*"

"*Will you shut up?*" Zola's voice interrupted. I knew it was a bad idea to pair them together, but I'd stupidly hoped Zola would keep him in line. Manage his mania.

The only other person I trusted was Madoc, but he was currently occupied with frog-marching our hostage into the room.

Olivia.

A short, heart-faced blonde with shockingly toned legs and a backpack full of secrets. Stormy gray eyes that brimmed with lies. I knew a swindler when I saw one. Hell, we were the masters of it. I didn't trust a single thing she said. I definitely wouldn't be moved by those crocodile tears (even if it made her face screw up in a strangely endearing way).

Madoc dropped her into the chair at the end of the table, directly opposite me at the head. Callum remained by the door, his arms crossed like a hired guard. Ryle hesitated, catching Madoc's maskless face, and shot me a hopeful look.

I nodded. Ryle pulled back a chair and collapsed in a heap, then swiped off his mask. His pallor was still concerning. The seasickness had probably wiped him of all his electrolytes.

A chocolate bar was thrown across the table as Madoc took his seat to my immediate right. Ryle gave it a wary look as he caught it beneath his palm. I didn't blame him.

"Eat," Madoc said.

Ryle opened his mouth to argue, then his eyes flicked to our guest, and he promptly took it without complaint. We didn't fight in front of outsiders. Not even Nate broke that cardinal rule.

Plus, Madoc never shared. It wasn't a gift to be taken lightly.

I dumped the binder onto the table. Olivia's whole body flinched. It was clearly important to her, and that gave me leverage. Her face hardened, like she knew what I was thinking.

Of course she did. Like recognized like.

Might as well show her my true colors. I reached up and yanked my mask off. Her eyes widened, then dropped quickly. I was programmed to spot fear—to exploit it where necessary—and she was terrified.

"Are you going to kill me now?" she asked in a small voice.

"Depends if you behave."

Her lips puckered in. "That's not reassuring."

"Watch me not give a fuck." I jabbed my finger hard on the binder. She winced, then glared at me like I struck her instead. "The girl, Molly. Who was she to you?"

She lifted her head and glared at me coolly, clearly concocting another bullshit story.

"...My sister." She said stiffly. But her voice cracked. "She went missing two years ago."

Silence fell thick and heavy in the room.

If it was sympathy she wanted, she'd be sorely disappointed. We all had sob stories.

"That it?" I asked bluntly.

She scowled at my insincerity.

"You have five minutes," I warned her. She recoiled in her chair like preparing for a blow. "Don't mince your words. Convince me not to kill you."

Don't lie, I added in my head.

She didn't know about Callum, who could read body language like a natural profiler. Or Madoc and his eidetic memory.

Olivia stood and smoothed down her shirt, as if she were about to conduct a business meeting. I sat down and kicked up my boots on the table. She glared at them like they personally offended her. Good.

"My sister, Molly Wood, went missing in October two years ago," she said in a clear voice. "There has been no contact since. Not a single text, phone call, or online post. And no ransom."

"You think she was kidnapped?"

She nodded. "I think there's a reason she hasn't come back."

Beside me, Madoc straightened.

Olivia chewed her lip and then caught herself and straightened. She gave me preppy good girl vibes, the kind of girl who preened and fussed over her image. But in the next breath, she sighed loudly and said: "I'm probably fucking crazy for doing this."

My brows lifted in surprise. Her swearing was like hearing a toddler swear. *Adorable*. "Doing what exactly?"

"This," she said, gesturing around us. "Breaking in. I was desperate. I didn't—I had no other options. I went to the police, and they opened a case, but nothing's come of it. They think she's just on some long-winded vacation."

Girls like her probably did spontaneous shit like that all the time. Something on my face must've tipped her off, because her eyes sharpened. "She's *not* on vacation," she said shortly. "Nobody just decides to cut off everyone and disappear. Especially not her. She had a fellowship at Columbia. She worked hard for that spot."

"Three minutes. Get to the point."

She huffed irritably. "I need more than three minutes."

I rolled my eyes to the ceiling, then held up my fingers, counting down.

"I decided to investigate it myself," she said, quicker now. "I managed to piece together some of her last known whereabouts."

"Here?"

She hesitated. "Yes."

"You hesitated."

"I'm nervous!" she snapped.

I liked her nervous. My lips twitched into a grin. "Two minutes."

"God!" She hissed in frustration, then collected herself. "I found Molly's diary. She wrote about some guy she met at a party a few weeks before she went missing. He offered to take her on a trip. Somewhere warm and private."

"But she never wrote his name or what he looked like. She just left early Sunday morning and took a car service to the airport. The driver said she was acting weird. Squirrelly, like she was on something."

I arched a brow. "Was she?"

Her face pinched. "Not a chance. Molly wouldn't touch drugs with a ten-foot pole. She doesn't even trust caffeine." She took a breath. "I think she was scared. I think she didn't want to go, but maybe he had something on her."

She paused, then, and the room waited.

Her eyes bounced up. " So I bribed a cop—"

"You *what*?" I burst out laughing. There was no way.

The little con artist shrugged, like it was nothing. She had money, a cute smile, and perky tits. She'd be hard-pressed to find a man who wouldn't fold.

"The cop managed to track her cellphone to a tower in Puerto Morelos. That's where she disappeared."

"A hostage with a cellphone," Madoc spoke up for the first time. Olivia's eyes slid to him, looking nervous. Madoc had that effect. "Sloppy."

That made her glare. "Molly is the responsible one. She never went out, never did anything. It doesn't add up."

Her shoulders dipped. "I'm the only one looking for her. My parents are in denial. I'm all she's got."

Slowly, I slid the binder over to Madoc. Her head snapped up, tracking the movement with diamond cutter intensity.

"And that brings you here," I summed up. "With a backpack full of secrets and a stolen watch."

Her cheeks flushed hot with shame. "Obviously, the watch was a mistake. I had a moment. That moment has passed." She bristled. "I was going to put it back eventually."

Callum's fingers flexed on his bicep. *Lie.* I didn't call her out on it.

Olivia opened her mouth, then froze, looking alarmed. She glanced toward the door right as Nate swaggered in. His eyes were bright, and his hair was mussed. Zola swooped in after him, perfectly immaculate, like they hadn't just fucked somewhere in the mansion.

Nate opened his mouth but caught my pointed look and wisely shut his trap. Zola manhandled him into a chair. He gave her a sappy, lovestruck look.

The painting was notably absent.

The look Olivia shot me was ten streaks of betrayal. "I didn't realize there were more of you."

I shrugged. "You didn't ask."

"I don't want to repeat myself."

"Then don't. I'll catch them up."

She didn't like that, but I didn't care. We were on a timer. And my patience was wearing thin.

"Fine," she said, speaking to the room, but fixed on me. "I did some more digging. Found some other missing girls who were last seen in Puerto Morelos. Open the binder, near the back."

Using his new knife, Madoc flipped open the binder. There was a bunch of news articles and official-looking reports in the back. A glance confirmed they weren't public documents.

What exactly did she *give* this dirty cop?

"Look at the news article," Olivia prompted. "A luxury yacht capsized a few years ago, not far from here. Six females and two males drowned. All between the ages of seventeen and twenty-three."

Madoc scanned it quickly, downloading it into his super-brain. His face gave nothing.

"I cross-checked it with the autopsy reports," Olivia went on, bouncing on her toes. My mouth twitched again. "Those girls had bruises on their wrists and ankles, like they'd been restrained. But not the men."

"And Salvadore?" I pressed her.

Olivia jutted her chin smugly. "The yacht was leased from his company."

"That's a reach," I said, disappointed when that made her stop bouncing. "He probably owns half the companies in the peninsula. The guy is a rainmaker. It's not enough."

She huffed in anger. "It's more than anyone else has! Keep reading. You'll find investigation reports from the families of the missing girls. Two of them mention this island." She flapped her hands dramatically. "Coincidence? I think not."

Madoc gave me a look. He agreed. Not that it changed anything.

"So what's the plan here?" I asked her. "Walk me through it."

"I'm here to find proof," she said confidently. "I know he won't be back until Sunday morning. That gives me enough time to search this place."

"And if you find nothing? What then?"

That made her pause.

Then her eyes found mine, hard and determined. "I will find something."

My gut twinged. I didn't believe in fate, and I wasn't superstitious. But something was off about her. The pain flared deeper in my gut. *Listen to it.* My instincts were rarely wrong.

I swung my feet to the floor and stood, my chain toppling over with a loud bang. Olivia flinched, crossing her arms nervously.

"You complicate things." I heard my father in my voice. His quiet baritone of fury.

She swallowed. "I know," she said. "But I'm not asking you for anything. You can just pretend I'm not here."

"It doesn't work like that."

"Why not?"

"You've seen our faces."

She bristled at that. "I didn't ask you to take off your masks. Besides, you're all totally forgettable. Just faceless blobs to me."

Nate jerked in offense while Callum snorted a quiet laugh into his fist.

"You like to play rogue detective." I raised my brows pointedly. "How do I know you won't start hunting us?"

A wry smile crossed her face. "I can only hunt one monster at a time."

"That's—" My throat clicked as bile rushed up. Shit.

"Don't move," I growled at her and retreated to the door. "I'll decide what to do with you when I get back."

"Do with me?" I heard her only faintly as I rushed to the nearest bathroom. Luckily, there were a dozen of them. The porcelain clattered as I dropped to my knees and finally purged the demon-sandwich. Sweat dripped into my eyes as I heaved myself into oblivion.

The bathroom door opened. A large body muscled in, closed the door, and leaned against it.

"You good, chief?"

"Fucking ace."

"You look it." Callum shook my shoulder gently. "Don't worry, Jax. I got a plan."

7

OLIVIA

God, this was awkward.

Without the leader breathing down my neck, I was left in silence so thick it suffocated me. None of them resumed the interrogation, but I sensed their questions, their doubts. After a minute, the big one at the door also dipped out, his absence only heightening the tension. I almost wanted to do something absurd, like break into a chant, just to provoke a reaction.

Real mature, Molly said.

The dark-haired menace who'd stolen my chocolate proceeded to flip through my binder with agonizing indifference. Everything I had was in that binder. Not just Molly but my own doodles and pathetic footnotes. I'd even painted little broken hearts on the back cover with nail polish because I was feeling sorry for myself. At his quiet huff of amusement, I resisted the urge to leap over the table and tackle him. I wanted to guard my binder like a mother dragon, but I knew that was stupid. And likely suicidal.

Also not mature.

Shut up, I snapped. With a small huff, I sat down in my chair and placed my hands primly in my lap. I would be good. Prove I wasn't a threat to them, whoever they were.

But then the dark-haired menace chuckled again, and my temper flared. Molly's diary wasn't exactly flattering for me. She'd been downright brutal sometimes, recalling every pimple-related meltdown and awkward-puberty mishap like she was studying me. I was the primate to her perfect.

I sat on my hands before I did something drastic. Finally, after a long agonizing eternity, I broke.

"Did he invoke a code of silence or something?"

There was a beat where I thought no one would respond. Then the girl spoke. "Or something."

The look she gave me was dripping with disdain. I was no stranger to that look—usually it was accompanied by a sweet smile and empty compliments, right before they stabbed me in the back. I'd been popular all my life. I had security, money, and privilege. I didn't blame them for hating me, but I also wasn't a pushover to it.

"You guys here for business or pleasure?" I asked sarcastically.

It was the pretty boy who spoke. He was closer to my comfort zone—well-groomed, aristocratic-looking, with really good teeth. "Oh, pleasure. We're here to catch some sun, surf, and sex." He flashed his perfect teeth at the unimpressed girl beside him. "We were long overdue for a vacation, right, babe?"

"Don't call me babe."

"I thought you liked it. Fine. Love of my life, sun of my galaxy, buster of thy mighty balls—what would you prefer?"

"Silence." But there was fondness in her voice. She accepted the loud smacking kiss he blew her before she returned her attention to me. "We're not telling you anything until the boss comes back."

"You can't even tell me his name?" I kept my tone light, like I didn't care either way. The look she gave me, all eyebrows and pursed lips, told me I wasn't fooling anyone.

Her fratty boyfriend shrugged. "He-who-shall-not-be-named will be quite miffed if we did. You are still a threat to our whole operation. We usually eliminate threats."

My mouth went dry. It must've shown on my face because the kind guy with the sunflower bandana on his neck scooted over to the chair beside me. "You can call me Ry."

"Like the bread?"

"Sure." He grinned at me. He was like bottled sunshine, and I felt myself thawing on the inside. "And don't worry. We're not killers. Well, not...intentionally."

"What does that mean?"

Fratty boy leaned forward and laughed. "It means if you trip and, say, fall down the stairs, it's ruled as an accident."

"Oh." Funnily enough, that didn't inspire much confidence. I dragged my eyes to the large window at the head of the room. The sun was high, the green alien world thrown into bright technicolor. I could see the ocean on the horizon, a dark blue lip that was both taunting and comforting. I was losing precious hours. There were still the lower floors to search, plus the creepy basement. I shot a discreet glance at the chocolate-thief—I wanted my knife back. I felt naked without it.

Not moving won me some brownie points because when the leader returned, I was gifted the smallest of smiles. Well, it was more a grimace than anything, but I would take it. My stomach flipped like it did every time I looked at him. He was attractive in a roguish way, with his blond hair falling into his eyes, his two-day stubble, and his sharp, angular bone structure that made him look effortlessly intense, almost feral. He was a guy who didn't put people at ease, who probably had a foul temper and punched walls, and who never settled down. I imagined bringing someone like him home to my parents, just so they could combust in shame.

He didn't sit down again. "We're going to talk."

"Isn't that what we've been doing?"

His smile returned, a bitter imitation but still a vast improvement. "Alone," he said. He patted his pocket. "Come on. I need some fresh air."

Fresh air was apparently code for chain smoking. He led me to a nearby balcony just off one of the handful of sitting rooms and lit up a cigarette without saying a word. I wondered if it was some kind of obscure interrogation tactic—the longer he smoked, the more anxious I felt, the harder I stared at the purse of his lips as smoke curled between them.

Catching me in the act, he offered me one.

"Oh, no, thank you."

He snorted. "She doesn't smoke. Shocker."

"Is it?"

He leaned forward, bracing one elbow on the railing, and turned toward me. "You're clean," he said. "Prissy."

My mouth dropped open. "Excuse me?"

"Exactly." His grin was cocky and savage. I wanted to punch it.

I crossed my arms, and his eyes dropped to my chest shamelessly. *Prissy*, he said, but it didn't stop him checking out the goods. "You don't know anything about me."

"I'm good at reading people."

"Go on," I said, goading him. I knew it was a bad idea, like inviting the stalker into the house for tea. My instincts told me to run. His arrogant grin made me stay. "Give it your best shot."

He took the challenge, cerulean eyes raking over every inch of me. I didn't move, didn't blink, didn't even breathe.

"Money," he said. "Lots of it. Gated community. Trust fund, a big one." His brow quirked up tauntingly. "Prom queen."

My cheeks flushed. "Lucky guess."

"Not a virgin," he went on, blowing smoke in my face. "But not anything crazy in the sack. Probably fucked the same dude since high school. Jock type. Meathead."

I scrambled. "That's—"

"You want me."

My jaw clicked shut. It took a full minute to pry it open. "I do not."

"You do. You want me the same way a Stepford wife wants the barely legal pool boy. You want to earn the attention instead of it being handed to you."

I swallowed my retort, refusing to rise to the bait. I wanted to. God, I wanted to hiss and snarl and tear him to shreds.

Eager to prove him wrong, I stepped into his space and watched his eyes widen in surprise. I plucked the cigarette straight from his mouth.

"You forgot head cheerleader," I said sweetly, taking a hard drag. Truthfully, I did smoke occasionally, usually after a delightful dinner with my parents, so I didn't do something drastic, like set the house on fire. But I hadn't had a cigarette in a few weeks, and it showed. My throat burned. "So, what are you going to do with me?"

He recovered quickly, looking bemused. "What do you want me to do with you?"

I rolled my eyes. "Knock it off. It'll never work."

His answering grin was full of mischief. "Careful. That sounds like a challenge."

"Not in a million years."

He laughed and looked up at the sky, swiping his hair from his eyes. He went quiet for a moment, thinking.

"I have a proposal for you," he said, and my brain shorted, smoke clotting in my throat and making me cough.

Stupidly, my mind went to a fantasy of him on one knee. *Idiot. Not that kind of proposal.*

He fished out another cigarette and lit it up.

"What proposal?"

"I want to buy you."

"Are you—what the hell?" I choked again and decided the cigarette was too much of a hazard. I'd made my point anyway.

But when I tried to flick it away, his hand snapped out and caught my wrist. I watched in bewilderment as he stuffed the butt, still warm, into his back pocket.

"It's how it sounds," he said.

"Why did you just do that?" I waved my hand at his ass. It was a nice ass. Firm, muscular—*stop.*

He hesitated. "It's... nothing. Just a habit."

"Are you worried about DNA?" I knew that couldn't be the case since I was pretty sure he had already thrown up in the bathroom.

"I'm trying not to litter," he said, but he avoided my eye.

I laughed, because *what?* "How very eco-conscious of you."

"Fuck off," he groaned.

"Do you also recycle? Invest in renewable energy?"

His shoulders tightened defensively, and I knew I should stop. He wasn't someone you wanted to push too far.

He took a deep breath, tension bleeding away bit by bit.

"I'll be blunt," he said, sounding calm even as his hand tightened on the railing. "We work for a dangerous guy. He sent us here to steal a painting worth a hundred million."

"Okay," I said.

He looked at me expectantly. Was I supposed to be impressed? I shrugged. That much money was probably shocking to someone who didn't grow up like I did.

"We usually receive a portion of the loot. It's dependent on the big guy's mood, if he's feeling generous. Usually it's around ten percent."

He watched me for another beat. "Ten percent of a hundred million is ten million. We split the money between us after we launder it. Use what we need when we need it."

"Wait a second." My eyes bugged out as it finally sank in. "*You* are a millionaire?"

He smirked. "Didn't think we were in the same tax bracket?"

"Please. Like *you* pay taxes."

He laughed at that.

I snorted, exasperated by him. I returned his sweeping assessment with one of my own. "You look like you shop at the dollar store."

He shrugged. "So what if I do? Socks are socks."

I knew he wasn't someone who shopped ironically, not like the frat boy hipsters who thought it gave them an edge. I eyed him in a new light, the ripped jeans and thin black t-shirt that clung to his muscled torso like a second skin. His boots were so discolored it was hard to tell whether they were originally black or brown.

A traitorous part of me liked it.

He shifted closer, swiping back his hair when the wind blew it into his eyes again. When that failed, he shoved his skull bandana up and over his forehead, pinning back his hair and exposing the harsh plains of his face.

Damn.

I noticed the scars first, the tiny white lines that crossed his cheek, another dipping over his jaw line. His skin was tanned under the sun, but it didn't erase the tired bruises beneath his eyes. This was a guy who lived hard and played harder. It was hard not to feel intimidated.

"Why are you telling me all this?"

"I'm offering you a cut." He blew out a harsh plume of smoke. "I'll give you fifty grand, and you keep your pretty mouth shut. We never cross paths again."

"Why give me anything?" I asked, reeling. "You could just kill me. Not that I'm, like, vouching for that. It just seems suspicious."

"What, you don't trust me?"

I shot him a pointed look. He grinned again, his fingers toying idly with his cigarette. I couldn't help but notice his arms, the way his bicep flexed. There was ink scrawled on it. Callum. Was that his brother? A son?

"We don't kill people," he said evenly, damn near casually. "At least, not anyone who doesn't fuck with us first."

"How noble of you." I bit my lip, wondering why the hell I hadn't fled yet. He'd just admitted to killing people. Self-defense or not, his morals were clearly murky.

Instead, I asked: "So, then, what's the catch?"

"I just told you. You forget us. We forget you." At my dubious look, he rolled his eyes. "And she said she bribed a cop. You couldn't hurt a fly, princess. I'm surprised you made it this far."

Indignation swelled in my chest. I knew he was deliberately provoking me. Testing my reactions. He wasn't just flirting—he was unraveling me, trying to understand how I ticked. I took a calm, measured breath and gave him a cold look. Typically, that only made him grin wider. "I don't accept your terms, and I don't want your dirty money."

His grin didn't waver. If anything, he seemed unsurprised, like I'd just walked straight into his trap. "What do you want, then?"

I straightened my spine and made him wait while I considered my words carefully. He wanted to buy my silence and throw money at the problem. That was an average Tuesday in my social circles. I knew how to play the game.

The golden rule was never to show your interest. Never appear too keen. A person easily bought was just as easily conned.

"Salvadore is hiding something," I said. "I want you to help me find it."

He made a disagreeable sound. "I'd rather you take the money."

"I don't want or need it."

Smoke puffed harshly from his mouth as he considered it. "Fuck. Fine. I'll give you until sundown. But you hold whatever we find until my crew and I are in the wind. I don't want them anywhere near this dumpster fire."

"Deal." It took every morsel of my willpower not to preen like a fat cat.

My victory was pathetically brief.

"What will you give me?" he asked slyly, turning it around on me. And he called me a swindler.

"My silence."

"We both know I still hold the advantage," he said, licking his lips. Danger lurked in his eyes. "You're small and outnumbered. You have no power here. I could tie you up and leave you here. You'll stay silent that way."

I stared at him in disbelief. Despite his teasing tone, I knew he was dead serious.

"I'm good at knots," he added, like he couldn't help himself. His eyes dropped to my mouth. "And gags."

My face heated. "F-fine. What else do you want?"

His head tilted, considering it at length. I tried to see my worth through his eyes, but it was hard. He was right—I was at a disadvantage. He *could* very well tie me up and abandon me, or worse, shoot me. He practically oozed violence, and the feral look in his eyes unnerved me.

"So many things," he said slowly, heavily. "I'll let you know when I pick one."

That was unacceptable. "You can't just—"

"Times up."

I stuttered. "What? I—"

"We're burning daylight, princess. You want my help, you got it. I'm done with the foreplay."

'Foreplay?' I mouthed incredulously. He was unbelievable. My head was still reeling when he extended his hand. I stared at it dumbly. Eventually, he laughed and took my hand and placed it in his own for the world's limpest handshake.

When I realized what was happening, I snatched back my arm like he had an infectious disease. "I don't like you."

"I'll get over it." He turned to the doors, but I couldn't let him leave just yet, not when I felt so wrong-footed. I needed to tip the scales back in my favor. "Can I at least know your name? You know mine."

His grin bordered on filthy, like he knew exactly what I was doing. "You can call me Jax."

8

JAX

Damn.

That went better than I'd expected. I'd been gearing up for a fight, or at the very least a righteous speech about how stealing was bad, bad, bad. Not that Olivia struck me as particularly righteous, what with her petty thieving and trespassing. She just...surprised the hell out of me.

She was so prissy and perfect. It made me want to prove how bad I really was.

"I want my knife back," she said as she rushed to catch up to me. I liked that, too. Her following me, eager and helpless. I ignored her demands—more to keep pushing her buttons than anything—and was rewarded with another prissy huff at my back.

Callum was still at the door, hovering over Ryle without trying to be too obvious. Nate and Zola were locked in another foreplay match. Madoc was gone. So was the binder. Olivia clocked it with a frown and leveled accusing eyes on me. "Tell Count Chocula to keep his thieving hands to himself."

I frowned at her. "You mean Madoc?"

"Madoc." She made a face like she'd just swallowed something rotten. "That's the cretin."

"He wants your knife," I said, resisting the sudden urge to poke her cheek. I suspected she would bite me, just latch on like a furious chihuahua. "And I don't tell Madoc anything."

Madoc lived in a world of his own. Usually, it felt like a privilege just to be part of it.

"What's the verdict, boss?" Nate perked up in his chair, one arm slung over the back of Zola's. "We making it like the wind and blowing this crypt?"

"Not yet," I said, catching Callum's eye. "We made a deal."

Callum grinned and whispered something to Ryle, who snorted loudly into his hand. I shook my head at the pair of them. Morons, all of them. I glanced at my watch, the black face turned in on my wrist. "I want to be at the extraction point by nightfall. We'll set up camp on the beach. That gives us six hours to do what we need."

"What deal?" Zola asked, zeroing in on Olivia by my shoulder. I knew that look. That look meant I'd have a fight on my hands after all.

"Olivia won't talk," I explained bluntly. "In exchange, we'll help her dig up some dirt on Salvadore."

"Will we now?" Zola said, her eyes dangerous. I raised my brow at her tone. Her face was blank, leeched of any emotion. Nate shuddered beside her.

"Not now," I warned her.

Zola smiled coldly. "Fine." It wasn't a win. Just a temporary cease-fire. I knew I'd cop an earful later. "Since we're apparently bringing in outsiders, you should know the painting is a cover."

I frowned. "A cover for what?"

Her smile sharpened. Sometimes I forgot who she was before she joined my crew. Then she smiled like *that*, and my balls shriveled up into my stomach. "Go see for yourself."

That was how we ended up in Salvadore's office. Like the rest of the house, it was charmingly rustic, with panoramic windows on one side and floor-to-ceiling timber shelves on the other. A large, Narnia-style wardrobe stood next to the door, clearly antique and very expensive. But that wasn't the main attraction.

Fixed on the wall behind the large mahogany desk was our painting. It wasn't as large as I'd expected, though it was no motel art. It was also bright and abstract, and a bit of an eyesore compared to the rest of Salvadore's collection.

I found Madoc sitting cross-legged on the desk, looking up at it with the kind of rapt attention most would devote to their favorite soap. I was overly aware of Olivia, the unknown addition to our party, examining the bookshelves with the same level of attention.

My thighs hit the desk as I stood behind Madoc. "What's the verdict?"

"Ugly," Madoc said without turning. I leaned over his shoulder and saw him fiddling with Olivia's knife. It didn't bode well for her if he'd claimed it. "You threw up."

I reared back, abruptly self-conscious. Madoc turned his head and smirked at me. "Feel better?"

"I won't until we're gone."

"That could be a while." Madoc's gaze zeroed in on Olivia, who had turned away from the books and stood at the window looking out. I didn't blame him. She was nice to look at. The sun made her skin glow and found the streaks of copper in her hair. Her legs were something else. Long, shapely. Weapons in their own right. I forced myself to look away, straight into Madoc's cutting, glass-green eyes. The same weird heat boiled between us and, as usual, I backed out.

Zola bumped into me hard and pointed at the painting. "Go on. Take it down."

Callum did the honors. As soon as he lowered it gently to the floor, we stared, speechless, at the wall behind it. No, not the wall. *The safe.*

"Huh," Ryle said with a slow nod like it was exactly what he expected. "I guess he does have some secrets."

"It's digital," Zola said, even though we were all familiar with safes. In fact, we'd made a decent living from cracking them. I slanted her a look, and she met my eye smugly. "Waterproof, fire-resistant, pry-resistant with a three-strike lockout mechanism."

"So we need the code." Ryle started to root around the desk. "What are the chances he wrote it down on a sticky note?"

"Slim." Zola crossed her arms and leveled Olivia with a cold look when she wandered over. "He used a hundred-million-dollar painting as a cover. Whatever's inside is clearly very valuable. There's no way we can crack it in under six hours."

To her credit, Olivia didn't look perturbed. "I thought you guys were, like, professional burglars?"

"This isn't some spy movie," Zola scoffed, examining her claws. Us men in the room exchanged wary glances, gonads mutually retreating.

Clearly, Olivia didn't have the same instincts. She met sass with sass, cocking her hip against the desk. "Really? A band of thieves? A locked safe? A hundred million dollars? Seems pretty 007 to me."

"Bond girl," Nate whispered. He flinched back at Zola's dead-eyed glare.

"We don't just turn up and crack a safe, sweetie," Zola said, smiling. "It requires weeks of planning. Manufacturers' instructions. Meticulous background research on the mark."

A flush stained Olivia's cheeks at the patronizing tone.

Smelling blood, Zola went in for the kill. "But who am I to stop you? Please. Go ahead. You'll have three attempts before the lockout mechanism is triggered."

"How..." Olivia's voice cracked. She straightened, clearing her throat. "How long does the lockout last?"

"Could be a few hours," Zola said. "Could be days. It could also send an alert to the owner's phone. In fact, I'm certain it does."

Olivia's mouth twisted into a thoughtful frown. I half-expected her to burst into tears (Zola could make grown men cry), but Olivia proved once again that she wasn't predictable. She broke into a wide grin, appearing positively chuffed by the news. "He's definitely hiding something."

"It could be anything," I said, hating the way my gut twinged at dampening her happiness. *Buzz kill.* "It doesn't prove he kidnapped your sister."

"It might," Olivia said, practically bouncing on her toes. Then she noticed Madoc and her knife, and landed flat on her heels, her eyes storming over. "That's mine."

Madoc flipped the knife casually in his hand like a toy. "This old thing?"

"Give it back."

"Take it."

Olivia clearly possessed enough self-preservation not to rise to the challenge. I was still confused by Madoc's need to antagonize her. It was rare that he found anything remotely interesting enough to annoy to death. With a huff, Olivia joined Ryle and ripped open the drawers on the desk, sifting through paperwork and stationery with furious intent. Meanwhile, Callum, with a frosty Zola, carefully secured the painting in the hardshell casing used for transport. At least that was one problem solved.

I turned at the rustling noise behind me. Nate emerged from the wardrobe, looking disappointed. "No secret doors back here, boss." He hit the liquor cabinet next. "At least he drinks good whiskey."

"Bingo!" Olivia produced a sleeve of old receipts and waved it proudly above her head. She frowned at our lack of enthusiasm. "He keeps a paper trail. That's a good thing."

"I doubt he filed 'kidnapping' under goods and services," Ryle said, giving her a sympathetic smile. "It's probably just household stuff."

Olivia shrugged and tucked the sleeve under her arm, undeterred. "It's a start. Maybe he has a suspicious number of handcuffs and chloroform on back order."

"You know chloroform doesn't actually work," Ryle said, the fun fact of the day. "It's more likely to kill someone than knock them unconscious."

"Something tells me you're speaking from experience." The fact that Olivia only seemed mildly alarmed by the topic was surprising.

Ryle clicked his tongue in disappointment. "Nah, Jax won't let us experiment anymore after we blew up our first workshop."

Olivia's eyes widened. "Blew up?"

"Nate has a thing for explosives."

Nate raised his hand in proud admission when Olivia looked around, unsure which one of us hellraisers was

Nate. There hadn't been much time for introductions. I wanted to keep it that way. The last thing I needed was for any of them to get attached to her. It wasn't a problem for Madoc or Zola, but the others were giant suckers for a lost cause. I could already see the dumb look forming on Ryle's face, like when he found that old cat living under the porch steps.

Olivia was certainly proving she had claws. "Where is my binder?" She glared at Madoc, unmoved by the weapon he wielded as effortlessly as a dinner fork. I'd seen him spear targets from a hundred feet away. Olivia didn't know that.

I hoped she wouldn't find out.

In response to her question, Madoc simply smiled. It was chillingly cold, vacant behind the eyes. It only made her glare intensify. "Seriously," she huffed. "What is your problem?"

Madoc remained silent. Olivia sighed in annoyance and turned to me with flushed cheeks. "Can't you take away his toys or something?"

"I'd rather keep my fingers attached, thanks."

Olivia looked on the verge of stomping her foot. On top of being stubborn as hell and easily corrupted, she was also kind of bratty. A total princess. It shouldn't appeal to me as much as it did. It shouldn't make me want to pull on her hair and watch the flush spread all the way down her chest. Madoc was doing enough of that on his own.

The realization stopped me cold.

Madoc *was* pulling on her hair. Figuratively, at least. He was riling her up, getting under her skin. It made my chest tight and jealous as all fuck.

Whatever expression crossed my face had Ryle honing in like an emotional support wasp. "Jax? You okay?" Before I could utter a response, my throat dry as sand, he stepped around the desk and eyed me up close in concern. "Is it your stomach again? I told you that sandwich had a weird look about it. Never trust airport tuna."

"I'm fine."

"You're sweating, dude."

"And you're fussing." I patted his cheek and shoved him away in the same motion. Then I pushed back my hair—it was pretty sticky—and addressed the room. "Listen up. We do a full sweep of the mansion. Buddy system. No one goes anywhere on their own."

"There are seven of us now, Jax," Zola reminded me sweetly. "Who gets stuck with the spare?"

Olivia frowned and then scoffed a second too late when she realized what Zola meant. "*I'm* the spare? You guys hijacked *my* mission. I was here first."

I slapped my hand on the desk before Zola could retaliate. "Olivia is with Madoc and me," I said, though it might as well have been a declaration of war from the betrayed look that crossed Zola's face. "We have a deal. You don't have to like it."

The way Zola withdrew into herself made it very clear that she didn't.

"And the safe?" Olivia asked, chewing her lip. "Three attempts, right? I know his birthday."

"It's never so obvious, lass," Callum said. "Let us find his skeletons. They'll be here somewhere. That might give us a better idea."

We all knew it was a long shot. Men like Salvadore were too smart and far too devious to be caught with their pants down. Anything illegal was likely iron-clad, offshore, and untraceable. The fact that Olivia had managed to find anything at all on him, even if it was mostly conjecture, was impressive.

That didn't mean anything would stick. And even if by some miracle it did, men like Salvadore with power and wealth didn't just fold. They fought back. They crushed the little guy. Obliterated the enemy.

Olivia had no idea what she was up against. Or how much she still had to lose.

9

OLIVIA

The full sweep took less than an hour and yielded some surprising—and disturbing—results.

I'd just started to feel disheartened by the lack of anything incriminating (and I even dug through his literal underwear) when Madoc opened a random door at the back of the utility room and made a soft "aha" sound that immediately put me on edge.

Madoc was a piece of work. I hated him more than I hated my neighbor Donovan, who found excuses to loiter around the fenceline whenever I was in the pool. I knew I wasn't the most likable person on the planet—I was no Molly, after all—but Madoc's icy demeanor felt personal.

All of that vanished the moment I peered around Madoc and into the secret room. It was too dark to see much, but the location was pretty suspicious. My heart thumped at the possibilities. Was this the room where he kept Molly? A shiver wracked through my body, and I knew Madoc felt it because his head snapped toward me.

"Calm down," he said flatly.

"I am," I lied. "So calm. The calmest."

Madoc rolled his eyes like I was being overdramatic. God, I hated him. The surge of anger I felt toward him was welcoming, a grounding force that I latched onto like a lifeline.

Jax pressed behind me. "Wait here. We'll go in first."

I scoffed. "You've got to be kidding me."

His hand latched onto my wrist in a bruising hold. "It could be bugged. A trap."

"Or a place to store detergent."

Then Jax was rolling his eyes. With pathetic ease, he pulled me away from the door to stand behind him. "We don't just run headlong into the unknown," he said, as if lecturing a toddler who wanted to jam a fork into the electrical socket. "Madoc will go first." I opened my mouth, but he cut me off: "It's not a sex dungeon."

My eyes bulged. Jax's mouth flattened in amusement as he tapped his ear. Right. The earpieces. I forgot he was communicating with the rest of his crew. I was hideously out of the loop and only got snippets of information. I tugged on my arm, still caught in his grip. "What sex dungeon? Who said that?"

"Scooby," Jax said with another eye roll. Who the hell was Scooby?

Movement caught my eye as Madoc lifted his shirt, exposing pale tattooed skin across his lower back, and removed a gun from his waistband. Of course he was armed. He didn't need my knife. He just wanted to screw with me.

He walked confidently into the darkness, and I viciously hoped it was a trap and it involved something sharp and pointy.

Jax gave me one last warning look before he followed.

What felt like an hour went by without a signal, so I crept to the door and squinted into the darkness. Tall shapes moved within, and for a heart-stopping second, I thought there were more than two of them. Then I heard a switch flick, and sinister red light filled the room.

"Oh," I said. The one word stole my remaining air.

Lo and behold, it was a sex dungeon.

The walls were painted black, hosting various tools like paddles and whips, and leather handcuffs. One side of the room had a wall-length mirror and an elevated platform with an honest-to-god stripper pole. The furniture, ultra-masculine leather, and low pine wood tables, were facing the stage like a high-end private strip club. There was a small bar in the back corner, the red light coming from a bright neon sign above that spelled 'Sinners'.

I didn't realize I was making any sort of noise until Jax was standing in front of me, gripping my chin and wrenching my face up to him. "It's just a playroom," he said.

Just a playroom? I blinked at him owlishly. I didn't think I was a sheltered little lamb, but the way he said it, like it was inconsequential, like it was *normal*, made me question myself. Did most people have a playroom? Was I too vanilla? Should I know what that long, curved rod with the bristles was used for?

"I'm…" I started, but stopped. I didn't know what to say. My stomach was full of withering snakes. Not fear, exactly, but something in that family for sure.

Jax's fingers flexed on my face. "You're panicking."

"Am I?" My voice was high and reedy.

"It doesn't mean what you think," he said, and I wished he would tell me what I was thinking, why I was panicking. "Come on, princess. You grew up in this world. Don't tell me you've never seen a playroom before."

"Do *you* have one?" I wasn't sure where that came from. I wanted to stuff the question back into my mouth.

His answering grin made my mouth dry. Hot, calloused fingers tapped my chin like a taunt. "I've been around," he said, and how was my poor brain supposed to compute that? "There's no shame in it. It doesn't mean he kidnapped your sister and brought her here."

I recoiled like a slap. He'd put words to the tight pressure in my chest. I was thinking about Molly, imagining her on the stage, forced to perform against her will. Then I looked at Jax and considered what he said. *No shame.*

"It's just a playroom," I repeated quietly, needing to give truth to the words. Meaning. "He's just a nice, normal sex deviant who wants to be paddled."

"Exactly." Jax's teeth flashed red. He stepped back and glanced at Madoc, who was examining the whips with a curious tilt of his head. Jax looked away jerkily. There was definitely color on his face now.

Interesting.

"We'll sweep the room," Jax said, back to business. He gave me a considering look. "You can wait outside if you want."

But I didn't want that. Not anymore. The panic was ebbing away, replaced by a new curiosity. I pushed past him and beelined straight for the stage and the wall-length mirror behind it. My reflection was demonic in the red light, but I could see how it could be appealing. It sharpened my edges, highlighted my cheekbones and lips, and deepened the natural copper in my hair. My white linen shirt turned pink and nearly transparent on my frame. I could see the outline of my underwear, the slight swell of my lower belly, and the cradle of my rib cage above my hips.

Behind my reflection, I saw Jax watching me. Madoc was lurking at the bar, messing around with the bottles before ducking out of sight. I became overly aware of them in the room, *this* room, full of sex toys and stale desire.

On a whim, I stepped up onto the platform. I didn't touch the pole (who knew how often it was wiped down), but I circled it slowly, feeling a strange sense of power overcome me. I'd never considered stripping, and evidently, I was *way* too sheltered to ever dabble in the bedroom. But I could see it suddenly. The flashing lights and body glitter and thumping music. I eyed the pole consideringly—I had the core strength to work it, thanks to my cheer regimes.

Madoc popped up suddenly behind the bar like a jump scare, and I was wrenched out of my daydream. Our eyes locked, and Madoc's widened just slightly. It was the most expressive I'd seen him so far, and it was gone so quickly that I thought I had imagined it.

Jax stepped toward me with a predatory expression. He didn't even try to pretend he wasn't eyefucking me to death. I flashed hot all over, that same tingly power turning my brain to mush.

"Go on then," Jax goaded.

Insecurity and a little bit of fear stopped me in my tracks. "I already said you can't buy me."

"I'm not about to start flinging singles." He approached the stage at a saunter. My heart thumped with renewed fear. "We both know you don't have what it takes."

I knew what he was doing, and I wouldn't buckle. I wouldn't play his game.

"Guess not."

He didn't look surprised, or even that disappointed, which bothered me. "Get down, then. It's just mean."

"*You're* mean." It was a childish retort, and I wasn't proud of it. Mulishly, I shuffled to the edge. By then, he'd reached me, and instead of stopping, his boots thunked hard into the stage and made me stumble. I gripped the pole for balance.

Ew, ew, ew.

"Asshole," I spat at him.

"Priss," he shot back.

Then his hands snapped out and grabbed my waist, lifting me to the floor. I was used to being flung around, thrown into the air, tossed and tumbled, but it had never made my stomach swoop so violently.

It never made my toes tingle.

"There's nothing here," he said, smirking at whatever dumb expression I failed to hide. "Scooby?"

I heard no reply, but Jax's face suddenly darkened. "You did what?"

Madoc prowled toward us, his expression blank as always, even though I knew he was also listening to whatever was happening over their communications. When he neared, I swallowed my anger enough to ask: "Who is Scooby?"

Madoc waited a beat, then turned toward me, his own eyes like pitiless black holes. He belonged in the shadows, but he was downright sinful in the red light. "Guess," he smirked.

The anger surged up like word vomit. "God, can't you just—"

"Shut up," Jax snapped, pressing a finger to his ear, trying to listen. "No, not you," he said a beat later as he turned away. "Fine. Meet us back in the war room."

Jax stormed out, pausing at the door just long enough to shoot me an impatient glare when I took too long to follow. Whatever had happened had turned him into a broody thundercloud. I treaded carefully as we returned to the utility room and through to the service corridor. When we came to the spiral staircase, I stared down into the basement, stomach clenching.

Apparently, Jax's crew had already searched it and found nothing. I was both relieved and disappointed.

When all else failed, I was counting on the basement to give me some answers. So far, all I had was an uncrackable safe and a bunch of receipts that were definitely useless.

I was running out of time.

The others were already seated at the dining table when we walked in, their voices dropping to a hush. I was surprised to see various items in the center of the table, like they'd shaken out the pockets of the mansion itself.

Jax took the head spot but didn't sit. His shoulders were bunched tight near his ears. Like him, I was also too restless to sit, so I leaned against the wall by the door. Madoc stood on the opposite wall, watching me with his unfathomable eyes. Slowly, without breaking his intense gaze, the bastard took out my knife and flipped it lazily in his hand.

It was the giant red head, Callum, who broke the silence. "Playroom that bad, huh? What did the old dog have in there?"

Jax waved his hand dismissively. "Nothing. Standard shit. Nate?"

I almost missed the way Nate flinched, head bowing, hair falling into his eyes. When he didn't speak, Madoc kicked the back of his chair hard. Nate went rigid, as if hit by an electric shock. "I found merch."

Merch?

"Drugs," Jax supplied automatically. He wasn't looking at me.

My stomach clenched. That wasn't what I expected. A grim tension filled the room. Then Zola snorted, breaking it.

"Relax. It's not heroine," she said with an eye roll. She was holding a tablet and tapping away on it distractedly. "It's a drug called Montroploze. It was used to treat severe insomnia and anxiety before it got banned. Dangerous side effects."

"Let me guess." Ryle's smile was a little strained as he tried to lighten the mood. "Anal bleeding? It's always anal bleeding."

"Actually, no," Zola said. "More like memory loss, psychosis, temporary paralysis. And that's just page one."

"Where did you find it?" I asked, my voice breathy with a hope that I couldn't squash.

Zola looked at me dead-eyed. "In his medicine cabinet. Where else?"

"How much did you find?"

Zola used her finger to push a small, clear vial across the table. "Single use," Zola said. My heart sank. For a moment, it felt like *something*, but I knew I was probably grasping at straws. I eyed the rest of the items: a shopping list, some books, a long cord with weird prongs at the end—a whip, I realized with a flush, my eyes automatically bouncing to Madoc, the whip inspector. I felt a bolt of awareness when I found him still looking at me. Smiling that unnerving smile.

He was definitely unhinged.

Zola spoke again, thankfully drawing my attention. She waved a tablet in front of her. "Found this squashed between a sofa cushion on the top floor. Dumbo here thought it was a high-tech TV remote."

Nate grinned dopily at the nickname. He must be Scooby.

"Well, what is it?" Jax asked, leaning forward, his hands braced on the table. I tried not to ogle his muscled forearms or the swell of his impressive biceps.

"It might as well be a remote," Zola said, clacking her nails across the screen. "I managed to override his password, but so far I've found nothing but porn, online shopping browsers, and some calendar reminders to take his medication."

Awareness zapped up my spine. "Is that drug on it? The Monopoly one?"

"No," Zola said with a derisive look. "It's not prescribed to him. It's more like a free sample, the kind pharmaceutical companies push on GPs."

"Were there any others?" Jax asked, clearly directed at Nate.

He jolted again, shooting Madoc a nervous look over his shoulder. Madoc bared his teeth in warning. "N-No. Just some painkillers and old heart pills." Nate hesitated, clearly wary. "I was just being thorough, Jax. I wasn't...I wasn't looking for anything. Honest."

Jax stared at him for a long minute, not saying anything. It didn't seem to matter because Nate cringed and hunkered down in his chair like a scolded school boy. His eyes were bloodshot, his skin somehow both pale and splotchy.

Jax sighed and rubbed his forehead as if warding off a headache. Gone was the playful deviant. He'd slipped back into the role of grouchy leader with a short fuse. Weirdly enough, I wanted the deviant back.

Forcing myself to look away from him, I spotted my backpack slung over the back of Callum's chair. I reached for it eagerly, surprising the big man who leaned forward so I could slip it off. My fingers groped the pockets, and I breathed a sigh when I felt the hard ridge of my phone.

At least Madoc hadn't confiscated that.

Returning to the wall, I discreetly opened the hidden zip and glanced at my phone. With a soft tap of my finger, the screen lit up. *Two missed calls.*

Shit. I'd missed check-in. I needed to call him back before everything went to hell. I needed—

A rush of air, and a knife embedded in the wall by my head.

I cried out and ducked instinctively. My eyes searched the room and landed on the slow, pleased smile that slithered over Madoc's face.

The asshole had thrown a knife at me?

My knife?

"What's in the bag, princess?" he purred.

The room watched tensely.

"You're a psychopath!" I hissed, straightening. The knife had struck mere inches from my ear. I glanced at Jax in disbelief. He just looked amused, like we were putting on a dinner show. This evening's entertainment—my brain splattered on the wall.

"It's nothing," I spat at Madoc, who started to advance. I tried not to cringe into the wall like a cornered animal. "You already took everything."

Madoc stopped in front of me. Venomous green eyes searched my face. Then he shrugged, like he didn't care either way, and reached up to pluck the knife from the wall.

Was this all just a game to him?

I clutched my backpack tightly and spun to the door. "Bathroom," I shot at Jax, not caring if he approved or not. No one stopped me, so I figured I was safe and fled to the furthest bathroom I could find.

As soon as the door locked shut behind me, I took out my phone and returned the call.

"Olivia. Finally." His warm, British accent was music to my ears.

I sagged in relief. "Preacher." My heart twisted, tears prickling at my eyes. "You are not going to believe who I found."

10

JAX

The pain in my head was relentless.

It felt like shards of glass were stabbing into the backs of my eyes. The cherry on top was the roiling nausea, the tuna-sandwich returning for an unwanted sequel.

My patience was razor fucking thin.

"There's nothing else here," Ryle was saying, his tone bordering on a whine. I was impressed that his attention span had lasted this long. "We've looked everywhere. Whatever he's hiding—*if* he's hiding anything—it's probably in the safe or kept off-site."

"I agree," Zola said, unsurprisingly. "This is a giant waste of our time. We've done our part. It's time to lie low and forget this weird crusade."

I grunted and jammed my knuckle into my throbbing eye. "Is that how you all feel?"

There was an incomprehensible murmur. I blinked hard and focused on each of them. Nate was avoiding my gaze, Callum was suspiciously quiet, and Madoc was staring at the doorway where Olivia had fled moments ago. Whether they admitted it or not, they were rattled. The mansion *was* freakishly clean. There were no photographs on the walls, no certificates or sentimental tokens to Salvadore's name. Everything was so impersonal that you'd be forgiven for believing it was a giant setup. A trap. Hiding the real operation somewhere behind it.

I wasn't one for conspiracy theories. I was practical, relying on hard facts. We had nothing on Salvadore, just a kink room, a safe, and a possible drug problem. But I relied on my gut as well, even when it was acting up like a fucking asshole.

I turned to Callum. "Tell me to leave."

Callum grimaced. "We should. Whole fucking place has me hackles up." He rapped his knuckles hard on the table. "Rooms are sterile. Even the staff quarters are clean. Old dog runs his house like a military camp."

As a disgraced Royal Marine, Callum would know. He scratched distractedly at the giant anchor tattoo across his forearm.

Next, I turned to Madoc, who appeared lost in thought. Then his hands stilled on Olivia's knife. "She's not working alone."

My gut twisted. "What do you mean?"

"She has a benefactor," Madoc said, returning his intense gaze to the doorway as if it were enough to summon her back. "Someone fed her the information to get her here."

"So they took advantage of a sad girl," Zola said, dropping the tablet on the table with a resigned *thunk*. "It's a dick move, but it's not our problem. Salvadore probably has enemies far and wide."

"You think it's a setup?" I asked Madoc. He knew the true gravity of my question and its implications. Madoc was a predator in his own right. He could slip into the minds of monsters and not lose himself, at least not where anyone could see it. He was rarely wrong, which was why he took his time to respond. He considered his words carefully.

One word and we'd blow the place to smithereens.

"Yes," Madoc said. "And no."

Callum snorted. "Unambiguous as always, lad."

Madoc ignored him, his mind a thousand miles away. I knew it was a fragile system and didn't want to interrupt, even if my headache was quickly eating up my patience.

Finally, Madoc tilted his head, coming to a decision. "She is meant to be here," he said, holding the knife to his face and examining it affectionately. "I don't believe in coincidences. We want to rob him, she wants to ruin him. It seems our interests are aligned. And so are those of our overlords."

"What are you saying exactly?" Zola asked with a suspicious frown.

Madoc smiled. "What if it's the same overlord?"

"Dr. Z?" I frowned at him. That couldn't be true.

"Either him, or someone in direct competition. A new player." Madoc's eyes snapped up as we heard footsteps approaching. "Meet the new recruit."

When Olivia walked in, the room was silent, and everyone swiveled toward her, unblinking. She hesitated, one hand twisting the strap of her backpack. "What's going on?" she asked nervously, looking at me. "Did you find something?"

"Not yet." I shot Madoc a hard look. He returned it, unsmiling. "Alright, fuck it. We'll do another sweep, be more thorough this time."

"How thorough?" Olivia asked.

"Crawlspaces and vents," I said. "Everything but the foundation."

Ryle jerked to his feet and hefted his pack onto the table. "First, a small recharge. I can't hear anything over Cal's stomach. Here." He tossed two protein bars and a packet of granola at me. "Sharing is caring," he said, shooting a meaningful look at Olivia.

A swell of gratitude rose in my chest. I could see the renewed determination on their faces—Zola even picked up the tablet again, laser focused on the screen—taking Madoc's words to heart. If Olivia were working for Dr. Z or someone in direct competition, it was better to keep her close. Find out what we could. Prepare for the worst, hope for the best.

"Come," I said, and like an eager little lamb, she followed me back to the balcony.

It was cooler than before, with the sun partially obscured by a new formation of greyish clouds. I didn't like the look of them, even if the fresh wind felt heavenly on my feverish skin. I breathed it in while Olivia watched me in bemusement.

"You're actually getting fresh air this time," she said at my questioning look. "I thought it was code for smoking."

"It can be both."

I started on the granola as Olivia beelined to the patio furniture and tried to arrange the chairs closer together. I watched her struggle for a moment, trying not to laugh, and then I leaned over and dragged them toward me one-handed.

Her eyes widened, lingering on the bulge of my arm. "Show off," she said. "Here I was convinced they were just show muscles."

I flexed, and she purposely looked away, but not before I caught the faint flush on her cheeks. I wasn't usually a show-off, but for some reason, she brought it out in me. I wanted to go full caveman on her, grunt and beat my chest like a silverback gorilla.

"Were you talking about me before I walked in?" she asked as she sat delicately in the chair and crossed her legs. This wasn't a tea party, so I purposely sat too close to her, knocking my knee into hers.

"Yes." I grinned at her answering glare.

"I knew it," she said crossly. "It reminded me of high school."

"Poor misunderstood prom queen."

She bristled, like I knew she would. But she regained her composure, leaned back, and hugged her knees to her chest. Her skin was so smooth, so unmarred by scars or tattoos. She probably had the same ridiculous skin care routine as Nate.

"Something tells me you didn't finish high school," she said, all snooty.

"You calling me stupid?"

"Am I wrong?"

"About me being stupid? No. About high school? Half yes."

"What does that mean?

I ripped open the protein bars and handed her one. "I got my GED in prison."

She inspected the bar with a vaguely disgusted look before my words clicked, and she blanched. "You were incarcerated?"

"Well, I wasn't there for meatloaf Mondays."

"No, I mean, yes, obviously. I'm just...surprised." She blinked at me owlishly. "I've never met an ex-con before."

"Technically, you've met three."

"What?" Her eyes went impossibly wide, still holding out the protein bar like a dirty sock. "Who else?"

"Not my story to tell. Eat before it melts."

She made another face before she took a tentative bite and chewed like she expected it to bite her back. "Huh."

"Meathead boyfriend never shared his protein?"

"Ex-boyfriend. And Heath isn't a meathead."

I choked. "*Heath?* Fuck, you can't make this up."

She flushed again but finished the bar and stared at her sticky fingers in distress. After a minute, she gave me a defiant look and wiped her hand on my shoulder. I made a point of licking my fingers clean before reaching for my cigarettes.

"Are you going to tell me what you did?" she asked tightly, like she hated that she was curious. Or maybe she was scared. I considered lying, pretending I did something truly egregious, just to get her riled up.

Then my head throbbed, as if punishing me for my impure thoughts. Better not push it. "I punched a cop."

"That's all?"

"I had priors. Petty thieving, grand larceny. Got me two years inside because the judge didn't like the look of me."

"That's understandable." She smirked at me. "Bet you wore sweatpants to court and, like, hit on the jury or something."

I pressed my hand to my chest. "You have such a low opinion of me. I've been nothing but nice to you."

"You've been everything *but* nice," she said with an eye-roll.

"Do you—" I cut off with a hiss. My head exploded; the pain was so sharp that I was convinced my brain was oozing out of my ears. I slammed my eyes shut, riding it out.

Vaguely, I heard the sound of a chair scraping back, then a soft hand settled gently on my forearm.

"Are you okay?"

Gritting my teeth, I squinted up at her, where she was suddenly standing over me. "Need a minute."

"Can I try something?"

"Unless it's a bullet, don't bother."

"Not a bullet," she said with a cute tinkling laugh. The sound didn't make my headache worse, which was surprising. The others knew to steer clear of me when I was suffering like this. I usually craved silence.

I didn't want her to be quiet. I wanted her to laugh again. I wanted—

Suddenly, delicate hands landed on my shoulders. I tensed automatically, which didn't help the pressure cooker in my skull. "What are you doing?"

"Helping." She sounded so confident, so sure of herself. I allowed it for no other reason than I was already in Hell. What more could she do to me?

Then she started rubbing me, digging her thumbs in the valley between my shoulder blades. It was phenomenal. Fucking biblical. A guttural groan punched out of me, my head rolling forward at the exquisite pressure release. Her gentle breath brushed the back of my neck.

"Jeez, you're so tight."

"I live with morons."

She laughed quietly. Mindfully. My chest cracked a little. "You should stretch more," she said. "I learned that lesson the hard way. Your body will snap like a rubber band if you don't." She paused, then added: "Not that you'll listen to me, of course."

"Keep doing that, and I'll sell you my soul." Or whatever was left of it.

Her tiny, glorious hands worked their way down my back, unknotting my spine, rearranging my very core. Unbelievably, the pain in my head started to ease, allowing other sensations to surface. Like the throbbing between my legs.

I shifted, trying to adjust without alerting her to the fact that a twenty-second massage had me popping a boner like a preteen. I didn't want her to stop. Pretty sure I'd start begging if she did.

She returned to my shoulders and started on my neck. That shitty motel mattress had done a number on it, which spoke volumes about how precious I'd become. Gone were the days when I could sleep rough on the sidewalk or park bench; those volatile years when anywhere was better than home.

Then her fingers brushed the crow tattoo behind my ear, and I stiffened for a whole different reason. She lingered, not rubbing but examining, tracing its shape. "It really *is* you..." she breathed.

I reacted like a spring trap. My hand locked on her wrist, the bones so delicate that I fought the urge to snap her like a twig. I tugged her forward harshly, so she had no choice but to bend over my shoulder, her breath hitching in shock.

"What do you mean it's *really me?*"

Her hair tickled my cheek as she spluttered: "N-nothing, really. I've just, um, heard about you."

Madoc was right.

"You mean you lied."

"What? No!" She started to struggle, trying to free her wrist, but all it did was press her body against my back. I was still hard as rock, which was annoying but not un-expected. I had more rage boners than normal ones and knew it wouldn't go down until I beat it like it owed me money. "You're hurting me," she complained.

"Who have you been talking to?"

"Lots of people!" She snapped. "You think I just stum-bled across everything in my binder? I had to get cre-ative. Find some shady characters with access to shady networks."

Like the dark web. That made sense. Most of our scores were sold on the black market, and our reputation was known among the sordid circles who funded it. Still, I didn't like it. Not one fucking bit.

I snapped to my feet and shoved her hard against the glass doors. The frame shuddered dangerously. For a second, I imagined pressing her against it for an entirely different reason, and the answering throb in my cock only heightened my anger.

"Jax—"

"No." I reached up and gripped her ponytail tight in my fist, using it to wrench her face up towards mine. She liked to hide, but I wouldn't accept that shit. "Did you know we were going to be here?"

She made a pained noise, but her eyes were burning with defiance. "Of course not."

"Convince me."

"Fuck you."

My grin was menacing, and I knew she regretted those words when her face paled dramatically. "Is that what you really want, princess?"

"I—no."

I snarled as I used her ponytail to turn her head sideways and pressed into her body. Her eyes widened at the jut of my erection, followed by a beautiful flush that spread all the way down her neck. "So predictable," I growled, dragging my lips over her ear. "Uptight little rich girl wants to be fucked by the trash."

Oliva bristled and tugged uselessly at my fist in her hair. "Let. Me. Go." Her mouth said one thing, her body something else. "Now." She was arching toward me, her hips seeking mine before she wrenched herself backward. Her glare was an added aphrodisiac. She wanted to murder me, and God, I wanted to let her try.

But I didn't trust her. And I sure as shit wasn't about to let her get under my skin.

"No more lies." I gave her hair a final warning tug. "Do it again, princess, and I'll kill you. Put my crew in danger, and I'll take my time with it."

She went still. Her lashes fluttered, tears dampening them beautifully. "I'm here for Molly," she said. "That's it. Don't put your trust issues on me. I've been nothing but transparent. *You've* been shady as hell."

"I'm the bad guy, princess. Shady comes with the territory."

Her jaw clicked shut. She glared and cried and promised vengeance with her eyes, and I almost kissed her. Instead, I released my grip and took a step back. She immediately sagged in relief, then turned to the doors, opening them with a violent snap.

Of course, she had to have the last word. "Touch me like that again, Jax, and I'll dig up every dirty skeleton you have."

It was only once I was alone that I realized my headache was gone.

11

OLIVIA

I was done.

Done with distractions. Done with pointless war rooms. Done with Jax. And I was definitely done with Madoc.

Unfortunately, he wasn't done with me.

"I want my binder back," I demanded as I stormed into the main bedroom on the top floor, where Madoc was doing God-knows-what. He was standing at the foot of the massive king bed, head cocked like the answers to the universe were stitched into the duvet. He didn't react to my entrance—not even a twitch—and I was starting to suspect he was some sub-human cyborg, unfeeling and unattached. Here for the kicks and nothing else.

Very slowly, he straightened. "Why?" His soft, inflectionless tone made me bristle. God, between him and Jax, I was at risk of developing a stomach ulcer. Or worse, frown lines.

Then why are you turned on?

I wasn't. I couldn't be.

I was, and I hated myself more than I ever had. Jax was an unhinged boiling pot of issues, and I shouldn't be fixating on the way his eyes had flashed electric blue, or the way his muscles had bunched tight across his ridiculous shoulders, or the way he'd pinned me to the glass, the hard jut of his erection...

I shook my head, banishing the thoughts. He threatened to kill me, and I knew he meant it. Just like I knew he would enjoy it because he *was* a bad guy, and somewhere I'd forgotten that.

I suspected Madoc was even worse.

"It's mine," I reiterated firmly, crossing my arms. "You have no right to keep it."

His cheek lifted in a smirk. "Finders keepers."

"Are you five?"

He angled his head toward me, so I was stuck glaring at his side profile, the slope of his cheek, and the smiling curve of his jaw, the dark hair that curled behind his heavily pierced ears. He had stretchers, and I wanted to find them repulsive, but I didn't. My brain was working against me, and I needed to get it back on track.

"What happened?" He asked, sounding amused. "Did the bad man hurt you?"

That *would* make him happy. "Don't try to distract me."

"You're crying. It's distracting."

I wiped my eyes harshly with my sleeve. "The deal is off. I want my binder back. And my knife. Take your stupid painting and leave."

"No."

My mouth dropped in outrage. "No?"

"No," he repeated softly. I was about to lose it. Before I could do something extreme, like a repeat performance of lamp javelin, he added: "You were right."

My mind went blank.

It was the last thing I expected him to say. "Right about what?" I asked warily.

"Him."

My temper flared back to life. "Jesus fucking Christ. Can you break character for just a minute and finish a whole sentence?"

That made him laugh.

Again, my brain stuttered in shock, not expecting it. It was a rough sound, not at all comforting, like it'd been scraped up from somewhere forgotten inside him.

He gestured to the bed, and my stupid brain latched onto it like an invitation. I planted my feet and clenched my fists, not trusting myself. "What's wrong with this pic-ture?" he asked, like a game.

"I don't know."

"Try."

I huffed, fully aware I was being distracted. "The night-stands are empty. And the bed was perfectly made before you assaulted me on top of it."

He happily ignored that. "What else?"

"I don't know. The pillows clash with the curtains?"

He glanced down at me, lip quirking up in a ghostly smile. I hadn't realized I'd come to stand next to him and purposely stepped back. "There is no art in here."

I glanced around, noting he was right. "So?"

"There's space for it," he said, pointing at the sizeable patch of wall above the huge headboard. "Every other room has one except this one."

"Okay, Sherlock. What does that tell us?"

"He doesn't sleep in here."

I frowned, not buying it. Madoc rolled his head with an unnerving crack, like he was about to deliver a final blow. I scanned his tattoos quickly—he had the same crow as Jax but bigger, wrapped around his equally impressive bicep. "All his clothes are in here," I said, wrenching my eyes back to the bed. "And his toiletries. Why would he use the bathroom but not the bed?"

"Gold star for Watson."

"Maybe he has a fear of heights," I deliberated, chewing on my lip, breaking the skin. Blood welled on my tongue, and I licked at it absently. "We're on the top floor. There are seven other bedrooms, plus the lower staff quarters, not that he'd likely choose them—what are you doing?"

Madoc had stepped into my space, his eyes so dark they held my white-faced reflection. He stared at my mouth intently. "Show me," he demanded in a quiet, deadly voice.

I froze. "S-Show you what?"

His intensity didn't waver. "Open your mouth."

Fear-dumb, I did. His jaw clenched, and his nostrils flared, his eyes flat and furious and terrifying. Then his own tongue snaked out, a silver ball piercing catching on his top teeth with a gentle click. Like a demented vampire, he stared at my bloody lip like he wanted to devour it—

Just as suddenly, he snapped out of it, turning away so abruptly that I was left standing, open-mouthed, like an idiot.

What the hell was that?

While my brain caught up, I heard the creak of floorboards, and then Ryle bustled in. "Hey—oh." He stopped short, looking between Madoc and me like he'd caught us with our pants down. I felt as mortified as if he had.

Ryle grinned impishly. "What's happening in here?"

"Nothing," I said too quickly. Typically, Madoc stayed silent.

"Riiiiiight," Ryle drawled, wriggling his eyebrows. "Then why do I have total FOMO right now?" He looked meaningfully at Madoc, who returned his gaze blankly.

Clearly used to Madoc's brand of apathy, Ryle turned his attention back to me. "Cool, well, I'm just going to ignore the weird as fuck tension in here and tell you that Zola found something."

I straightened. "What did she find?"

"You have to come downstairs."

That made me tense. Downstairs meant seeing Jax, and I wasn't ready to confront him yet. Not with my chest so tight and my legs so wobbly and my nipples so achingly hard that they were at risk of chafing.

For the first time in a long time, I missed Heath. For no other reason than that he made me feel safe, normal, and in control. Not enough to ever go back to him—I didn't hate myself that much—but at least I could count on myself not to act so stupidly helpless.

Movement in my periphery made me snap into hyper-awareness, but it was just Madoc heading to the door. He left without so much as a backward glance.

Dick.

Left alone with Ryle, I felt awkward again and smoothed down my ponytail (Jax had utterly destroyed it). He watched me unabashedly, head cocked like a puppy.

"Can't you just tell me what she found?" I whined a little.

"You avoiding Jax?"

A bit helpless, I nodded.

Ryle nodded like he understood perfectly. "Yeah, he's a super intense guy. Not as bad as Madoc, though, so good luck with that."

I blinked at him. "What?"

Ryle nodded again and kept nodding. He was practically vibrating with energy. "Don't worry about Jax. He can be a giant asshole sometimes, but he's got a squishy center underneath all that angry muscle. You just have to be patient with him."

"I want nothing to do with him."

His head kept bobbing. "Smart."

I watched him curiously, and when he started shifting from foot to foot, I couldn't help myself. "Are you...okay?"

He groaned. "The boat made me sick, and I threw up all my Adderall, so I'm a bit twitchy. Sorry." He forced himself to stop moving, but then his foot began tapping. "It's worse if I try to control it. You must think we're all completely unhinged."

"Not all of you," I murmured unconvincingly.

He snorted. "Yeah, well, you wouldn't be wrong, I guess. We've done some shit."

"Even you?"

"Oh, I'm the worst."

Having spent an unwilling amount of time with both Jax and Madoc, I found that hard to believe.

Reading my doubt, Ryle sucked on his teeth and exhaled like a confession. "I killed my parents."

I froze.

Ryle stared hard at the ground between us. "Didn't mean to just blurt it out like that, but yeah. I hit my dad with a brick when I was ten. Just popped him right when he was asleep in his favorite chair. Luckily, he was blackout drunk, so it was easy to pretend he tumbled out and brained himself on the TV unit."

Easy?

I tried to school my expression so he couldn't read my horror, but he wasn't looking at me anyway. He had gone completely still, his face soft and eyes faraway in hideous memories.

My voice broke. "And your mom?" I asked tentatively.

His mouth flattened. "Died in childbirth."

"That's not your fault."

He shrugged limply. "Dad certainly thought so. He hated my guts." The shadows on his face darkened. It made him look older, less like the sunny energy ball that had flounced into the room. "I planned it," he said abruptly, almost defensively. "It was totally premeditated, so don't go thinking it was, like, self-defense or anything."

I had no idea what to think anymore. But there was definitely more to the story.

The room felt stifling suddenly, and my head was too full. I wanted to move on and forget everything he just said; I wanted to hug and squeeze the hell out of him. Both impulses left me conflicted, so I offered a stilted: "My parents are shitty sometimes, too."

His head snapped up, eyes wide and concerned. I quickly backtracked. "Not like—they're not abusive or anything. They're just super toxic."

"Nate's family is like that. Is it a rich people thing?"

"Not all rich people are jerks." Though if I had to throw a rock, I'd be hard-pressed to hit anyone in my life who *wasn't* terrible. The only person was Molly. And I didn't even have her anymore.

The reminder of Molly sent a sharp dagger into my chest. "We should go downstairs," I said. Face the music.

Ryle nodded, looking relieved. The darkness on his face faded, no longer eclipsing his infectious sunshine. "Race you down the stairs?"

I absolutely did not race him.

Somehow, we made it to the dining room in one piece, where I immediately locked up at the sight of Jax. He was seated at the head of the table, boots kicked up, and ankles crossed, hands linked behind his head like he was soaking up a tan. He didn't look at me. Not even a glance as I shuffled into the room.

Ryle abandoned me instantly to launch himself at Callum's back, where he stood staring out the window. The large man barely flinched at the surprise attack, as if it were a common occurrence. Knowing what I now knew about Ryle, it probably was.

Nate sat at the opposite end, face buried in his arms, apparently snoozing. Madoc was staring at him from his post against the wall, twirling my knife like he was considering giving the sleeping man an impromptu haircut. I glared at him just because, and, like Jax, Madoc pretended I didn't exist.

I wasn't sure if that was better or worse.

And then there was Zola.

She walked over to Jax and leaned far too close to him, practically kissing him as she showed him something on the tablet. Jax grinned up at her, no hint of malice or mistrust. He didn't look like he wanted to rip her hair out and call her a liar.

Wait. Was I seriously jealous? What was wrong with me?

"Well?" I snapped.

All eyes, barring Nate, swiveled toward me.

"Well, what?" Zola asked with a sneer. With great reluctance, Jax rolled his head toward me and smirked.

"Tell her highness what you found."

Zola scoffed. "Why should I? I've been busting my ass doing her dirty work while she's been, what? Admiring the silverware?"

"I'm not a magpie," I said, refusing to cower under her hostility. "Have you actually found something useful or not?"

Zola shoved the tablet into Jax's chest, hard enough to make him fumble it. "You tell her. This is your deal, not mine. I don't give a fuck what happened to her whorish sister."

Acid burned in my mouth. "She's not a whore."

"So, no family resemblance then?"

My fists clenched, nails biting into familiar grooves. The room waited for my retaliation. In a physical fight, I knew we would be evenly matched. She might've been world-weary and street-hardened, but I was a goddamn varsity cheerleader. It was more than just pom-poms and chants—it was ruthless strength and conditioning, endless flexibility and endurance training.

I would not be underestimated.

"Do not," I warned, my voice sugary and sweet, "talk about Molly."

Zola's eyes flashed, her grin sharpening. "Or what, Nancy Drew? You'll trip over here and break a nail?"

"Don't try me."

Zola started to prowl around the table before Jax shot out his arm, halting her. The asshole just looked amused by the whole thing. "As much as I'd love a bitch fight right now, we're on the clock."

"Aw, come on." The tension had apparently revived Nate. His glassy eyes bounced between his girlfriend and me eagerly. "The Hacker versus the Cheerleader. This should be televised. Let's take bets."

Zola's dangerous eyes snapped to him. "Who are you betting on, babe?"

Nate shrank back fearfully.

I took a deep breath, pushing down my temper. It was hard. I was strung out and wired, and my head hurt just as much as my heart.

It was Callum who took pity on me.

"Come on, lass. Take a beat. I'll show ya' what we found." With Ryle still clinging to his back like a happy spider monkey, Callum pulled back a chair and gestured for me to sit. I plonked down gratefully.

"What did you find?" I asked wearily.

Jax handed the tablet to Callum but spoke to me. "Zola hacked his email. A purchase order was issued to a pharmaceutical company here in Mexico. A big one."

"How big?"

"Two hundred units."

My eyes widened. "So, big, then."

Ryle whistled over Callum's shoulder. "That's a whole lotta product. Was it the same drug Nate found?"

"Yeah," Jax said, rubbing his shoulder—the same spot I had worked on earlier when I'd apparently lost my damn mind. "Either the old dog has a severe fucking anxiety disorder, or he's pushing it somewhere else."

"Cartel?" Nate asked.

"Doubtful," Zola spoke up, unable to help herself. "The market value is shit. It's not exactly addictive. What's suspicious is that the pharmaceutical company lost its funding two years ago. They're not even registered anymore."

"So, it's a cover for something else?"

"Or they're manufacturing illegally," Zola said, reaching for the tablet, which Callum relinquished easily. "The last order was made two weeks ago. It's a repeat order, delivered directly to the coordinates of this clown house."

"So where is it?" Ryle asked. He wriggled until he slid down Callum's back and landed wobbly on his feet. "We've checked every room. You'd think we'd notice that much product."

Something gnawed on the edges of my mind, like a memory that wasn't solidifying. Why would Salvadore invest in an illegal anti-anxiety drug? Was he experimenting? Had Molly been some weird lab rat?

I pushed my fingers into my eyes. It didn't make any sense.

Unless...

"What else could the drug be used for?" I asked, then repeated it when no one heard me.

Madoc smirked at me. "Got something, Watson?"

I scowled at the nickname. "Stop calling me that. The drug is non-addictive, and it clearly doesn't work for anxiety. So, it must do something else, right?"

"I suppose it could be a light sedative," Zola said, not looking at me. "The temporary paralysis and memory loss—you'd be a vegetable but not completely out."

"Like a date rape drug," Nate said, his head buried back in his arms. His flyaway comment landed like a dagger into my chest. My stomach plummeted.

Jax hummed thoughtfully. "A date rape drug hidden in plain sight. Smart fucker."

No.

No. No. No.

My throat tightened, and a lump formed that I couldn't swallow. My hand flew up, clawing at my throat, the skin breaking under my nails.

Not Molly.

Around me, the voices ebbed and faded, like they were speaking from very far away. Or maybe I was disassociating—that was a thing, right? My fingers tingled, but everywhere else went numb, and I didn't hate it. In fact, I wanted to chase it.

I didn't want to feel anything.

For a time, I just existed. Staring at nothing, feeling close to nothing. Then something tugged on my ponytail.

It didn't hurt, but the abrupt sensation drew me back into myself. My head fell back, so I was staring up at Jax with blurred vision.

His brow furrowed. He looked almost concerned, so I knew I'd truly lost touch with reality. He said something I didn't hear. His hand tugged again, a bit harder, the pain shooting like fire down the back of my neck.

"Olivia."

I blinked at him dumbly. "You remember my name." Here I was thinking he'd forgotten it.

His eyes narrowed, then flicked up to the rest of the room. "Everyone out."

There was movement around me, and then we were alone. Jax's fingers moved up my ponytail and sank into my hair. His nails scratched soothingly across my scalp.

"Not a cat," I murmured, blinking wetly.

His lip quirked. "Bet I could make you purr."

My cheeks went hot. I scrambled after my dignity and tried to squirm away, but he wasn't having it. His fingers clawed, gripping my hair possessively, refusing to let me go.

"I want a new deal," I gasped up at him.

That got his interest. "I'm listening."

"Stay."

"I'm right here."

"No, I mean, stay *here* with me until Salvadore comes back."

His hand tightened. "Don't be stupid."

Fresh tears prickled at my eyes at the brutal hold.

Jax considered me, lingering on the exposed jut of my neck. "You're angry."

"Yes," I hissed.

"You want revenge?"

"More than anything."

His eyes darkened, burning with that unnerving vio-lence that made me shudder. "You want to become a killer, princess? Make him suffer?"

Wordlessly, I nodded.

Jax leaned over me, his face so close that I felt his breath on my mouth. My own lips parted automatically. Heat licked up my spine, igniting more and more with each purposeful tug of my ponytail.

Then his lips brushed mine, voice soft and deadly. "You don't have what it takes."

And that, finally, made me snap.

12

JAX

Insanity looked good on her.

I knew it said something about my twisted mind when my cock twitched at her furious expression—that burning indignation in her eyes that promised bloodshed. I saw the hit coming. Hell, I hungered for it, craving the harsh slap of her palm across my face. My head whipped to the side, copper in my mouth.

Give me more.

She went soft instead, sinking into the chair in defeat. I didn't like that. Her anger was perfect. It was important. Defeat wasn't an option.

I wouldn't let her give up on herself.

I gripped her ponytail, my apparent newest obsession, and used it to force her to her feet. She cried out in pain, clawing at my wrist. But her fury returned.

Good.

I could take her anger. I could take whatever she gave me, so long as she didn't turn it on herself. It was a slippery slope, how easily helplessness turned into self-loathing.

"Let me go!" she snarled, her nails digging into my flesh. "I'm not your fucking puppet to pull around."

"Make me."

Her anger flared, then simmered into a new expression. I searched it curiously, then grinned when I realized what it was: *determination*. A shiver actually went down my spine when she spoke in a cold whisper: "I warned you not to touch me like this again."

I tightened my fist. "I'm a slow learner."

With that, she twisted in my grip and kicked me straight in the guts. I doubled over with a groan. For a pint-sized beauty queen, she packed a surprising punch.

I didn't try to defend myself. It was too much fun.

My cheerleader let loose on me, an eruption of everything she'd been holding back. She punched, kicked, and scratched. She thrust her knee into my balls. She fought hard and dirty, and I was fucking impressed.

And so turned on, it made me dizzy.

"Come on," I egged her on, shoving aside a chair when it became an obstacle between us. "That all you got, princess? Here, I won't even move."

I planted my feet and spread my arms.

She pounced at me like a feral cat, not purring but hissing and seething and going for blood. She busted my lip and gauged my shoulder. Between one punch and the next, I hooked my hands under her knees and lifted her up against me. Her legs snapped around my waist automatically. I stepped forward and pinned her down against the table. She clawed at my back, but it was futile—she was mine.

After a few beats, she stilled. We stayed like that, pressed together, breathing heavily.

"I hate you," she seethed, sweat glistening on her neck and chest. Then she went limp, not in defeat, not anymore, but in pure exhaustion. Her head thumped against my shoulder, nails loosening on my back. "You didn't even try to stop me."

"Feel better?"

"Not really. Feels like I just went three rounds against a tree."

I adjusted her slightly, accidentally brushing her against my erection. She went stiff in shock, then reared back and stared at me with wide, incredulous eyes. "Seriously? *This?*"

I smirked unapologetically. "What? You're not even a little bit turned on?"

"Not even a little bit," she lied, looking suddenly bashful.

Man, I was in deep shit.

I made an effort to extract myself, but her legs tightened around my waist. Her eyes glared pointedly at the wall behind me.

Testing the waters, I dragged her against me, a slow, torturous grind of denim on denim. Her lips parted in a silent gasp. I did it again, harder, more forceful. I made her feel every hard inch of me, the steel rod I was packing because of her.

Her lip quivered. Her hands moved behind her, seeking balance on the tabletop. Her head rolled back, eyes looking anywhere but me. I made her shameful and I decided I liked it. She was a priss and a good girl, and I was the devil she didn't *want* to want.

"Stop," she said weakly.

"Your mouth says one thing," I said, flexing my hips, mindful of my gun lodged in the back of my waistband. "Your body says something else."

"I don't want you."

"Then why can't you look at me?"

With visible effort, she snapped her gaze to mine. Instantly, her eyes dropped to my busted lip, and she looked so fucking proud of herself that I groaned.

My hands dragged down her thighs, memorizing the lean muscle, the goddamn rapture that was my cheerleader. "Tell me to stop."

"I did."

"Actually mean it." I jutted forward hard, nailing her with my throbbing erection. Already, precum was dampening my briefs, testing my shaky restraint. My hands tightened to a bruising lock.

Olivia shuddered and said in a breathy whisper: "Stop."

Clenching my eyes shut, I stopped.

My balls were tingling. It had been way too long since I got off. I was hard up and angry, and there she was, splayed across the table like a sinful banquet.

Was she a test from God or a gift from Satan?

"This is wrong," Olivia said, sounding unconvinced. I opened my eyes and took another serving. She was flushed and shaking, her ankles knotted at my lower back, heels digging in. Drawing me in. Her eyes were still wet, still brimming with hatred.

I expected her to chicken out.

I did not expect her to sit up and reach for my belt.

Jesus.

The clink of metal was deafening between us. Her fingers were trembling, and she was back to avoiding looking directly at me. Fine. That was fine. Hate me and fuck me—I was used to it. I'd never loved anyone, and I didn't need the warm and fuzzies to do my part.

I was going to ruin her.

She flicked open the button of my jeans and reached in. Despite her obvious nerves, she found the mark instantly. Her fingers curled over my cock, giving it a testing tug.

"Oh," she said. Then her thumb pressed directly in the vein beneath my head.

I jerked so hard, I nearly pulled my lower back.

"Jesus, fuck," I groaned.

Her answering smile was small and bratty. Her touch was searching, too soft in some ways, too hard in others. Her chest heaved, and her lashes fluttered. She bit her lip in determination.

Me? I just held on.

I was too amped, already on the edge of an embarrassing oblivion. I blamed the stress of it all, the aching months since I unloaded properly, the way she pushed all my buttons. She dragged her palm over my head, gathering the slickness, and gripped me harder, twisting to the base.

She giggled at my reaction.

That wouldn't fucking do.

Regaining control was easy. I gripped her hips and dragged her closer, so she had no choice but to cling to me. But her defiance was just as clingy to her—she was battling with herself, with her own desires and reactions—and I wanted her to lose.

Give in.

I gripped her chin and forced her to look at me. Then I dipped my head, prepared to seal that mouth shut once and for all—

"Jax!" A voice bellowed from the doorway.

Olivia flailed in panic, ripping her hand out so fast that I flinched at the potential castration. I knew it had to be important—Callum wasn't a shouter—but I was also pissy at his interruption.

Meanwhile, Olivia was trying to disappear into herself, her cheeks rosy. I didn't let her pull away completely as I glared over my shoulder at Callum in the doorway.

"What?" I barked.

Callum didn't so much as balk at our position, and I knew that was a bad sign. "Chopper," he said gravely. "We have company."

13

OLIVIA

What was wrong with me?

I barely registered Callum's words as Jax quickly retreated, extracting himself from my body with awkward, jerky movements. I watched him with wide eyes as he stuffed himself back into his black briefs, then buckled his belt. Disappointment crashed through me. My heart was pounding, adrenaline surging, core throbbing in a way that felt bad for my health. I was so wet, I was nearly sliding off the table like a puddle of needy goo. I'd been so close, not just to a surprising orgasm, but to a total sexual awakening.

I wasn't a virgin, but damn, I had missed the mark somewhere. Sex was always good, except for those first few times, but those didn't count. I was good at sex. I moaned at the right times, took my fair share of the work, and toed the line between sexy and demure that made Heath go nuts. It was never mindless, never boring.

But, god, it was never *this*.

Raw, dangerous, heady with sweat and a bit of terror, the risk of being caught, the wrongness of it being Salvadore's dining room table. It was Jax and his huge body, his bracketing biceps and near-pained groans, his trembling restraint. It was my hatred of him, powerful and electrifying, making everything more intense.

My therapy bill was going to be huge.

"Come on," Jax snapped, gripping my face and jolting me back to reality.

A reality that involved twenty to life in a Mexican prison if we were caught.

Fear surged through me. "Shit. What—what do we do!?" I scrambled to my feet, smoothing down my hair, trying to regain my bearings. My backpack was tucked beneath a chair. I grabbed it and slung it over my shoulder. I didn't have my binder, and for a second I was relieved—I didn't want to be caught with a backpack of evidence that could be used against me. Or a knife that could be classed as an aggravated burglary.

Was that why Madoc took it?

I shook my head, unable to split my focus with that infuriating green-eyed sadist. Jax grabbed my hand and led me into the foyer, where the unmistakable beat of helicopter blades filled the space.

"Scatter!" Jax barked at his crew. Like cockroaches, they split off in different directions, with Nate and Zola taking the stairs and Callum and Ryle disappearing into one of the many guest bedrooms. I couldn't see Madoc, but I wasn't worried. He probably enjoyed curling up in the drywall like a demented possum.

Jax dragged me up the stairs to the third floor.

"What are we doing?" I hissed when Jax eyeballed a few rooms and then dismissed them. He ignored my question and tugged harder on my hand when I tried to pull back. I felt like a lost little kid in a shopping mall, overwhelmed and directionless.

Finally, Jax stopped at a walk-in linen cupboard directly opposite Theodore's office. He snapped open the door and shoved me inside. "Stay," he commanded.

I gaped at him. "For how long?"

"Until I come back."

"What if it's Salvadore?" My voice cracked. For all my talk of murder, the idea of being anywhere near him made me tremble. Girls like me didn't survive in prison.

Jax held my eyes, his face hardening. "I won't let him near you."

"Okay." I believed him. "What are you going to do?"

"Stay here," he said, ignoring my question again. His voice was like grated steel. "Don't move. Don't be a hero. I'll come back for you."

He shut the door, and I was enveloped in darkness. When my eyes adjusted, I looked around helplessly at the shelves of towels and linens, the soft scent of detergent somehow amplifying my dread. *I bet a funeral home smells like this*, my brain piled on helpfully. I slid down to the floor and hugged my backpack. At least I had my phone. Worst case, I called Preacher for an emergency extraction. But it was a last resort—he scared me as much as Jax did.

I strained my ears and caught the sound of footsteps creaking on the floorboards. Instantly, my heart rocketed, my stomach bottoming out. What if my intel was wrong and Salvadore had caught an earlier flight? Or what if he'd sent his staff to prepare the mansion in advance?

God, what if they insisted on changing the sheets first?

My linen cupboard just became a hot sauna of death. Sweat beaded over my temples, prickling down the back of my neck. The creaking got louder, confident steps, the steps of someone who belonged. I held my breath and squeezed my backpack when the footsteps neared, then paused. Shadows flickered under the crack of the door.

"Hello?"

Oh god oh god oh god

"Yeah, yeah, I'm here," the voice continued without a reply, sounding impatient. It was male, young. Not one of Jax's crew. Another pause, and he said: "Don't ask me. I'm just the errand guy. Maybe he's finally going digital."

The lack of reply meant he was talking on the phone. That meant he was distracted, and not scenting the air like some demonic bloodhound ready to hunt me down. Another minute later, the shadows moved on, his voice pitching in annoyance as it drifted away: "Cool your jets, Marcus. I'm headed to the safe now. There's a reason I'm the one holding it and not you. I'm fucking trustworthy."

Panic thrummed through my veins. The safe. The painting. As soon as he saw it was missing, he would raise the alarm. There was no time to delay.

I stood up and reached for the door, slinging my backpack over my shoulder. I waited, and waited, but there was no cry of shock, no sirens. Was there another safe we didn't know about?

More secrets, Molly whispered.

A fresh tear of grief ripped through my panic. I couldn't leave now. Not when I was finally onto something. With trembling fingers, I opened the door and peered cautiously across the sun-lit hall into Salvadore's office. The stranger was in there, speaking in low tones. I expected him to sound angry, like he'd just discovered a hundred-million-dollar hole in the wall.

Could he be so distracted that he hadn't noticed? That didn't seem likely. His conversation made it seem as if he were a frequent visitor, someone trusted with the safe. I stepped forward, pressing my sneaker delicately onto the floor so I didn't trigger a creak. The new angle let me see the stranger, his back to the door, half-perched on the mahogany desk, his phone pressed to his ear. He was wearing a lime green shirt and black jeans and—

My brain stalled.

The painting was in front of the safe.

I blinked hard, thinking it was a trick of the light. But no, it was the same painting I'd seen Callum and Zola slip into a travel-friendly case. The stranger waved his hand, and my heart stopped, but then he grumbled, "You know how it is. He's got a taste for it now. He'll be back."

Before I could second-guess myself, I skulked across the hall and into the office, immediately beelining for the huge wardrobe next to the door. Luckily, it was partially opened, as if the latch didn't quite work anymore. I squeezed myself inside, nearly choking on my tongue when I was engulfed in fur.

"Hang on a sec."

I froze, my heart pounding in my head, my mouth full of slaughtered mink. As I eased back, the hangers above me made a terrible clinking sound. I froze, my eyes plastered to the crack between the doors, waiting for him to come over and investigate.

Stupid, Molly said.

I know, I replied miserably.

There was a shuffling sound, like papers being sorted, and then he was talking again: "Do you know if he keeps his cigars in the top drawer? What? Since when?"

I released a winded breath. I couldn't move, not without setting off the hangers, a task that became increasingly difficult when the fur stuck to my sweat-slick skin, making me itch. This was a stupid idea. Stupid and reckless and desperate.

"Brunette? Meh, I prefer blondes."

My stomach made a low, grumbling complaint. *God, not now.* The rollercoaster of adrenaline was wreaking havoc on my digestive system.

More shuffling, a sound of a drawer being opened and shut. "Senator who? Never heard of him."

He let out a short, barking laugh. "You know what? I wouldn't put it past him. Nothing like good pussy to sway the vote. He can have the brunettes."

A ghost of air brushed the back of my neck.

Terror bolted through me. I stiffened, a scream budding in my chest before a firm leather hand clamped over my mouth from behind. Solid warmth pressed to my back, a terribly familiar voice in my ear: "Don't fucking scream."

Madoc.

The overwhelming relief was short-lived. His other hand latched onto my throat, cutting off my air supply. I realized I was making noises, small gasping whimpers against his palm. The squeeze of his hand stopped all sound from escaping. It also sent sparks shooting behind my eyes.

Would he kill me to maintain his cover?

Probably. Out of all of them, I suspected Madoc was the most ruthless. Jax was the only one who didn't fear him. Plus, he clearly hated me, and the fact that I kept finding myself under his hand was like tempting fate.

"Stop moving."

Hard to do when my muscles were spasming with oxygen deprivation. His hand on my throat loosened, enough that I took in a long, silent breath.

His lips brushed the shell of my ear. "Move one step to the left. Make a sound, and I'll slit your throat."

Jesus.

Madoc wasn't playing around. His voice was terse, clipped. I could smell his sweat, woodsy and masculine, tinged with the sweet notes of stolen chocolate. The space was extremely limited, so I felt all of him—the press of his thighs on the back of mine, the clip of his belt in my lower back, the hardness of his abs, the sharp butt of his gun. His leather glove was clammy on my mouth from my desperate gasping.

On his command, a hard nudge to my ribs, I moved one careful step to the left. The hangers didn't clink, the fur coat slipped slowly off my shoulder. Madoc slithered around my body, his chest dragging against my shoulder, before he took up position in front of the crack and peered into the office.

He had to have put the painting back as soon as he heard the chopper. It didn't lessen my vehement dislike of him, but I admired his quick thinking. I stared at his profile, the sliver of light slicing across his left cheek and turning his eye emerald. His jaw was tense.

"Yeah, yeah, I got it, man. I'm not on the clock, you know. I might just stick around for a while, take advantage of those double showerheads." The stranger barked another laugh, then said: "Man, this painting sucks ass."

The sound of the safe clicking made my pulse kick. I stared at Madoc with wide eyes, hoping he had super vision that could see the combination. Madoc was so still, I was pretty sure he wasn't breathing.

"Alright, it's in. Tell the boss man he can relax."

Footsteps approached, and my hand snapped out to tangle in Madoc's shirt on instinct. I held on to him, taking comfort in his solidness. His stillness. When the footsteps receded, the annoying voice with it, Madoc reached down his side and gripped my wrist. It took a herculean effort to unpeel my fingers from the material. Madoc didn't rush me, perhaps suspecting I was right on the edge. Once he was free, he slipped out. I made to follow, but he shot me a dark warning look. Somewhat sheepishly, I stepped back into the wardrobe and watched him scope out the corridor. He disappeared for a few minutes, but I knew he didn't go far. His return was as silent as the grave, his face just as cold.

"He's in the shower."

I burst out of the wardrobe, nearly tangling myself up in the coats. "What—did you get it?" I pointed frantically to the safe.

Madoc's face didn't change. "What do you want?"

Was he for real? I flailed in exasperation. "What do you think? I want you to open it. This is our chance."

"Ask nicely."

My teeth ground together. "Please," I managed.

His mouth quirked up in a smirk. "Please, what? Be specific."

I hate him, I hate him, I hate him.

"Please open the safe. Quickly, before he comes back."

Madoc watched me for another long, frustrating moment before he shrugged and went to the safe. I sagged in relief. I knew I couldn't make him do anything, but god, I was glad I didn't have to try.

He lifted the painting and placed it carefully against the wall at his feet, ready for transport. Then he started on the dial of the safe, turning it with such confidence that it was like he'd done it a thousand times. I was begrudgingly impressed.

"How do you—"

"Eidetic memory," he said shortly.

I stopped asking questions.

With a click and a slight woosh, the safe yawned open. I tried not to step on Madoc in my haste to peer inside.

"Oh."

My world tilted once more.

14

JAX

Everything went to shit just like I knew it would.

I lunged up the stairs, doing a cursory sweep for anything we could've left behind. Despite the unexpected hiccup, I was calm, mechanical. Panic didn't shut me down; the opposite, actually. My mind cleared, my instincts sharpened. I was in my element, a predator set loose from its cage.

Except I wasn't hunting.

I was running.

Our guest came up the stairs behind me, still jabbering away on his phone. Quickly, I ducked into the nearby study nook, inwardly groaning as I folded myself beneath the tiny desk.

Served me fucking right.

My neck panged at the awkward angle, my knees smashed against my chest. I'd never been good at hiding, not even as a kid when I'd tuck myself in small spaces to avoid my old man during one of his violent rampages. He'd always find me eventually, and the pain of uncurling after hours in the same position was almost as painful as his fists. Well, not really.

Stop whining, boy.

I squeezed my eyes shut like I could expel him from my head forever. He loved to pop up at the most inconvenient times like a patronizing ghoul. As the footsteps retreated into the main bedroom, my father goaded me into jumping on the man's back and twisting his neck until it snapped. It sounded easy, but I knew it wasn't. Humans didn't just die quietly. My father had groaned and flailed like a fish when his heart gave out. They said it was instant—nothing could save him—but man, did it go on forever.

Still thinking about me, boy.

Right. Think about something else. Like the fact that I was still ragingly hard. Every time I shifted, trying to adjust, my weeping tip jutted against my zipper and sent a bolt of heat through my lower half. It was a stress boner. Or a rage boner. Fuck if I knew the difference anymore. I'd spent most of my turbulent youth jacking off, even when I was angry—no, *especially* when I was angry.

And, what do you know, I was still thinking about my dad.

My mouth went dry, and my hands started to tremble where they were fisted around my shins. Now wasn't the time for my mega daddy issues to screw me over. They were too distracting, just like her.

Thinking of Olivia made my chest tight in a good way. I chased the feeling greedily, replaying the feel of her body against mine, the burning hatred and desire as I gave her what she desperately wanted—a rough, emotionless fuck. She could deny it all she wanted, but I knew the truth. She was guarded and clean, not pure but unspoiled. I wanted her to kneel at the altar that was my angry outlaw cock.

Fuck. This wasn't helping.

Trying to be quiet, I jammed my fist into my dick. I wasn't a sadist—I suspected that was more Madoc's thing, which I could not think about right now—but the pain was grounding. In the main suite, I heard the shower turn on, a door click shut.

Time to end this nightmare.

I crawled out with a silent groan and took the stairs two at a time. When I reached the third landing, the first thing I saw was the door of the linen cupboard, open. My heart hammered into my sternum. *Of fucking course.* I knew she wouldn't listen. I just knew it.

My head snapped to the right when I caught movement in the doorway.

"Where the fuck is she?" I growled.

Madoc tilted his head softly as he leaned against the frame, like I was late to some standing appointment. Normally, I appreciated his unwavering calm—now it only fed the wild animal in my chest.

Silently, Madoc stepped aside, giving me a glimpse into Salvadore's office. I immediately clocked Olivia curled up on the floor, her back to me, her shoulders hitching in silent sobs. I shot Madoc a questioning look, which he returned flatly. Right. Too many emotions for him.

"Take watch," I told him quietly. "We bounce in five."

I didn't hear his acknowledgment, but he was gone before I'd made it halfway across the room. Olivia didn't react as I knelt beside her. She was blank-faced, despite her trembling frame. In her lap was a thick, leather-bound notebook with a gold-woven spine. It was fancy and well-used, like a relic or tome. My eyes shot up to the safe.

"It's not enough," Olivia mumbled, her voice thick with tears. Then she glanced up at me, rosy-cheeked and eyes like molten silver. "You came back for me."

I didn't acknowledge the shock in her voice. I kept my promises.

"The hell is it?" I gestured to the notebook.

She handed it to me despondently. I flipped it open to a random page, then paused at the list of handwritten scrawls. Names and dates. A guestbook. It was no signed confession or serial killer scrapbook, nothing blatantly incriminating like Olivia obviously hoped it would be. I scrutinized the names, pressing my side against hers. "Do you recognize any of the names?"

"No," she said, sniffling. "It's weird, right? He must host some big parties. Why else would he need a record of attendance?"

My mind went to underground orgies and sex clubs—discreet, undocumented. If Salvadore was manufacturing date rape drugs, he had to be using them somewhere. But the guestbook didn't make sense.

Perverts didn't typically keep records. Not unless...

My brain stalled on the dark red smears by each name.

"It looks like blood," Olivia observed with a cute wrinkled nose. "God, it's so archaic. Like voodoo or something."

"Or collateral." My brain was piecing it together quicker than I could communicate. "It's like a blood signature. DNA. Indisputable proof that they were really here."

"Ew. But why?"

"Blackmail. It buys their silence." A sharp emotion daggered into my chest. "Fuck this. We're leaving."

"What?" Her eyes widened. "No, you can't! Not yet. Jax—"

"We had a deal," I reminded her firmly. "You hold what you find until my crew is far away from this place."

"But I don't know what any of it means yet!" Olivia clambered onto her knees and shuffled closer until she could grab onto my shoulders. My hand automatically went to her waist to steady her. "This isn't enough. You owe me until sunset. That was the deal."

At my furious glare, she softened. "We can wait and hide until he leaves."

"You're not so good at the waiting part."

Her expression turned sheepish. "I saw an opportunity. I'm not sorry for that." She waved the guestbook between us. "This proves there is something fishy going on. We haven't looked outside the mansion. He might have other hiding spots."

I shook my head and extracted her claws from my shoulders. "Not happening. This was already too close. Others could be coming."

Olivia chewed her lip, looking stubborn.

"I'm not leaving," she decided. "Not yet. I owe Molly that much."

I bared my teeth. "Don't be fucking stupid."

"Better than being a coward."

A harsh, bitter laugh escaped me as I got to my feet. The word was a trigger, a hatchet to my aforementioned daddy issues. It took every ounce of willpower not to grip that pouty mouth and force her to take it back.

I stood over her instead, taking sick satisfaction in the way she looked up at me, eyes fluttering nervously at the danger on my face.

My voice was dark. "Good luck then, princess."

"Wait," she said, softly, regretfully. "I didn't mean—I'm sorry."

I faltered.

"I'm just—shit." She scrambled, clearly flustered. "I can't think when you look at me like that."

My lips twitched, despite myself. "Like what?"

"Like you want to murder me and flush me down the toilet."

"This your first apology?"

"Shut up," she said, sighing defeatedly. "I'm just so over-whelmed. I thought I was ready, that I was prepared. But I'm not. I have no idea what I'm doing." Her eyes met mine. "Without you and—god, *Madoc*—I would've never have gotten this far."

"Better." I grinned at her.

Her cheeks warmed. "Please stay."

My grin dropped. I turned away, unable to look at her, at those grey-blue eyes so wide and sincere. I liked it when she begged, but not like this.

Did I have a weakness for cute girls who needed saving? Or was I simply preying on that weakness? Devouring it?

Grinding my jaw, I turned back to her. "I'm not hiding."

She frowned in confusion. "What do you mean?"

"You want answers, I'll get them. But you won't like how I do it."

In my ear, I heard my crew latch onto my words and the meaning behind them. As if on cue, Madoc reappeared in the doorway, eyes alight with hunger that made my insides lurch.

I gave him a solemn nod. "Root canal."

His lips curled up slowly.

"You sure about this, chief?" Callum asked in my ear, his voice hitching as he came up the stairs.

My eyes flickered to Olivia. She stared back at me questionably. "No."

But fuck it. I was doing it anyway.

Ryle arrived next, looking pale but determined, gun already in hand. I took one look at him, all his twitchy glory, and said, "You stay with Olivia."

Instantly, his face dropped. "I'm not a kid."

He was, but I knew better than to point that out right now. "Someone needs to make sure she doesn't get tangled in the insulation."

Olivia chirped in outrage. "That is so—"

Ryle's protests were louder: "I hate when you treat me with kid gloves. It's bullshit." He pouted and shuffled into the room like a moody teenager.

Madoc kicked his shin as he passed, a solitary reassurance that made Ryle hiss and hobble. "Dick."

I met Callum, Zola, and Nate on the landing, all of them masked and armed, which made my chest swell up all prideful.

"Secure the painting."

Zola nodded, dark eyes glinting dangerously above her pretty rhinestone mask. Madoc slipped out behind me and prowled up the stairs. His eagerness for bloodshed should've been alarming to me—instead, I found it strangely arousing. My own blood started to boil, my heart thumping hard.

I shot one last glance at Olivia. She met my gaze steadily, even as my demons unleashed from their brittle chains.

She wanted a savior. I'd give her a monster instead.

As I lunged up the stairs, I sank deeper into the crimson-tinged fog. By the time I made it to the bedroom door,

I was feral. Callum stood on my left, Madoc on my right. Nate covered my back, for once, utterly still and silent.

We didn't say a word.

And when the door opened, we attacked.

15

JAX

"Wha—?"

He didn't have time to react, short of gripping the towel around his waist, an unconscious clutch for safety as he was set upon by masked strangers. The fact that he was naked was a point in our favor. Not that I particularly enjoyed seeing his flaccid cock bounce around as we forced him to his knees, but it made him more compliant. More vulnerable. His hair was still wet, slicked back from his paling face. His eyes bounced fearfully between us, then landed on me with fervent desperation. "W-Who are you?"

I stood over him, grinning behind my mask. "I'm nobody. Answer our questions, and I'll stay nobody."

His tongue darted out across his lips. His chest heaved, droplets still clinging to his flushed skin. He didn't look much older than me. He was well-groomed, lightly toned, with the kind of douchebag haircut that Nate called the *'frat boy freshie'*. He'd been sporting one himself when he joined our crew.

"W-What do you want to know?" He spluttered out. His hands clutched valiantly at his towel, trying to preserve his modesty. He was shaking all over. That was good. That meant he would break easily.

"Let's start with a name."

"K-Kane."

"Last name."

"S-Smith—"

My fist struck before he finished stuttering. His head whipped back, my knuckles throbbing from his jawbone. He fell back gracelessly, towel forgotten, and moaned as he stared wide-eyed up at the ceiling. Beside me, Madoc twitched. I didn't dare look at him.

"Every time you lie, I deliver another blow." I held up my fist, then my gun. Naturally, his eyes fixated on the gun. "I won't use this," I said. "Yet."

"Please, man. What the fuck?" He cried, anguished as he rubbed his jaw and tried to sit up. I noticed the pile of clothes on the bed and gave Callum a nod. He stepped over the quivering man and began picking through the pockets until he struck gold.

I caught the wallet he tossed me, followed by the cellphone. I flipped through the wallet carelessly. "Kane Davies. Twenty-seven years old. Lives at Forty-Nine Baker Street, Newark."

His eyes bulged in panic as he scrambled onto his knees. Callum moved instantly, grabbing his arms and pinning them hard behind his back, causing him to buck, but he was no match for Callum. Realizing he was wildly outnumbered and overpowered, he started to babble: "Listen, man, whatever it is you want, just take it. I won't tell anyone, I swear to god."

I flashed the phone at his face so it unlocked with facial recognition. Then I scoured his call log, finding mostly local numbers, including a recent one with a London area code.

I tossed the phone over to Nate. "Go through his camera roll."

"Bet I'll find a million dick pics," Nate muttered, settling into the task. He gurgled in laughter not a minute later. "Called it."

"Please." Kane thrashed. "Whatever you want. Just don't fucking kill me, man."

"I want to know everything," I said. I took a menacing step toward him and inwardly preened at the way he instinctively recoiled into Callum. Between two predators, he feared me the most. "Starting with what's in the safe."

He opened his mouth, and I lifted my fist, causing him to choke in fear. "Don't lie."

"Nothing, man," he blurted out. "Just some fucking—I don't know—documents, the usual stuff. Man, it's nothing. Its—oof!"

The cartilage of his nose cracked under my knuckles. Callum, in the firing line, didn't so much as wince as blood splattered across his face, some beading in his eyebrow. For a second, I worried I hit Kane too hard—his body flopped, then spasmed as he fell back in a limp daze, groaning loudly.

"I warned you about lying."

"I wasn't—okay, wait!" His body thrashed wildly. "Okay, shit, alright." His voice was thick and nasally, his nose crooked. "It's just a book, man. People sign it when they visit so that the old man can keep a record. That's it, I swear."

That was far from it. He knew it as well, judging by the nervous flick of his eyes to my hands, expecting my fist.

"Why?" I asked.

He hesitated, then his tongue lashed out and licked at the blood gushing over his top lip. "It's n-nothing. He's just a quirky old dude, you know. I don't get how he thinks."

"Another lie."

His whole body trembled, sweat beading over his brow and joining the blood that was already messing up his face. It was a gruesome sight, but it clearly wasn't enough. Whatever secret he was guarding had apparently worse consequences than getting the shit beat out of him.

That meant we had to take it up a notch.

"Bathroom," I grunted.

Callum wrapped his burly arms around our hostage, who flailed in confusion as we moved our party into the bathroom. It was still steamy and damp, faintly floral from expensive shampoos. Our boots squelched against wet tiles as we maneuvered into the space. There was a teak artisanal-style bathtub in the corner, raised on a step like a stage. For our next act, Callum dumped our hostage into the tub, his naked body smacking and sliding wetly along the sides. He whimpered and cupped his nose, his eyes wild and horse-like.

We stood around him, masked pillars to his humiliation. The steam dampened my hair, and when I swiped it back, I knew I smeared blood on my forehead. It didn't bother me, since we were about to get a whole lot messier.

"Last chance," I said. He jerked and stared up at me fearfully. "Tell me the truth. What is really going on here?"

"N-nothing, man. I swear."

"Boss." Nate motioned over at me, then thrust the phone in front of my face. My stomach dropped like a stone. A couple was posed on a sagging couch, both of them grinning and saluting the camera with red cups. Without all the blood and sweat, our man Kane was effortlessly handsome, with his douchey hair and thousand-watt smile, but it was the girl who stole my attention. The long blonde hair, the achingly familiar gray-blue eyes.

My vision went hazy, and the drip-drip of water from the leaking showerheads suddenly deafened my ears. A dull ache in my knuckles tugged me back to earth, where I was clenching my fists at my sides, the gun strangled in my grip.

It wasn't Olivia. I had to repeat it to myself three times before I could unclench. It wasn't her.

It was Molly.

Snatching the phone from Nate, I stepped up to the bath edge and snarled. "Who is this?" I shoved the phone in his face. He squinted at it blearily, uncomprehending.

"Wha—I don't know, man. Just s-some chick I met at a party."

"When?"

"Couple years ago. What the fuck is the big deal?" He scrambled up, as if prepared to fight his way out of the tub. My fist knocked him back, hitting his temple and causing him to slide back into the tub.

The sight didn't alleviate my fury. It was beyond me, consuming me. My body felt too tight, my muscles bunched up with tension, like I could snap at any moment.

"Sparrow," I heard myself grunt hoarsely. It sounded like a plea—it was—but it was also a threat. Madoc, who'd been a silent observer until now, snapped his gaze toward me. Green eyes were bright and lucid, unblinking, waiting. "Make him talk."

Like a snake uncoiling, Madoc moved with deadly precision, stepping up to the tub and looking down at his prey with hungry curiosity. I could stomach a lot of things, but Madoc had a particular talent for brutality. Kane looked up at him with the same blank panic, and it wasn't until I stepped back and gave Madoc center stage that it dawned on him: Madoc was the real predator. Kane blanched, turning white, and went very still.

"Hi," Madoc purred softly. "This is going to hurt very much."

"Wait." Kane looked over at me desperately. "Alright, it's—it's not my thing, okay? I'm just the scout. I wanted out a long time ago, I swear to God."

Madoc didn't move, but there was a distinct click sound, and I saw Olivia's switchblade appear in his hand by his thigh. Kane clocked it and paled even more.

"Who are you scouting?" Madoc asked in the same soft, silky voice. I purposely ignored the shiver that went up my spine at the sound of it. It should be terrifying, and it was, but it was also fucking mesmerizing. Like pillow talk.

I wondered if Madoc sounded like that during a good fuc—

Stop. I wrenched my mind to a halt, refusing to let my demons win. I needed to stay in the moment. Keep a tight lid on my control so I didn't snap and kill him.

Kane choked for a moment, fear clogging up his windpipe. He couldn't see Madoc's smile behind his rose bandana, but I could. I knew it intimately, the slow, deadly shape of it, the promise.

"It was just—they wanted—I never."

"You sound like you are missing your tongue." Madoc raised the knife, his grip loose, almost playful. "Try to find it before I remove it."

Kane trembled, his knuckles bleached on the edges of the tub. "Girls!" he exploded in a desperate burst. "I find girls."

"Why?"

"I—it's just—we pay them. L-Like an escort service. It's all legit, I swear."

"Legit, he says. Why don't I believe you?" Madoc pressed the tip of the blade to his thumb, testing the sharpness. "Ah, well."

Quick as a viper strike, he gripped Kane's hair in one hand, gave it a sharp yank so Kane's face was tilted up toward him, then pressed the knife into the mangled cartilage of his broken nose. Kane went still as death, then seized up in terror. The acidic stench of piss permeated the air.

"P-Please."

"Walk me through it," Madoc purred. "Slowly."

Kane jerked, and that small movement caused the blade to slip into his wound and blood to gush down his face. He quivered and groaned, his words thick and stilted. "T-they pay me to f-find girls to bring to the island. M-most of them are willing, I s-swear. They k-know what's g-going to happen, some even want to come back!"

Madoc's bicep flexed, and the blade dug in just enough to make Kane scream. My heart palpitated at his admission. My fingers twitched on my gun.

"And the others?" Madoc asked.

"W-What?"

"The unwilling ones."

Kane balked, his naked legs flailing out, slippery with blood and piss. "T-They a-always come around. O-Once I explain it to them."

I stepped forward, my voice guttural. "Explain what?"

"The r-rules." Kane's eyes wheedled to mine, watery and pain-hazed. "I-I don't m-make the rules. T-They do. I just b-bring them here."

"Why?" Madoc asked softly. At Kane's hesitation, he twisted the blade like a screwdriver, straight into the bloody lump of his nose. Kane screamed again, the sound echoing from the tiles, likely traveling through the mansion. My thoughts drifted briefly to Olivia before I dismissed them. She had no place here.

"Say it," Madoc urged when Kane's voice grew hoarse and whimpering. "Why do you bring them here?"

Kane sobbed wetly. He was so pale, he looked almost alien in the wooden tub, an unsightly creature. "T-T-They..."

"Yes?"

"T-They t-take turns...w-with them."

My gut rolled and my vision wavered. Everything became dreamlike for a second. I knew the details were important—we owed the victims that much—but the more Kane spoke, the more detached I felt, and the harder it was to resist putting a bullet between his eyes. I'd only ever killed two people in my life, both of them in self-defense, but I knew I was more than capable of acting out in anger. *Sensitive*, my old man would say, right as he drove his fists into my ribs.

I was drawn back to Madoc, who, aside from the faint sheen of sweat on the back of his neck and shoulders, appeared utterly unbothered. Not even Callum achieved such stoicism; the larger man squinted every few seconds as sweat dripped into his eyes. Nate was vibrating against my shoulder, muttering "dogs" under his breath.

The bitter tang of blood and piss and sweat became unbearable, even through our face masks.

Finally, when Kane regained consciousness after briefly passing out from shock and pain, Madoc yanked his head back at an unnatural angle and pressed the blade under his jaw. "Where does the old man sleep?"

The question was odd, so much so that Callum and I exchanged a quick, puzzled look. "I-I don't know. P-Probably downstairs," Kane gasped out.

"Why?"

"I-I don't know, man." Kane started to wail. "P-Please. I-I'm nobody. D-Don't kill me."

Madoc sneered and jabbed the knife harder into his tender jugular. "Did you join in?" Kane blanched as Madoc started to twist. "Don't lie."

"I-I didn't w-want to, I swear."

"Tsk." The blade pierced the skin, a rivulet of fresh blood streaking down Kane's chest.

My tongue was thick and uncooperative. "Wait."

Immediately, Madoc released him and stepped back, causing Kane to sag in weeping relief. For a split second, I almost pitied him. He looked ruined, his face mangled, his blood pooling in the tub and dripping slowly down the drain. Then I thought about Olivia, who was likely the same age Molly had been when Kane "scouted" her. I wondered if Kane would recognize Olivia. Then I wondered if Kane had his turn with Molly, and I saw fucking red.

"Where did he keep the girls?" I asked, trying and failing to remain as cold as Madoc, but I was burning up from the inside. "You said downstairs. Where?"

Kane hiccupped wetly, his eyes shooting fearfully to Madoc. "The basement."

Madoc didn't react, but Callum shook his head. "The git's lying."

"N-No, wait!" Kane frantically thrust up his hands toward Madoc, who wouldn't move an inch unless I told him to. "I'm not—I'm not lying. There is a door in the basement, behind the wine racks. I—if you let me go, I'll show you."

Madoc's eyes flashed to mine. I considered him with stones in my chest, then turned to Callum and then Nate, who were wordlessly waiting for my call.

There was no doubt we had to check out the basement. We were in too deep now. Holstering my gun in my waistband, Kane released a premature sob of relief, then choked on it soundlessly when I leaned menacingly over the tub.

"Do not mistake me," I drawled in a low voice. "You are going to die. How long it will take, how much it will hurt, will depend on what we find."

The way Kane's eyes widened and then fluttered in fear told me everything I needed to know.

We headed down to the basement.

16

— · —

OLIVIA

The screams bled through the walls.

With each one, I curled up a little tighter, rocking like a mental patient in the middle of a psychotic break. What made it worse was Ryle's total indifference to it all. He moved around Salvadore's office like a curious puppy, sniffing this, nudging that. He'd poured us both a drink from Salvadore's liquor cabinet, but I was nursing mine, watching the amber liquid slosh around the crystal, thinking of blood.

"What is root canal?" I asked him during a prolonged stretch of silence.

Ryle sank down opposite me, his back against the bookshelves. "It's a painful but necessary extraction."

"Oh."

"Callum, the big sexy redhead, used to be in the Royal Navy." Ryle adopted a misty smile. "He taught us all these cool code names and phrases."

"Did he also teach you how to shoot?" My eyes lingered on the gun resting by his knee like a discarded toy. No offense to Ryle, but his overall twitchiness wasn't what you wanted when holding a loaded weapon.

"Nah. That was Madoc." Ryle took a hefty swig. "No idea where he learned it. Madoc doesn't talk about his past. It must've been super fucked up, though."

"Because he's such a barrel of laughs?"

"More like a trainwreck of trauma." Ryle saluted me. "Let's hope we don't swing too far off the rails."

I took a sip. The heat scorched down my throat and settled in my stomach. It wasn't unpleasant, so I took another. Then I returned my attention to the guestbook in my lap, trying to recognize any of the names.

There were hundreds of them.

All printed and dated, going as far back as eight years. Some were recurring, some were foreign with long names, and some had actual suffixes, like Carlisle De Arthur III.

I looked for Molly and was both relieved and disappointed when there were no females listed.

Another wretched scream filled the room.

I squeezed my eyes like I could ignore it. My mind betrayed me like it always did, flashing back to Jax right before he left—the violence in his eyes, the tension in his frame, the deadly promise in the sharpness of his grin.

You dry humped him, my brain reminded me, like the catty bitch she was.

Denial was my friend, and I clung to it now, tuning out the satanic symphony that played on a loop.

Ryle was tipsy and rambling about his vehement dislike of banana-flavored things (*"It's not even based on real bananas anymore! It's just false advertising!"*) when Zola swooped in, sans painting.

She spared me a cold look and perched on the desk, admiring her cuticles like an aloof royal.

"Painting secured," she said, clearly not talking to me.

Ryle staggered awkwardly to his feet. He opened his mouth, only to be cut off by another gut-wrenching scream. When it was over, he said: "You agree with me, right, Zol?"

"Sure," she said, not even bothering to ask for clarification.

Ryle turned to me smugly, as if I'd been disputing his very random tirade, when he suddenly went still.

I perked up, instantly alert.

There were no more screams, just a thick, awful silence.

Even Zola froze, her brow scrunching delicately. Then her eyes snapped up to mine, and my stomach sank.

"What is it?" I demanded with a rasp.

Ryle touched his ear, the tiny bud of communication that I wasn't privy to. Not that I wanted to be. The screams were enough—I definitely didn't need them in high definition.

"Madoc is finished playing with him," Zola said, trying and failing to remain nonchalant. "It won't be long now."

I sensed there was more to it, especially when Ryle refilled his glass like he was gearing up for a fight.

When he suddenly spluttered into a coughing fit, I knew I'd regret pushing it. "Okay, you need to tell me. What is going on?"

"N-Nothing," Ryle lied badly while Zola rolled her eyes.

"Madoc broke him."

"Broke him how?"

Zola smiled, and I cringed at the sight of it. "He blabbed. You won't like what he said, Nancy Drew."

A terrible part of me was counting on it.

Zola slipped off the desk. "Come along, then. Let's dig up those skeletons in the basement."

At my visibly paling face, Ryle offered me the rest of his drink. I gulped it down without thinking, then coughed until my lungs stopped burning. "I thought you checked the basement," I forced out.

Ryle scowled. "Turns out, we missed a doozy."

The trip to the basement was quick and daunting. I kept the guestbook clutched to my chest like a cursed teddy bear. At one point, my sneakers squelched on the stairs, and I glanced down in horror at the trail of fresh blood.

Of course.

Of course, the blood led to the creepy basement.

I lost my nerve right near the bottom, unable to cross the short hallway into the unknown. I could hear voices, notably Jax and his deep rasp, and I wasn't ready to face him.

"You can stay here," Ryle said kindly, offering me a way out. Zola huffed impatiently and shouldered past me.

"I just need a second." And more whisky. Lots more.

"You're scared," Ryle observed, cocking his head. "Me too."

"You are?"

"And hungry. And a little drunk." He grinned sheepishly. "You just have to push through it. Learn to keep going." He made a rolling motion with his hand. "The river will twist and turn, but it keeps going forward."

My brows pinched together. "That's...inspiring."

His eyes brightened. "I fucking know. And to think, Jax wants to revoke my cookie privileges. I'm basically Gandhi."

Unbelievably, I did feel a little better.

The feeling returned to my legs, and I pushed forward, striding into the basement before I could chicken out.

Only to be immediately set upon by Jax, who swooped in front of me and blocked my entrance.

"Stop," he said.

I blinked up at him, adjusting to the low light. He wasn't wearing his mask, the material bunched under his chin, and his expression was tense, his eyes too wide, the blue dark and unreadable. His hair was stuck with sweat to his cheeks and temples. I continued downwards, unable to stop myself—his t-shirt was soaked to his torso, with either sweat or blood (god, I hoped it was the former), and his arms were bulging with tension, all the way down to his slightly trembling fists. His knuckles were bruised and bloodied, and that did something to me.

My stomach whooshed.

Not in a bad way, but in a totally inappropriate, borderline crashing out kind of way.

I was *not* attracted to men who punched walls, chain-smoked, and wore ripped jeans and discolored boots.

I was not. I was not. I was not.

"You should wait outside," Jax said, in his usual patronizing way. "For your own good."

"Why?" I shot back. "Did you kill him?"

His brow ticked up, the very faint scar on his cheek tugging at the movement. "So what if I did?"

I gulped. "I didn't ask for that."

He shrugged. "You don't have to like my methods. They're effective. I got what you wanted."

My stomach twisted in fear. I tried to glance around him to the others, but his huge body blocked my view. I shoved his chest half-heartedly. His heart was steady and strong beneath my palm.

"He's not dead," he said, sounding disappointed by the fact. "But I will kill him. Probably. First, we got some show-and-tell."

"Please move," I said. At his stubborn expression, I scowled. "I can handle it. I'm not going to break down now."

"We'll see."

His lack of confidence in me stung. I tried to ignore the tightness in my chest as he stepped aside, and I got my first real glimpse at the basement.

It was...underwhelming.

Not the haunted, cabin-in-the-woods I expected—there were no creepy mannequins or suspicious moving dolls or cursed mirrors. It was basically empty, with a low wood-paneled ceiling, some whiskey barrels in the corners, and a wall of wine bottles slotted into built-in brackets. A dusty tusk chandelier offered tepid light, just enough to make out the naked figure hunched on the floor.

A high-pitched noise escaped me before I could stop it. Jax's rumbling laugh answered beside me. "Fucker doesn't deserve your pity."

I said nothing as I stepped toward the bleeding man, trying to be quiet so I didn't spook him. It didn't work. He flinched at my approach, his head snapping up, and glared at me from a mangled face.

I froze at the flash in his eyes. It was fleeting, a mere second before it was replaced with panic.

Did he recognize me?

My heart iced over. Not me. Molly. We looked similar enough that people used to mistake us.

Slowly, I turned and faced Jax again. He smirked back at me, all insufferable and smug.

"Molly," was all I managed.

He nodded.

I felt no triumph at the confirmation, no bitter victory. I went numb, my fingers tightening on the edges of the guestbook pressed to my chest. Our hostage watched me with nervous eyes, which widened in fear when he realized what I was holding.

Strike two.

"H-How did you g-get that?" He stammered out.

I ignored his question and leaned down, bringing my face close to his. His nose was mangled, bloodied, and swollen between his cheekbones. His eyes flickered over my face, mapping it with dawning horror. I sensed movement to my left and, without looking, knew it was Madoc. The man trembled, his gaze flickering left, his lip wobbling.

"Please," he whispered to me. "P-Please d-don't let them kill me."

I held up the guestbook. "Explain this to me, and I'll consider it." I was lying. I knew there was nothing I could do to stop Jax or Madoc. The evidence of their unleashed brutality was staring me in the face. I couldn't tell which damage belonged to Madoc and which to Jax—they obviously tag-teamed it. Took turns.

The thought made my insides woosh again. *Down girl. Jesus.*

Between hiccup and sobs, the broken man explained how guests signed the book on arrival to the island, and how they pricked their fingers and pressed it to their names, ensuring their silence if they ever tried to speak out. When I asked rather reluctantly why their silence was so important, he broke down until he was near incoherent, and only Madoc's looming presence made him talk.

I listened in hollow silence at the girls he scouted on behalf of his bosses, the way he'd drug them and smuggle them onto the island, the month-long orgies, the disposal once they were done. "W-We don't k-kill them," he sobbed, like that made it better somehow. "T-they get paid, and some even agree to come back."

"Because you break them," I said in a hollow whisper. "You make them forget. You brainwash them."

"No," he denied vehemently.

I stepped back, my jaw clenched so tight that I tasted metal. A hungry, vicious anger swirled in my gut. I wanted to break him. I wanted to hurt him, tear him apart, rip him limb from limb. I saw it vividly, and it didn't scare me, not like I thought it should.

Was this how Ryle felt when he bludgeoned his father to death? My face tilted up, finding him. He was standing by Callum, his arms folded, his face dark. My gaze slipped to each of them, even Zola, who was tucked into Nate's side as he swayed on his feet. I knew they understood, and I was suddenly grateful they were here. I skimmed over

Madoc, who was always watching, and looked at Jax, my heart thumping wildly.

"You can kill him now."

Jax searched my face, then grinned. "I'll get right on that."

"Not yet," Madoc said. "It's just getting interesting."

What more was there? I swallowed dryly, not sure if I could handle it. Jax nodded at Callum, who stepped forward and easily hefted the bloodied man to his feet. His nudity shocked me, his bits and bobbles hanging out, his chest streaked with blood and thighs stained with—

My nose wrinkled, and I turned into Jax's chest. "Gross."

His hand settled on my lower back.

"No more delays," he said, his voice hardening, making my insides flutter. "Show us what's behind the wall."

"P-Please."

Jax gestured to Madoc, who gave the naked man a small mocking wave, my knife clutched between his fingers. I made an affronted sound, and Madoc's mouth hitched in an evil smile. The asshole.

"Either you do what we want, or green eyes over here will happily cut off your dick and balls."

Happily being the key word, judging by the manic gleam in Madoc's eyes. I searched the walls, wondering what the hell could be behind them. Was it some kind of secret wing? A bat cave?

The man quivered as he was frog-marched over to the wine wall. Callum loosened one arm just enough so that the man could reach out and twist one bottle like a door-knob in disguise. There was a great shudder, a long groan like a sealed crypt being opened after many decades, and the whole wall swung forward.

I stumbled over eagerly, nearly tripping over my own feet. A damp, rank smell infiltrated the space. I froze as the wall kept opening, revealing a wide-arched entrance.

"Oh my god." My breath caught in my chest.

17

OLIVIA

Behind the wall was a tunnel.

It was wide, with a low ceiling, and the walls sloped, exposing rock as if it had been drilled directly through the earth. It smelled like the sea, like fish guts and rust, like rot and misery. Naked bulbs hung from the ceiling and trailed off into darkness. I knew without a doubt that this was the sordid underbelly of the pristine mansion, the real place encased in the fake one.

I wasn't aware that I was moving until a hand wrapped around my upper arm and tugged me back. "I want to go," I heard myself whine breathlessly. I didn't think it was a lie, but my heart was pounding like I was about to jump off a cliff.

"Hang on," Jax said. My anger sparked like flint against rock, my eyes catching his heatedly.

But then he lifted his gun and pointed it directly at our naked tour guide. My mouth clamped shut, my protest drying up. Jax had that look again, the undercurrent of violence that made his eyes wide and his finger twitch on the trigger.

"What am I looking at here, Kane?"

Kane licked his lips as his eyes swiveled over each of us. He couldn't seem to look directly at the tunnel, as if it would somehow seal his fate. It probably would. "We call this d-downstairs," Kane said with a timid stammer. "He k-keeps them here. They never see the inside of the mansion."

"Any alarms?"

Kane trembled and shook his head frantically. He blanched when Madoc stepped toward him. "N-No, I swear. It's empty right now. I haven't—I was supposed to—shit."

"Right now," I repeated in a daze. Ignoring the gun now at my back, I stood in front of Kane. "How often does this happen?"

Kane blinked at me. He was becoming too fear-drugged, his eyes watery and unfocused. "There's a new shipment every month."

Shipment. Like they were nothing but product. Tools. Toys.

Molly had been a toy. Reduced to nothing but a warm body. Did Kane rape her? I glanced over his body, like I would see evidence of Molly on him. He was leanly muscled, completely hairless, pale beneath the streaks of blood. He wasn't very tall—in fact, they'd probably been the same height. Had Molly found him attractive?

We didn't often talk about boys. Molly was a deeply private person, and the very topic of sex used to make her screechy and flustered. She wasn't a virgin—I knew that much from her earlier diary entries—but I got the sense she didn't really enjoy it. She didn't crave it. The few times she'd noted had sated her curiosity enough that she didn't want to keep exploring it. Whoever she ended up marrying would be regimented in their routine, a sex once-a-week type of deal.

I flinched back, directly into Jax's feverishly hot body. The gun slotted over my shoulder, so I became the unwitting sniper. I couldn't stop picturing it. Molly held down. Molly gagged. Molly drugged. Molly cracked open. I stared at Kane with refugee eyes, and the pictures changed, so I was seeing his body over hers, between her legs, rutting, forcing. Bile burned up my throat.

I felt Jax's voice rumble through my body. "You first."

Callum forced Kane into the tunnel, deliberately knocking him hard into the wall so he staggered with a pained cry that echoed. And echoed. *This must be what Hell sounds like.* I shuddered, and Jax pressed harder into my back, almost like a reflex. Silent support. His heart was still steady, but his anger was palpable. His body was taut and spring-loaded, and it made my lower belly clench in that new, unhinged way.

Damnit. I liked his violence.

It was drawing out my own violence almost tenderly, bringing to the surface my need to break and hurt. My fist curled at my side. If it weren't for the valuable evidence against my chest, I'd probably be clawing out Kane's eyes from his skull. I might just do it anyway.

After Callum went Madoc, slipping into the hellmouth like a shadow warden. Then Nate and Zola followed, and Ryle with his face turned down at his shoes, and then it was just Jax and me.

"I hate this," I said miserably into the empty basement.

Strong hands turned me around. I stared unseeingly at Jax's collarbones.

"Look at me."

The firm command made me look up obediently. He was no longer smirking, his eyes intent as he searched my face. "Don't disappear yet."

I nodded, my head feeling too heavy for my shoulders. "I'll try."

"You can hit me again if you want."

That made me smile. Damn him for that. "Thanks. I'll keep that one in the bank."

His hand grazed the back of my neck, squeezing it. It was too much—too intimate, too familiar, too everything—so I stepped back, putting some much-needed distance between us. His hand dropped away.

"I still hate you," I said, because I needed to say it. I needed to keep the distance.

He smirked, but it looked tired. "You don't lie as good as you cry."

I glared at him. "Shut up."

"You ready?"

I wasn't. I nodded anyway.

The tunnel was empty when we walked in, the others already exploring whatever lurked ahead in the darkness. I could hear them, the acoustics making it obvious that we were in a long, cavernous place. Refusing to let my fear stall me, I marched determinedly ahead, Jax a solid presence behind me.

At the end, the tunnel split into opposite directions, which, at a glance, were mirror images of each other. Low ceiling, bulb lights, and doors. Dozens of doors, made of cold metal with little peephole windows like a supermax prison. On a whim, I turned left, away from the rest of the crew. At the first door, I arched onto my toes and looked through the mail slot window.

It was a prison cell. Worse, probably. If I could speak at all, I'd ask Jax if he'd had better conditions on the inside. In the dim light, I could just make out a single cot, a bare mattress, a bucket in the corner, a small, low table with little drawers that probably contained all sorts of nefarious things.

No windows. Just naked bulbs hanging from the low rock ceiling.

Numbly, I reached for the metal latch, unable to work the mechanism until scarred fingers reached around and slid it open effortlessly. I didn't spare him a look as I walked stiffly inside. The air was stale yet somehow damp. I could smell the mattress, the cold iron of the bed frame. For a moment, I just stood in the space, taking it in, dizzy and numb.

Jax hovered in the doorway, his arms crossed, biceps twitching with his undercurrent of violence. I walked to the bed and gingerly lay on it. The frame whined and creaked, the mattress wholly unforgiving.

"The fuck are you doing?" Jax sounded shocked, then furious. I stared up at the lights, thinking of Molly.

"She was here," I said in a small, distant voice. I felt so far away, and I thought that was how Molly had probably felt. Not here. Somewhere else. Somewhere better.

Jax was suddenly leaning over me, breathing heavily. "Get up," he snarled.

"She was here." It begged repeating. After all this time, all my efforts to dig up the truth, and I was lying in her casket.

Rough hands grabbed me and hauled me up. I fought him clumsily, still floating too far out of reach.

"I don't want to see you like that," Jax growled in my ear. "Not as one of them. Fuck, he's going to die slowly."

My hands curled over his biceps, anchoring me back to the grim present. He was so solid. So alive.

A tiny flash of red above his head caught my eye. I froze, then withdrew with a slow blink, uncomprehending. A few seconds later, I pointed. "Is that what I think it is?"

Jax turned, his body vibrating against mine. We were pressed together so tightly that I felt when his heart skipped. "Shit," he muttered. He pressed a finger to his ear. "Zola. We got eyes."

Whatever reply came didn't seem to surprise Jax, but it made his face downright surly. He cursed again, then man-handled me out of the room, not bothering to shut the door behind us. I went willingly, if not a bit shocky, my feet tripping over nothing and only his firm grip preventing me from eating dirt.

The tunnels went on forever. I lost count of the doors after seventeen. We arrived at the end of one tunnel to a set of double doors that hinged inwards, a grand opening to another cavern of Hell.

It was a bedroom, a proper one, with a plush king-sized bed in the middle, polished dark wood side tables, and another tusk chandelier hanging from the ceiling, the light warm and soft against the rough cavern walls. I knew with certainty that this was Salvadore's real bedroom, not the pristine showroom upstairs. The room was still neat, but it had signs of life—the mug on the side table, a pair of reading glasses beside it, a box of tissues and lotions, and the artworks on the walls. They were decidedly more sinister than his upstairs collection, more flesh and bone, wailing mouths and twisted bodies contorted in agony. Whoever painted them was probably less disturbed than the reclusive billionaire who hung them up in his underground rape dungeon.

The thought, bizarrely, broke through my shock and made me laugh. It was a quiet, desperate noise that made Jax falter. The others were waiting in the bedroom, and on our arrival, they each turned and stared at me like I'd grown a second head.

I barely smothered my laughter, pushing my knuckles into my mouth. "Sorry," I muttered.

Nate shot me an amused look. "She's cracked."

"She hasn't cracked," Jax said, at the same time Ryle punched Nate in the shoulder. "You're one to talk, dude."

Callum dragged our naked hostage to the bed and forced him on top of it. He had gone weak and rubber-limbed, the blood flaking where it had dried on his chest. "M' not allowed in here," he mumbled without prompting. "He don't let anyone in here."

His lids fluttered, and he started to slump over on himself. Callum caught him, and then Madoc leaned over and slapped him hard across the face. Kane jerked upright, blinking, the pain spiking his awareness.

"Not nighty night time yet," Madoc sang. He was enjoying this. Of course, he was, the weirdo. It was probably one of the few reasons Jax kept him around. It wasn't like his personality was winning any points.

It was then that I realized that Zola was missing. My stomach clenched hard, and as I turned to alert Jax, he said, "Zola, don't watch it."

There was a beat. Then Nate shot out of the room, and Jax rubbed his forehead with a resigned expression. I noticed Madoc watching him intensely. And then Madoc noticed me watching him, and I couldn't seem to look away from his pitiless stare.

It was Ryle who broke our staring contest.

"Hey," he said with a grim smile. "Zola found the surveillance room. There are videos. She's watching them now."

His gentle words doused me in ice. "Videos?"

Ryle's mouth pressed into a hard line. He nodded to something over my shoulder. I followed it, finding a wall of TV screens mounted there, facing the bed. "The sicko liked to watch," Ryle said.

And so the depravity continued.

"It's a good thing," Ryle went on, and then balked at my incredulous expression. "I mean, obviously not the videos themselves, but the evidence. It's what you wanted, right?"

Right. I nodded robotically.

Jax inhaled sharply behind me. Ryle's eyes flickered to him, then his brow furrowed, and he looked concerned. He always seemed to look like that when it came to Jax.

I turned to the door. "Show me."

Ryle hesitated, still watching Jax. "I—are you sure?"

"I need to know if Molly is on them."

"You can't unsee that."

"I know."

After a moment, Jax nodded at Ryle, but seemed determined to stay in the room. His cold blue gaze was fixed on Kane. He was going to kill him, probably the moment I stepped out of the room. I searched my feelings, but they were a confusing tangle, too confusing to unravel. Did I care? *Should* I care?

Thankfully, Ryle took the lead, so I followed him dazedly out of the room. A last glance over my shoulder saw Jax cracking his knuckles, and the white flash of panic on the soon-to-be dead man's face.

18

JAX

"What are we thinking?" Madoc mused as he stalked like a feline around the bed. "Kill him here or in one of his little torture rooms?"

Kane whimpered and twitched against Callum's hold. He still had some fight in him, and it excited me. I was one sick puppy.

Distantly, I knew that I was losing touch with reality, becoming mindless with rage and violence. Seeing Olivia on that bed, her face pale and withdrawn, looking far too fucking vulnerable, made me see red. I was still seeing red; the blood on Kane's face, on my knuckles, on the tip of Madoc's (Olivia's) blade. Even the sheets on the bed were silky crimson, a bed of blood.

Pressing the heel of my hand hard into my forehead, I steered myself back to sanity. "You find anything else?" I asked.

"Found the stash." Madoc revealed two glass vials from his pocket. He dropped them on the bed beside Kane, who flinched away from them like live grenades. My eyes met Madoc's, our thoughts syncing in the way they sometimes did.

His answering smile was slow and deadly. "I'll find a syringe."

With him gone, I released a breath I hadn't realized I was holding and gave Callum a quick once-over. My stoic giant was unflappable as always, his hands steady where they locked around Kane's naked body. Like all of us, Callum had his own demons, but he managed to keep his shit together. I knew when we returned home, he'd lock himself away in his library to escape his rancid memories. I tried it once—desperate times and all—but my head was too loud, and only keeping my hands busy kept the bad thoughts away.

Kane withered on the bed, then went very still when I loomed over him. "How many girls, Kane?"

His lip trembled. "I—I don't—I didn't want—"

I backhanded him, his jaw clicking shut in the most satisfying way. The sound of his pathetic pleading was grating on my nerves. "Answer the question, moron."

"I-I didn't k-keep count. I'm not like that."

My anger spiked. "You're just the victim here, right? You had no choice but to lure in those girls."

"I'm sorry," he said in a small voice. "I'm sorry, I'm sorry. I'm so fucking sorry."

"Too little too late."

Footsteps crept up behind me, then the faintest brush of fingers across my lower back. Madoc knew I hated being snuck up on, and he was the master of it. I appreciated his warning, even though I still stiffened at the contact.

"Found one." Madoc held up a clearly used syringe. The tip was rusted, all nasty and shit. Perfect. "It was under one of the beds. Should we have a go?"

Kane balked in distress. "Oh god, please, man, no."

"Hush." Madoc picked up a vial and filled the syringe. He handled the drug expertly, as if he'd done it a thousand times. It shouldn't have been as attractive as it was. I definitely shouldn't be popping another boner over it.

You're so fucked up, cap.

I wrenched my eyes to the far wall, trying to redirect the blood flow to my brain and not my traitorous dick. It was clearly just punishing me for earlier. I told myself it was a bad case of blue balls and that was why I was reacting to everything. Fuck, a light breeze would probably set me off.

Just as I was getting myself under control, Madoc went and kneeled on the bed, wrenching Kane onto his back. In quick, precise movements, he used his knees to trap Kane's arm and jammed the tip of the dirty syringe into the crook of his elbow.

Kane released a harsh, throaty cry that echoed throughout the chamber. Madoc wasn't gentle, and soon blood began spurting from the injection site. I grabbed Madoc and pulled him back, ignoring his pissy look. I didn't want that dirty blood anywhere near him—well, more than it already was. Madoc sidestepped me but kept close, the three of us watching as the man started to convulse on the bed. A fresh stream of urine arched into the air. It was as undignified and humiliating as he deserved.

Madoc hummed in amusement. "Like a human fountain."

Callum and I shared a bemused look, and that set us off. We laughed until our sides hurt, until Callum was rubbing his chest and I was leaning on him like I was drunk. Madoc's mouth twitched upwards, hysterics by his standard. Our twisted amusement soothed some of the pressure in my chest. It reminded me that we were together for a reason. Dr. Z, as much as I despised him and his creepy recruiters, had known what he was doing when he hunted us down. My madness was his madness was his madness. We were broken, twisted beyond repair.

Ryle's voice in my ear sobered me up: *"What are you lunatics laughing at?"*

Right. Back to business.

Our dear friend Kane had slipped into a foggy delirium, his eyelids heavy and mouth slack. The only sign of awareness was the quick snap of his eyes when Callum moved to check his pulse.

"Strong but thready." Callum sneered down at Kane's pale face. "I'd say he's still too alert, lads. Probably feels everything."

Most date rape drugs worked like that. Madoc hummed and crawled onto the bed like a lover, causing me to feel a certain type of way. Then Madoc tortured us both by softly brushing aside Kane's sticky hair from his forehead, and I hadn't known he was capable of such gentleness, such *reverence*, until he purred softly: "You are completely helpless now. You can't run. You can't fight back. I'm going to cut off your toes, starting with little piggie, and there's nothing you can do about it."

As delightful as that sounded, we were running out of time. With a quick jerk of my wrist and a pointed cough, Madoc looked thoroughly disappointed as he took out his knife. "Or I'll just slit your throat, I guess."

Killing him was quick but messy, a theatrical performance that painted the room a deeper crimson. I ignored the way my cock stiffened and my gut pulsed, and I avoided Madoc's heated gaze as we sealed the bloody tomb. If all things went according to plan, it would be a long time before anyone found him. And if someone knew where to find him, they had a vested interest in hiding him and his sordid operation.

We entered the main surveillance room. It was darker than the rest of the tunnels, so I had to blink to find sense in the morbid silhouettes of Nate, Ryle, Zola, and Olivia against the glare of screens. None of them were moving, too focused on whatever was playing. I stole Madoc's move and gently brushed my fingers across Olivia's lower back. She flinched but didn't turn. A quick glance at her face revealed the shiny tracks of fresh tears.

"Which one?" I tried to keep my voice soft, but I couldn't. I sounded like I'd been gargling bleach.

Olivia swallowed thickly and pointed at the bottom left screen. "That one."

The picture quality was startlingly clear as two bodies thrashed on the single cot. Watching it made me yearn to resurrect Kane and follow through with Madoc's sinister plans, and then some. It called to the sickness in me, the dull throb between arousal and rage, the hunger for vengeance. Sick fucks like Kane didn't deserve quick deaths.

I suspected my proximity was unwelcome, so I stepped back. To my surprise, Olivia stepped with me, like we were inexplicably tethered. I gave her ponytail a soft tug, and her shoulders loosened just slightly.

"Have we seen enough?" Zola's voice was bright and sparkly in the dim room. She was a ruthless compartmentalizer, no doubt due to her many years working on the dark web. I doubted this ranked in her top five worst videos she'd seen.

Olivia stiffened against me. I knew Zola's nonchalance angered her. I waited for the eruption, but then she took a deep breath and said: "Yes. It is enough."

Her voice was steady. Her posture was perfect. But she was barely holding it together.

Something would break in her, and soon.

"I'll make a copy," Zola said, fingers clacking efficiently across the keys. "Then I'll wipe the last few hours."

"Any cameras in the main bedroom?" Callum asked. His eyes slid to mine, then dropped to Olivia with a knowing look. I didn't like that look—it made me bristle, made me defensive—but I didn't know why. Guilt and something sharper feuded within me. Nosy prick.

"Nope," Zola said, after a quick perusal of the options. "And none in the mansion itself. Good for us, bad for him."

"Not even in the first-floor hallway?" Nate asked, looking far too smug.

Zola smirked up at him, quick and gone. "Not a chance, babe. You know where I sit with sex tapes. They always get leaked."

"So? We're hot as shit. Bet we'd trend on the porn sites."

"You're an idiot."

I tugged Olivia out of the room.

"Come on. Let's get some fresh air."

She came with me without complaint, a temporary submission. By the time we reached the basement, some color had returned to her face. She was still clutching the guestbook like a lifeline. She couldn't look at me until we were back on the balcony.

"I get why people need fresh air now," she said in a small but clear voice. I offered her a cigarette, but she shook her head.

The sun was three fingers from the horizon, the sky streaked with violet amber. Thick rain clouds still hovered, the smell of rain teasing in the gentle salt-tinged breeze.

"I don't—" Olivia started, then stopped, frowning at the cruel paradise around us. "I don't know what to do with these feelings. I'm so angry, I might explode."

"So explode."

"I can't," she said. "Bad things happen when I do." Stormy eyes lifted, seeking mine. "How do I stop feeling like this?"

I took a careful inhale, sucking in the poison that fueled me. That was the problem. It never stopped. "No idea."

She nodded, accepting that, looking defeated as she watched the smoke dance around her. "Have you figured out what you want yet?"

I choked a little on my next puff. My mind went *there*, but I reeled it back. Not the time, dickhead. "Not yet."

Her smile was bleak. Strained. She was trying. Trying not to break. My chest cracked a little more. I looked at my bloodied knuckles next to her delicate ones, two worlds set on the same collision course. "I'm not good at this part."

"Which part?"

I curled my fingers up awkwardly. "Talking. Feelings. Giving reassurance." A whole parade of angry ex-girlfriends flashed through my head.

Olivia smiled indulgently. "You're not as bad as you think you are. At least you try. That's something."

I scoffed. "You need to raise your standards, princess."

"Probably," she conceded. She sighed and rubbed her eyes tiredly. "I don't know what I need right now. Probably therapy. Lots of it. Maybe I'll try that one with the goats."

I slid her a baffled look. She laughed weakly at my expression. "It's a real thing, I swear."

"If you say so." I waited a beat. "Do you eat the goats?"

She laughed again, all tinkly and cute. "No. You don't...never mind." She sniffled, but she wasn't crying. It felt like victory. "I know you're distracting me."

"I've never had goat before."

"Stop it," she snorted and slapped a hand over her mouth. "I shouldn't be laughing. Not after what I just saw."

"No judgment here."

She looked at me consideringly. Her eyes were soft. Too soft. It made me squirm. "You can't judge me," she said. "You're way more screwed up than me."

Facts.

I flinched in surprise when her fingers brushed lightly over my bruised knuckles. "I like this," she confessed like a dirty secret. "It makes me think you were right before."

"About what?"

"The Stepford wife thing. Wanting what I shouldn't want."

A dangerous hope ignited in my chest. "Careful."

"You're so bad for me," she said. "You're arrogant and dangerous. I wouldn't be enough for you. I'm too vanilla."

My hands tightened on the railing. I gave her a hard look. "Tell me where Meathead lives."

She flinched back, startled. "What? Why?"

"He clearly did a number on you." My voice dipped dangerously. "Nobody should make you feel like you're not enough."

Her eyes widened to saucers. "Oh my god." She slapped her hands over her face. "Damn you for saying that. Do you want me to cry? I hate you."

"Good."

With that, I dragged her against me. The dam broke, and she wept into my chest, her delicate fists twisting into the fabric of my shirt. My instincts screamed at me to run—for once, I ignored them, stroking her side until her sobs softened.

She pulled back after a few minutes. Her eyes were puffy, her cheeks red and splotchy. Her ponytail was off-center, golden strands stuck damp to her face.

My heart fucking skipped.

She sniffled and ducked her head in embarrassment. "I think my brain is broken," she admitted. "I just want to forget for a second about all of this—about Molly and that video and the—the dead guy. You killed him, right?"

I nodded.

She took a deep breath, steeling herself. "You should kiss me now."

My brain short-circuited, so I wasn't sure I heard her correctly. "What?"

She looked up sharply. "Kiss me," she repeated.

I hesitated. Just for a second. She held my gaze defiantly, daring me to deny her. My bossy cheerleader.

"Fuck it." I stamped my cigarette out on the balcony railing and cupped her face. "Crazy looks good on you, princess."

She licked her lips. "Prove it."

I crushed my mouth to hers.

19

OLIVIA

The kiss was rough, demanding, and a little bit feral. Just like him.

There was also something claiming about it, something possessive about the way his hand slid around my jaw, cupping the back of my neck and holding me in place. I couldn't move even if I wanted to. And I definitely didn't want to.

Weirdo, Molly taunted in my head. The sound of her voice was devastating in the wake of the truth. I pushed her aside, down deep where she couldn't reach me for a while. I needed to turn off. Breathe. Forget.

A breathless moan escaped my mouth when his lips molded over mine, his tongue immediately seeking entrance. I gave it to him, and the hot slide of him left me quaking in want, my body disconnecting and reconnecting in sharper agony.

God, he was a good kisser. Hard, unapologetic. Full of teeth and violence and cigarettes. I tried to keep up, but it was a lost cause. I was practically a virgin again, fumbling under his touch, trying to swallow my moans so he couldn't find them. Our teeth clicked once, and he pulled back, only just enough to bite down hard on my lower lip. My eyes sprang open in shock, and I was unprepared for the shock of blue, the icy fire.

Jax released me, his voice ragged. My own pants were loud and embarrassing between us.

I knew we needed to stop. Once was forgivable—anything more was a commitment. I fumbled for the words, finding them and losing them all over again when he leaned in, dragging his stubble across my chin and down my neck.

At my ear, he whispered huskily: "Stop thinking so much."

"I can't," I practically whined.

Then his teeth nipped my earlobe, and the pain was electric. His hands settled low on my hips, calloused thumbs rubbing my bare hip bones. "I'll just have to do better," he said.

He kissed me again, wholly, consuming. My brain was my brain, so I couldn't silence it completely, and I became overly aware of my limp arms. Wanting to regain control—wanting to prove *something*—I dragged my hands over his stomach, over the fabric, then dipped underneath. He was so hot. Feverish almost. His ridiculous abs tensed and rippled beneath my touch, and I just knew he was doing it on purpose.

I hated that it worked.

As payback, I scraped my nails hard against his naked sides, and he jerked in response, but not in a bad way.

In a very, very good way.

Then I went higher, across his ribs, over jagged scars, over his hard nipples. He jerked again, more violently, and slammed my body against his.

He was rock hard.

I made a startled noise, and he smirked against my throat. "Problem?"

So many problems. All the problems. But what came out of my mouth was the biggest one: "I want you to touch me."

A hungry growl rumbled from his chest. "Where?"

"Everywhere. Make me—um, finish what you started. Earlier."

His head dipped down, danger in his eyes. "You want me to make you cum?"

Mortified, I nodded.

"You can't even say it."

"Can so."

"Then say it." His brow quirked at my embarrassment. His teeth flashed, and he kissed me again, quick, dry. "Fine. Don't. Turn around."

Too eager, I did. My neck prickled with awareness at the heat on my back, the gentle brush of his breath on my neck. Those rough hands positioned me, so I was facing the orange-mottled horizon. Then Jax slotted in behind me, every line of his large body pressed against mine. I felt him—all of him. His thighs, his stomach, that unforgiving bulge in between.

Was he going to bend me over the balcony? My stomach swooped, my palms instantly damp. It wasn't that Heath and I had never experimented—we'd gone through all the positions, checked all the boxes (except well, *you know*, back door). It had been good. Nice. Fun.

It didn't threaten to unspool me like this.

My body moved independently from my mind, already arching over, wanting to accept him like a feral cat in heat.

Jax dragged his hands across my belly, then down my thighs, a groan building in his throat. "Fuck. Your legs."

"You like them?"

"You could say that." To prove it, his fingers clamped around my flesh tightly, hard enough to bruise. When I started to squirm, he loosened his hold, but his fingers continued upwards, blazing a path to the button of my shorts. With an easy flick, they came undone. I suffered a hot flush of panic, not remembering the exact type of underwear I'd picked, but then his fingers dipped down, and I decided it didn't matter. Softly, he parted me, exploring my tender core with near reverence.

"Have you been wet this whole time?" There was wonder in his voice. Admiration. I was too far gone to be ashamed by it.

"Shut up."

"Jesus. So eager." His fingers curled inwards, and I yelped, startled at the intrusion. Then I felt nothing but white-hot pleasure, the kind that thrummed down my legs and pooled in the soles of my feet. It wasn't an orgasm, but it was close enough that I worried the real thing would kill me.

There were worse ways to go, I supposed.

Jax kicked his boot between my legs, parting them further, giving him better access. His hand started a brutal motion, circling, pressing, releasing when my hips hitched forward, chasing my release. He was drawing it out, his lips on my neck, tonguing my rabbit pulse.

"You're already so close," he growled in my ear. "You need it, don't you? Admit it."

Lust-drunk, I nodded.

His finger stopped and hovered, right where I needed him. One more touch and I'd crash over that beautiful edge. He knew it, so of course, he held it ransom, his teeth grazing my ear as he continued his filthy observations.

"If all I get is this, my fingers won't be enough."

"They—oh my god—they are definitely enough." My chest heaved, my thighs twitching. I was not above begging. "Please, Jax."

His other hand slid over my waist, pressing on the cusp of my belly. I moaned, then balked at the sensation, as the pressure somehow increased between my legs. "What—"

"I'm good with my hands," Jax said, amused.

Good? He was goddamn biblical. With his hand on my belly, the other hovering above my throbbing clit, I was so close. Painfully close.

Then he removed his hand from my shorts, and I whined at the loss. "J-Jax!"

"I got you."

Quickly, he spun me around, the railing biting into my lower back. I barely blinked before he was gone, kneeling at my feet, his hands ripping down my shorts to my mid-thigh and exposing me to his hungry gaze. My breath stuttered in shock and arousal. I slapped my hands down in a loose attempt to cover myself, but Jax wasn't having it. He caught my wrists and pinned them against my legs.

"Stay."

And then he just…looked.

Stared, like I was a feast for his eyes. I squirmed, but he wouldn't let me go.

"So pretty," he purred, teeth flashing savagely. "Cute and pink, just like you."

"Will you just—oh." Words left me as his head bowed, his tongue lashing over my aching core. Mere seconds later, I gasped and came with such force that my ears popped and my vision whited out. He didn't stop licking, and that was a new torture, prolonging the waves.

Between a moan and a shudder, I caught movement through the glass doors in front of me, a flicker of a shadow. I squinted, half delirious, and told myself it *hadn't* been a pair of green eyes that I'd caught staring back at me.

Releasing my hands, Jax grasped my thighs and sank back on his heels, looking up at me with sinfully glistening lips. "You look ruined, princess."

"I—I think I swallowed my tongue."

"Here. Let me find it." He sprang up and kissed me hard, drilling his tongue into my mouth. I tasted myself on him and kissed him back just as hard.

An insistent prod at my leg drew me back. My hands were on his belt moments later, unfastening and freeing him. I knew from earlier that he was big, but seeing it was a whole different thrill. His crown was flushed and angry, a bead of precum welling on the tip. When I wrapped my hand around the base, he pulsed and pulsed.

"Can I...?"

"Yes," he groaned hoarsely.

Even though I wasn't entirely sure I was prepared for it, I slid to my knees and licked tentatively across his leaking crown. His hips flexed at the contact, and another moan chased with a curse. He tasted salty and masculine, and there was already so much of it. I twisted my hand around him, meeting my mouth where I wrapped it around his head, suckling eagerly.

"Jesus—fuck." His large hand dropped to my head, fingers latching around my ponytail.

I focused my tongue on the vein beneath the head, searching, learning. His response was encouraging—he gripped my hair tighter and pulled me in. He didn't gag me, his restraint obvious in the tension thrumming along his thighs. He was heavy on my tongue, smooth like warm velvet. I pulled back and gave him a soft kitten lick.

My other hand slid up his inner thigh and tugged once on his balls. They drew up quickly, his hips stalled, and he groaned: "Fuck—do that again..."

I pulled back and lapped at his slit, gently cupping his balls. His thighs clenched around me. I spared a glance upwards, blinking to clear the haze from my eyes, and saw him in erotic definition—his lips parted and head thrown back, all sharp angles and elegant columns. And then he snapped forward, his eyes finding mine, pupils blown wide and dark.

I saw the end in the way he stopped breathing. Without warning, he exploded in my mouth in hot bursts. I swallowed on instinct, not minding it as much as I thought. Especially when Jax staggered slightly, when his fingers tangled in my hair, when his eyes slammed shut, and his jaw flexed, his chest heaving.

There was so much of it. I swallowed twice before it slowed. Then I held him for a breathless moment. He softened and withdrew, tucking himself back into his briefs.

I wasn't sure what I expected to happen next (Jax struck me as a root-and-boot kind of guy), so I was surprised when he lifted me up and crushed me into his chest.

I mouthed dumbly at the fabric of his t-shirt, reeling from the embrace. He was...hugging me? His large hand stroked down my back, finding the tension. Easing it. My insides fluttered in a way that had nothing to do with what we'd just done.

"What are you doing?" I asked, my voice muffled.

His chest vibrated. "Just checking something."

"Checking what?"

"That you're real." He pulled back just enough to smirk at my suspicious expression. "I knew those pouty lips could do more than cuss me out."

"Shut up." My face flooded with heat. But my head was blank. Totally empty. It was welcoming, like a blanket of numbness.

"Don't tempt me." His bruised knuckles bumped my chin gently. "It's sunset."

His hair had turned copper under the bleeding sky. "I didn't take you for a romantic."

"I'm very romantic," he said with a quirked brow. "I just unloaded in your throat, and now we're watching the sunset. Tell me you've had a better date."

I recalled candlelight dinners and Heath's unironic movie nights full of horror and heavy petting and realized he was right. This was better. Not that I'd tell him that.

The reminder of sunset—our deadline—came prickling in like a slow poison, turning me cold. I shivered. "So what happens now?"

Jax hummed, staring over my shoulder thoughtfully. "We assemble the evidence you need. Wipe the place down. Scrub the surveillance and sit pretty on the beach until dawn. Our boat arrives at five."

"I meant after we leave."

His eyes found mine. "You want to know your future?"

I could tell from his tone that I wouldn't like it. But apparently I was a sucker for pain, so I nodded.

"The princess returns to her cushy little life with her meathead boyfriend and trust fund. She settles down, earns a white picket fence, a few kids. Cute kids," he added, giving me a fond grin. "All stubborn and uppity, like her."

I jabbed his shoulder. He caught my fist and squeezed it.

I looked away, my throat tight. "Sounds nice."

"It is," he agreed. "Nice and safe."

If that was the case, why did it scare me so much? That future was all but set in stone—he'd described Molly's ideal life, the one my parents had carved out for us. I hated being such a cliché. So predictable and boring and normal.

Jax wasn't normal. He'd never feel safe. He came with so many red flags I could start my own parade.

"And what about you?" My voice came out scratchy.

Jax lit up another cigarette. "Me? I'll be lucky to live to middle age."

"No plans to settle down?"

He puffed and smiled. It was just shy of bitter. "This life chose me. It won't let go until I'm useless and dead."

"That can't be true."

"It's true enough," he said with a shrug. "People like you get vigils. People like me get forgotten."

I won't forget.

Jax caught my expression. "No looking back. Only forward." He reached up and tugged on my ponytail gently. "I'm already your past, princess."

20

JAX

"Is this everything?"

"Yep," Zola confirmed, passing me the flash drive. "Four hundred and sixteen hours of pure snuff. I hope you know I'm going on a spa retreat when we get back."

A spa retreat or a bottle of Jack and a two-day power nap? I knew which one I'd prefer. "We bounce in five."

"Finally." Zola looked relieved as she gathered up her remaining tech. Then she paused, her fingers idling on the zippers. "What are you going to do about Nate?"

Right. That big idiot. I rubbed my eyes tiredly. "We could roast him over a fire?"

Zola grinned wickedly. The tension lingered, but her eyes brightened. "That would smell too bad. And attract too many predators. We could blindfold him and push him over a cliff?"

I smirked. "I'm not wasting the blindfold."

That made her laugh. Something in my chest loosened at the sound. We were a bunch of miserable assholes and needed to find our happiness somewhere.

Like pretty girls with big gray eyes and pouty lips.

My cock stirred, remembering all too well the sounds she made, the warmth of her tongue, the way she tasted. I knew it was only a one-time deal, but shit. I was ready to sell my soul to keep her.

"Seriously, though," Zola said, sobering up. "He's been acting weird for a while. Ever since we got this job." She shouldered her pack aggressively. "He needs rehab."

"The Compound has a basement."

"We can't just lock him in the basement and throw him protein bars for a month."

I rolled my eyes. "God forbid he doesn't have his ten-step skincare routine."

She laughed again, a bit rustier than before. "I don't think your unique brand of tough love will cut it this time, Jax. He needs a proper facility. Actual therapy."

"With goats," I mused.

Zola gave me a weird look, which flattened in distaste. "You've been spending too much time with little miss pom poms."

Little miss pom poms. I liked that. Uploaded it straight to my spank bank.

The others, minus little miss pom poms, were waiting for us in the foyer. Nate was slumped against the wall, crashing out. Callum was hovering, and Ryle was bouncing around him like a hopped-up jackrabbit.

I stopped. "Where's—"

Madoc appeared in front of me like a fucking apparition. I jumped about a foot and went warm in weird places. "Jesus. We need to get you a bell."

The look Madoc gave me was different from his usual ones. Something lurked beneath the mask, an unwanted curiosity. Green eyes lingered on my throat, and I reached up without thinking and gave it a scratch.

Had Olivia left marks on me?

Fuck, I should've marked *her*. The idea of her wearing my bruises while she returned to her perfect life was euphoric.

"Need something?" I asked him. My voice broke like a goddamn tween.

Madoc's mouth twitched. "Never."

"Good. Stop looking at me like that."

"Like what?"

"All knowing and shit."

Madoc hummed. There was a devious twinkle in his eye that usually meant one of us was about to get a pinecone to the head.

Had Madoc seen us?

It wouldn't be too shocking, I suppose. He saw way too much. He'd definitely seen me in more compromised positions, so I had no idea why my face was burning up like a bashful bride. I jabbed his shoulder, and he responded with a quick undercut to my gut.

"Oof." I bent over, relieved more than anything.

Pain was good. Pain was our love language.

Then Ryle bounced over with his dimples and hyper grin and said, "Aw, you two made up."

I frowned at him as Madoc shifted. I had deluded myself into thinking the rest of the crew hadn't picked up on the tension between us. Ever since that stupid night, those words I blurted out, the way I'd leaned in, heart in my mouth, only for him to withdraw completely.

"No. Not like this."

His words still haunted me. The flat rejection of them, like he'd been waiting for me to screw up for a long time.

My anger returned, sharp and unrestrained. "Don't," I warned Ryle.

The stupid kid only grinned wider. "But I've missed Jadoc."

An aneurysm burst behind my right eye. Madoc went still.

"What," I growled, "the *fuck* did you just call us?"

Ryle stopped bouncing, sensing he'd swam into infested waters. "Um...nothing."

"Did you give us a *couple name?*"

"No," Ryle scoffed. He shuffled back, hiding behind a bemused Callum. "No way. Nah huh. Never shipped you. Never will."

There were about to be two bodies hidden in this house.

Before I could pummel him to death, Nate made a startled noise and jolted, as if a hot poker had stabbed him. He shuffled forward and fished out Kane's cellphone. His glassy eyes widened. "Ah, shit."

What now?

"We might have to jump to the third act," he said, rising unsteadily to his feet. "Kane is expecting a delivery. ETA thirty minutes."

Callum frowned. "A delivery of what?"

Nate winced. "Well, I doubt it's a family-sized pepperoni."

"It's another shipment." My voice dropped, my gut sinking. More girls.

Part of me knew it'd been too good to be true. A clean death, a quick getaway. A hundred million dollars strapped to our backs.

A newfound urgency rippled through me. *Olivia.*

Madoc moved before I could. "I'll get her."

"She's probably still—"

"I know," Madoc said without turning back.

He knew.

Because he'd seen us.

There was no time for shame, or whatever confusing emotion wanted to tangle me up. The flash drive burned a hole in my pocket. The ghosts of the girls filled the room, demanding vengeance, urging us to act.

A hand settled firmly on my shoulder. Callum, the anchor I always relied on when I started to drift. "We'll do whatever you decide," he said.

He was giving me a choice. I looked at each of them, finding only acceptance. I could walk away, and they would follow. We could start fresh. Take our money, return to the Compound, drink until we forget.

Nobody expected us to be heroes. We weren't the good guys who swooped in and saved the day. We were thieves. Thugs. Whatever morals we had were loose at best.

I made the heinous mistake of catching Ryle's eye. He'd stopped smiling.

I groaned. "Jesus. Don't do that to me."

Ryle blinked. Then pouted. "I'm not doing anything."

"Menace." I stepped forward and locked my arm around him in a chokehold. His laugh filled the space, chasing the ghosts away.

"We're not running," Callum deduced, looking pleased.

"No."

"We're saving those girls."

"Yeah."

"Beauty," Callum said, rubbing his hands together greedily. The others stood taller.

Zola looked downright menacing. "Does this mean we can break out the real tech?"

"And the guns," Callum said, fist bumping Ryle.

Nate was uncharacteristically silent in the wake of promised destruction.

Ryle lunged toward the stairs. "I'll go tell Madoc."

"Careful," I said pointlessly.

There was no room for careful.

Not when we were about to pull off the toughest job of our lives.

21

— · —

OLIVIA

An existential crisis while standing on a balcony on an unmarked island after having my world rocked by an actual thief wasn't on my bingo card.

But it happened, and I was sure as heck having one. It wasn't just Jax, even though he was the catalyst. It was him and Molly and the future that awaited me, a future without either of them.

Panic clawed at my throat. It wasn't that I didn't want all those things Jax said—the white picket fence, the kids, the niceness. It was that I'd never permitted myself to want anything else. I was the girl who smiled at everyone, who got good grades and volunteered, who joined my sorority as a legacy, who became cheer captain by unanimous vote because I was organized and disciplined, and because my parents sponsored the team.

I wasn't as good as Molly, who thrived on my parents' approval. But I was good.

I was a good girl.

Who wanted to do really, *really* bad things.

Specifically to a six-foot-something deviant with dirty blond hair and busted knuckles and the kind of feral grin that belonged in a mugshot.

And then I just felt selfish. *More* than selfish. I was a terrible person who had just found out that her sister was the victim of a human trafficking ring. Grief had become my constant companion over the last two years. I missed her every day. Every second. The only time I didn't was when Jax touched me, when he literally brought me to my knees.

Without him, everything I'd been avoiding came crashing over me. The tunnels, the videos, the proof. The fact that my sister was probably dead—and that an awful part of me hoped she was.

But I wouldn't give up my search. I'd come too far—crossed too many lines—to stop now. I had Preacher waiting for me to deliver the proof. He'd take the video and the names in the guestbook and use his terrifying influence to bring them down. Bit by bit, we'd unravel the operation, and hopefully find whatever was left of Molly.

I wondered if Jax would be open to a new deal—

My thoughts were interrupted by the sound of the door opening behind me.

Somehow, I knew it wasn't Jax. My body tensed, sensing the demon at my back. "Of course it's you," I sighed.

"Thinking about jumping?"

He sounded more curious than alarmed. For some reason, it made me smile. There was something dependable about Madoc's assholeness. While the rest of us burned in the fires of our own making, he just stood back and enjoyed the warmth.

I shot him a resigned look over my shoulder. "Would you stop me?"

He cocked his head in thought. "No," he said after a minute. At least he gave it *some* consideration, I noted bitterly. "You wouldn't die. It's not high enough, and you're conditioned to land on your feet."

I fought another smile. God, I was broken.

"I wasn't going to jump," I said, even though my voice was shaky like a lie. "I was just...thinking."

"About Jax?"

"Yes. And no."

Madoc nodded like that made perfect sense. He leaned on the door, watching me curiously. I could probably live a thousand years and never understand what went on in that twisted brain.

Especially when he suddenly tossed my backpack at my feet. I could tell from its bulky shape that my binder was inside. I glared at it distrustfully. "There better not be a live snake in there."

His mouth twitched. "Open it and find out."

Against my better judgment, I knelt down and rifled through it. Everything was accounted for, minus my knife and chocolate. My binder was secured. My phone was in the hidden pocket. My suspicions rose.

"Did you go through my phone?"

"Yes," he said, shamelessly.

Brilliant. I scowled and refused to check it in front of him. Whatever messages he'd seen would've been cryptic. Peacher had drilled into my head the importance of discretion in his line of work.

"Thanks," I said sarcastically.

"Don't thank me."

"Whatever." I almost said 'sorry' before my brain caught up and reminded me that Madoc was still Madoc, the knife-wielding, throat-squeezing, murderous psychopath.

He also saw you cum.

Thank you, brain. Warmth spread like a rash over my body, pooling at my cheeks, stinging my neck. I hugged my backpack to my front tightly like body armor. With Jax, I needed to shield my heart. With Madoc, I needed to shield my secrets.

"What do you want?" I asked him.

Madoc pursed his mouth in thought. It was a pretty mouth. An unhelpful observation, but true nonetheless.

"How does he taste?"

My heart stopped. "W-What?"

"You heard me." His eyes glimmered with wicked amusement.

Suddenly jumping from the balcony seemed like the greatest idea I'd ever had. Anything to spare me from this.

I floundered, then stuttered out: "You can't ask me that."

"Why not?"

"Because!" My cheeks burned, even as I met his eye daringly. "It makes you sound jealous."

His lips pursed, as if to say *maybe*.

Oh my god.

He couldn't be...could he?

Abruptly, my brain was filled with visions of them...together. Madoc pressed against the railing, Jax kissing him like his life depended on it. The battle for dominance, the clashing teeth and violence. Madoc with his hand wrapped around Jax's throat. Jax fisting Madoc's inky dark hair, forcing his eyes up, daring him to—

"Something on your mind?" Madoc asked, still watching me intently.

My whole body was on fire. "Nope. Nothing."

He moved so quickly that I had no time to react. One minute, he was by the door; the next, he was looming over me. He was everywhere, yet not a single part of him touched me.

"He likes you," Madoc said in a soft, deadly voice.

I clutched my backpack tighter between us. "It didn't mean anything."

"I don't like liars."

I chewed my lip, and his eyes honed in on it with that same cutting intensity as earlier. I wasn't bleeding this time, but I wondered what would happen if I just...bit down. Cut into the skin. Bled a little.

Girl. What.

I wrenched my head back with such force that I gave myself whiplash.

Madoc hummed, the sound mocking and satisfied, like a cat who'd finally caught the tricky mouse. He moved slowly, precisely, lifting his hand and touching my throat. Unlike all the other times, it was soft. Caressing.

Searching.

"You felt him here," he said, ignoring the way I gulped nervously. "He's big, but he used restraint. Good for him."

My mouth dropped open. "You...?"

"Yes." His eyes flashed. "I know everything about him."

The possessiveness in his voice was unmistakable. The feeling it invoked in me was less so. My heart skipped, my face burned, and my knees were unsteady.

God, the absolute last thing I needed was to collapse at his feet. I didn't trust Madoc, especially with that unhinged look in his eye. He was a textbook psychopath. Pretty and softly deceiving, possessive to the point of suffocating. I didn't know if I was a threat to him or another toy for him to obsess over.

I wasn't sure I'd live long enough to find out.

"Stop," I said, my voice weak.

"Stop what?"

"Whatever game this is. I'm not playing." I lifted my chin, faking a confidence I definitely didn't possess. "You want Jax? You can have him. Our deal is over anyway."

Madoc tapped my chin in a light reprimand. "You have it all wrong."

"Do I?"

"I don't want anything."

For some reason, I believed him. He was smiling, but there was nothing behind it, a mask over a blank canvas. The only insight was his alarmingly sharp eyes, seeing everything, all my faults and lies.

I almost wept in relief when Ryle appeared at the door behind Madoc. He looked between us with a knowing grin that I immediately wanted to slap away.

"So this is a thing now, huh?" he said, leering at Madoc, who tossed him a lazy look over his shoulder. "Man, and I thought Jax had it bad."

I cringed as Madoc turned and headed toward the door like nothing happened.

"You tell her yet?" Ryle asked him.

Madoc, the jerk, just breezed on by without comment.

I was still trying to catch my breath.

"Tell me what?" I asked, winded.

"We got a new shipment arriving in thirty minutes. Well, less now."

That made my lungs seize all over again. Ice swept through my veins, chasing away the heat. "More girls?"

"Presumably so."

"How do you know?"

"Nate still has that dickhead's phone. Turns out he was here to prepare the house for the drop." But Ryle was still grinning, so I knew it wasn't all bad news. "Jax called another war room. We're going full Rambo on their assess."

I nodded robotically. Ryle gave me a friendly bop on the head as I passed him, clearly sensing my malfunction.

The mood was instantly different upon returning to the war room. The atmosphere was electric, the kind of excitement that prefaced a homecoming game. I felt detached from it, an outsider.

Would this day ever end?

There was no hint of exhaustion in the crew. Even Nate had apparently found his second wind. They crowded around the dining table, their packs and equipment spread out like a smorgasbord of chaos. It was nearly sundown, the chandelier encasing the room in a warm, anticipatory glow.

Jax looked up where he stood at the head and caught my eye. Whatever he saw on my face hardened his own. I deliberately didn't look at Madoc, feeling those laser eyes on me from across the room.

Jax crooked one gloved finger and beckoned me over.

Like a hopeless idiot, I went. When I stood before him, he faced me, and for a second I thought he was going to kiss me—a reassurance I'd gladly accept—but instead he reached for my hand and placed something cold in my palm.

"Yours," he said.

I unfurled my fingers slowly and found a silver flash drive. My eyes instantly burned, and emotion clogged up my windpipe.

Evidence.

The very thing I had traveled across the country for. The reason I'd exposed myself to skeevy fisherman and sex dungeons and mouthy thugs with piercing eyes and bruised knuckles.

It didn't feel real. Not him. Not any of it.

I closed my fist around it, the sharp bite into my palm a welcome sting. "Thank you."

The tender moment was broken by an enthusiastic Ryle reaching for a long-nozzle gun. "Dibs on the AR-15."

"No!" Callum, Jax, and Zola said at once. Callum reached around and plucked it from his grasp.

"Let's take it easy, boyo," Callum said, unmoved by Ryle's answering pout. "We all know you get a wee bit trigger-happy."

"Do not."

I stared, wide-eyed and unnerved by the spread of weapons. "So, uh, what's the plan exactly?"

Jax's shoulder bumped mine. "You ever seen Home Alone?"

"Only a million times." It was Molly's favorite movie.

"Well, it's like that, only more carnage." His hands were piecing together what looked like a complicated metal egg. "We rig up the house, wait for them to set off the traps. Then we take them out."

"And by *take them out*, you mean...?"

Across the room, Madoc dragged his finger across his throat.

Right. Murder. How cute.

The others were piecing together their own weapons. Zola's fingers were flying across tablets and keys with scary speed. *They've done this before,* I realized with a sudden pang of awareness, something that shivered like fear through my body.

I'd come too far to chicken out now.

"What can I do?" I asked, feeling pathetic as I stood there, limp and useless.

Jax didn't even falter. "What you do best."

My expression blanked, remembering the balcony and the way I'd taken him in my mouth. Swallowed him eagerly. Annoyingly, that memory was now tainted by Madoc, his finger on my throat as he taunted me. *How does he taste?*

Jax gave me a lewd grin like he knew *exactly* what I was thinking. "Not that," he said quietly. "Your other talent."

It was sad just how hard I had to think. I could tumble like a pro, read five hundred words per minute, and apply liquid eyeliner in a moving car. Not exactly a helpful skillset for the current situation.

Eventually, I landed on a deflated: "You want me to cheer from the sidelines?"

He winked. "Exactly." He handed me a small earpiece. "Put that in. Communication stays green at all times. And only use code names, no real ones."

I slotted it into my ear. "What's my code name?"

He reached up and tugged lightly on my ponytail. My cheeks heated, my eyes darting nervously around the room. But no one was paying us attention.

No one except *him*, obviously.

"Welcome to the crew, Princess," Jax said with a conspiratorial grin.

A confusing fizzle of emotions made me duck my head in embarrassment.

For all of two seconds.

Then Jax tugged my hair again, a bit harder, so I looked up, annoyed. "You're going to be our lookout," he said, and inclined his head to Madoc. "You'll be up in the trees with him."

Madoc gave me a disconcerting smile, like he couldn't wait to fling me out of said trees.

Next, Jax gestured to Callum. The big man unrolled sheets of construction paper with what looked like complicated architectural drawings. "We're here," he said, pointing to the bottom third of the page. "We can assume the tunnels run along here. They weren't included in the initial scope."

"Shocking," Ryle muttered.

"The girls never see the inside of the mansion," Jax reminded him.

Callum nodded. "Exactly. Which means we got a secondary access point somewhere on the east side of the property. It'll be discreet. Easy to miss unless you knowin' where to look."

"Why not just take them out on the beach?" I asked, then immediately felt stupid when six pairs of eyes swiveled to me. I crossed my arms defensively. "What? Is there some killing etiquette I don't know about?"

"Kinda," Nate said, perking up from where he'd started to slump against the wall.

"We want to minimize casualties," Jax said, scratching at the crow tattoo behind his ear. "These pieces of shit will use the girls as human shields under attack. They'll be heavily armed and likely outnumber us. It's better if we isolate them, lull them into a false sense of security."

Someone's device buzzed loudly.

Nate fished out a phone from his pocket and glanced at the screen. "Fifteen minutes until they reach land."

"Gear up," Jax said, and then his hands were on me, strapping a tactical vest onto my chest and tightening the straps and buckles. I immediately felt ridiculous, like a child in an adult-sized life vest, and judging my Jax's amused squint, I looked the part.

"Where are you going to be?" I asked him as the others left the room, like hungry wolves. Ryle's devious cackles echoed after him.

Jax slipped on his own vest, then holstered his many weapons. "Aw. You worried about me?"

I scoffed, flicking my ponytail over my shoulder. "No."

His answering smirk caught my lie. He glanced over my head, where Madoc was waiting with a bored expression. "Listen to Madoc," Jax said. "I mean it. If you two kill each other, I'll be pissed."

Madoc gave him a mocking salute and walked out without another word. Jax stared at the door for a beat, then sighed and nudged me gently after him. "He won't wait for you."

"He's such a jackass."

Jax smiled fondly. "Yeah." Another beat passed. Time we didn't have. Time I wished would slow down. There was still so much unsaid between us. The flash drive was already lodged in my pocket, the guestbook tucked on top of my binder. I couldn't shake the feeling that we were missing something. And that we were headed straight for disaster.

I searched Jax's face, soaking in his roguish confidence, the easy set of his frame as someone born and raised in violence.

The thought of him dying punched a gaping hole in my chest, right over my already-splintered heart.

"Don't die," I blurted out. Way to play it cool.

"Go," he said, and then grinned his usual cocky grin. "You can cry on me later."

My face heated as I turned to the door. "I hate you."

"Good."

I forced myself to walk away, to look forward and not back. There was no time for goodbyes, but it still felt like one anyway.

22

JAX

The traps were set.

In record time, Callum found the secret entrance to the tunnels, tucked behind a seemingly innocuous garden shed on the east side of the mansion. Ryle and Nate were in the basement, rigging up the trip wires and dye packs. Zola was in the control room, where Ryle would be joining her as backup. I was looping wires across the staircase, each landing becoming a death trap for the unsuspecting.

It would be quick and messy and loud.

It was also a bloody Hail Mary.

Bringing down what was likely a well-established operation would take more than a few handy parlor tricks. We didn't have our best equipment—our lethal explosives were stored safely back at the Compound, where Nate couldn't get his greedy hands on them—and our intel was flimsy at best. The plan had so many flaws and potential for disaster that it left a gnawing pit in my stomach.

But I was ready—more than ready.

I was fucking amped with nerves and anticipation, more awake than I'd felt in months.

My pulse was a steady thump beneath my skin. My mask was pushed up over my forehead, keeping my hair out of my eyes while I fingered the intricate pieces of my equipment. I'd hooked a crowbar into my belt loop, the metal thunking comfortingly against my outer thigh. When all else failed, smashing skulls proved to be pretty damn effective. Not as effective as, say, bullets, but I wasn't opposed to getting my hands dirty.

Well, dirtier.

"Basement set." Ryle's voice chirped in my ear.

"Scooby?" I checked in.

There was a pause. *"Affirmative, Alpha."* His voice was strained. *"Five minutes."*

Five minutes until they reached the shore. My pulse kicked. I returned to our makeshift war room, taking inventory of everything left behind. There was a forgotten pack shoved beneath one of the chairs. A glance at the inner pocket revealed its owner.

Ryle.

Sloppy.

With a sigh, I hefted the pack onto the table, pausing at the metallic thump it made. It was heavier than I expected. Biting off my glove, I unzipped his pack, finding the typical hazardous mess that followed Ryle everywhere he went. Beneath his clothes, snacks, and whatever else he'd deemed a priority (including a half-empty box of condoms) was something square and metallic at the bottom.

"Idiot," I muttered, reaching in to pull it out.

My hand stopped cold.

What the hell?

I lifted the device and examined it. It was the drone's battery pack, the one we'd supposedly forgotten.

Why the hell hadn't Ryle said anything?

"Sunshine!" I barked into my earpiece.

Ryle's voice returned chipper: *"Yeah?"*

I opened my mouth when something else caught my eye. There was another device at the bottom, a burner phone. The brand was different from the one we typically used. The screen lit up, and a single message appeared.

A familiar area code.

My blood turned to ice.

"Two minutes," Nate said urgently.

Zola's voice followed sharply: *"We've finished with the fuse box. Going dark in three...two...one."*

The lights went out in a single blink, plunging me into darkness. For a second, it was suffocating, my chest impossibly tight.

I tapped the screen again, squinting at the brightness, hoping I was wrong.

My fist clenched around it so hard that my knuckles cracked.

This was no longer a Hail Mary.

We were fucking doomed.

23

OLIVIA

It was official. Madoc wasn't human.

At least, not completely. The way he moved was unnatural, like a jungle predator stalking through the dense rainforest, marking his territory. He even tapped on the trunks of trees we passed like he was spreading his scent. It would've made me laugh had it not totally freaked me out.

Thankfully, he remained intent on ignoring me. I bumbled behind him, trying to mimic his grace and failing. I was too awkward in my too-big tactical vest, and my backpack slapped against my spine with every clunky step. Twice I lost sight of him, and just when I was convinced he'd ditched me for good, he reappeared like a jump scare. My favorite.

Eventually, the weirdo found what he was looking for. He came to an abrupt stop and looked up and around us with sharp eyes. Without so much as a nod in my direction, he climbed the nearest tree, swinging up with monkey-like efficiency. I gaped up at him from where I stood, helpless and exposed at the roots.

And then he was just gone, disappeared above the canopy. As soon as my brain registered it, I became acutely aware of the rainforest and all its hidden nasties—the humming insects, the crack of twigs, the things moving in the dark.

"Hey!" I hissed.

Nothing.

I knew he heard me, the jackass.

Cursing under my breath, I gripped the nearest branch and hefted myself over it. I'd never been so thankful for my upper body strength. I actually enjoyed the strain, my muscles engaging after days without a proper workout.

The splinters were a fun little challenge.

I persisted, gritting my teeth as I climbed up, and up, hoisting myself over branches, breaking through the first layer of canopy. I was sweating oh-so-attractively, the air hotter and stickier the higher I went. In my head, I cheered: *lift, hold, pose. You got this. Gooooooo*—

The fall was inevitable. I'd just gotten my hand on the branch above me when the one beneath my feet cracked loudly. There was a moment where I swayed, teetering on the edge of oblivion—*not like this, not like this, not like this*—when a hand shot down from above and gripped my wrist.

"Move," Madoc snapped.

I hugged the trunk as tight as possible and used the momentum of Madoc's grip to swing to the next branch. To my intense surprise, he didn't release me until we were settled at the same level. Madoc was straddling his branch easily, looking perfectly content, like I'd interrupted some private meditation.

I was still catching my breath when he let me go and reached for his pack. "Idiot."

"Screw...you."

"I'd have to get in line." I could hear his smirk, even though I couldn't see it through the fireworks exploding behind my eyes.

Madoc removed a pair of night vision goggles from his pack. I watched him slot them over his forehead before I did the same. Instantly, my vision flashed white, then settled on neon green, the shapes distorted and alien.

"Trippy."

When I looked at Madoc, he was looking back at me, his mouth quirked beneath his own goggles.

"Something to add?" I demanded.

"Rich girl does cosplay."

I crossed my arms, then regretted it when I started to slide. "Don't sound so shocked. I happen to dress up every year." Mainly for Halloween and themed sorority parties, but Madoc didn't need to know that.

Besides, his condescending laugh said enough.

I ignored the blush on my cheeks as I twisted the lens, trying to get better acquainted with my surroundings. Instead, I caught myself watching Madoc as he shifted into a crouch with his back to me, facing the horizon. My eyes dipped low against my will—he was ridiculously agile, his legs tensed and strong, his back rippling with muscle.

"Basement set." Ryle's voice in my ear made me jump. They'd been oddly quiet in their tasks, focused and intense. Now and then, I'd hear the odd chuckle, gasp, or muttered curse, and it comforted me in a way that I didn't want to explore too deeply. Like I hadn't known just how lonely my head was until it was full of them.

The ocean was a dark green lip on the horizon, broken by white streaks of waves. I turned carefully, finding the mansion easily in the distance, the bright pricks of light that almost hurt to look at.

I settled myself better on the branch, deliberately not looking down. I told myself it was only because Madoc happened to be in front of me, not that I was staring at him intently, that I noticed him tensing. I followed his eyeline and saw it—the flare of a boat approaching the shore.

"Five minutes," Nate warned in my ear.

Madoc's head snapped over at me. "Eyes up."

"What? Why?"

"They could have a bird." The unspoken idiot was heard, loud and clear. Gritting my teeth, I looked up, scouring the neon green sky.

"Two minutes," Nate said urgently.

Zola's voice followed sharply: *"We've finished with the fuse box. Going dark in three...two...one."*

Behind us, the mansion blinked out.

There was a moment of profound silence, like right before a storm.

Then...

"Sparrow?" Jax's voice was both a blessing and a curse.

Madoc, typically, bit back. "What?"

"What was the code for the safe?"

Madoc remained silent, focused intently on the approaching vessel, until I thought he was going to ignore Jax entirely. Then he murmured: "six, one, seven, nine, two, six."

Jax inhaled sharply. Madoc's shoulders tightened at the sound, his head dipping low.

"Why?" Madoc asked carefully.

"Just checking," Jax replied quickly—too quickly. Judging by Madoc's continued tension, he knew it, too. *"It might come in handy later. Princess?"*

I jolted, my thighs automatically clenching around the branch so I didn't topple off like an idiot. "Yeah?"

"I don't hear any cheering."

"Right, sorry. Um, all good here, I think. The yacht is approaching. It's about...fifty feet in size. Actually, from here it looks like a Princess yacht."

"A what?"

"It's a brand—never mind. Not important. I see a table on the top deck and, I think, someone is sitting at it."

"Two someones," Madoc corrected.

I glared at his back. "No signs of choppers or drones or UFOs."

"Good." Jax's voice warmed. *"Don't want you getting beamed up yet."*

I'd let you probe me, I added in my head, my cheeks burning beneath the goggles. Madoc shifted, adjusting his position, and I craned my neck up, feeling caught off guard. For all I knew, Madoc could read minds.

"The yacht has docked," I said, my voice becoming scratchy with nerves. I twisted the lens, zooming in. The first face I saw belonged to a thin, weedy man who started directing from the stern. He was armed, his gun holstered across his back. "I see, um, lots of men."

"How many?" Jax pressed. *"Try to be specific, Princess. You're our eyes."*

"Four—no, five."

"Eight and counting," Madoc cut in. "Armed thugs. No sign of the girls yet."

The silence pressed in my ears. Considering. Planning.

A few seconds later, Jax urged, "Keep talking."

Between Madoc and me, we relayed the scene unfolding—the numerous men who spilled out from the yacht cabin, sweeping the beach with militant precision. Once the search was clear, the girls emerged, climbing up from the belly of the yacht and onto the dock, solemn and quiet. Prisoners marching to the gallows. The swing of flashlights made me clench and duck, but Madoc remained unflappable, part of the landscape. I stared at the girls, committing them to my memory, searching for a familiar face. A set of shoulders, honey-blond hair, grey eyes.

"They're heading up," Madoc broke in with a murmur. "The party has split. First wave is six men and fourteen girls. They are taking the direct path to the mansion."

It was obviously a familiar path; the girls were herded like cattle around the twisty bends and obstacles by steady flashlights. Their route would bring them directly beneath us. Madoc adjusted easily, never taking his eyes off them. He settled his gun quietly across his lap.

"How many stayed?" Jax asked softly, whispering so we didn't startle.

I looked back toward the shore. "Six men guarding the yacht. Two are still sweeping the beach."

"Okay," Jax said, sounding settled, ready. *"You did good,"* he added a moment later, the praise washing over me like a warm hug. *"Now don't fuck it up. Listen to Sparrow."*

"You don't have to keep telling me," I mumbled, adjusting my grip. There was a pointed huff that came from too many directions, and I bristled at their amusement. *Assholes.* I could obey when I needed to, even from a giant prick like Madoc.

Any trace of amusement evaporated as the footsteps approached, voices low and closing in. The very air grew heavier, blanketed in dread. I swallowed thickly and looked down, tracking the girls as they shuffled dazedly around the trees. Their features were hard to distinguish—their heights and ages varied, but they all had one thing in common: *hopelessness.* It was the slump in their too-thin shoulders, the drag of their feet, the way their clothes hung off their frames like a uniform. They didn't speak, didn't acknowledge each other. When one of them stumbled, clearly drugged to her eyeballs, a man grabbed her roughly and corrected her. My fingers tightened on my goggles. In front of me, Madoc reached for his gun, not to fire, just a reminder.

It was a foolish thing to hold onto the desperate hope that I'd see Molly among them. I knew I wouldn't, and the brief flare of hope in my chest left me breathless.

I turned away, unable to stomach it. That was a mistake. My backpack shifted, and the branch beneath me creaked ominously.

All at once, the footsteps stopped.

Madoc's hand snapped up, closed in a fist. *Wait.* I didn't move, didn't dare blink, didn't breathe. The voices below traveled with the wind, foreign and sharp.

"What's happening?" Jax demanded in our ears.

Neither Madoc nor I reacted. Slowly, Madoc lowered his fist, settling it on his gun. Then a flashlight beamed across the trees around us, searching. I almost cried out, but clamped down at the last second, biting hard on my tongue.

They were directly below us. If they just looked directly up, if they moved their lights ever so slightly to the left, into the canopy that shielded us...

"Vamos!" The voice cracked like a whip through the night, impatient. The lights flickered, dropping away, and

the morose shuffling resumed. When they were no longer directly beneath us, Madoc loosened his grip on his gun.

"We're clear," he said, no hint of strain in his voice. "Hostiles approaching. East side. ETA Ten minutes."

"Roger," Jax said. In a quieter voice, he added: *"Sparrow, be careful."*

Madoc gave him no indication that he'd heard him. But I was confused by the sentiment, the warning laced with concern. Madoc shifted once more, this time angling toward the ground, as if preparing to drop down at any moment.

"What happens now?" I asked him, half-expecting he wouldn't respond.

Madoc lifted his night vision goggles and settled them on his forehead, his eyes black and unreadable beneath them. Following his lead, I did the same, squinting to adjust to the darkness.

"I'm going to take the beach," Madoc said, like it was simple. Obvious. He relayed his instructions with the same cutting dryness that he applied to everything. "You'll be my eyes." Madoc leaned toward me, making my breath hitch. "You talk to me," he whispered. "Only me. No one else. Don't let the others distract you, even when it gets loud."

I nodded gravely. "Got it."

He stared at me for a long moment, looking for weakness, for cracks in my resolve. He wouldn't find any. I schooled my expression carefully, ignoring the sweat dripping down my face and stinging my salt-cracked lips.

Finally, he nodded, apparently satisfied. "Follow me," he said, shouldering his gun. "Lose me again and I won't come back for you."

Nodding determinedly, I followed his careful movements as we descended from the tree to find a new post closer to the beach. My legs ached when we returned to the ground, rubbery from overuse. It made me clumsier than I liked, but I refused to let it hinder me.

Behind us, the mansion waited, dark and breathless, like the open jaws of a predator. Time dragged and rushed together, so by the time I climbed the next tree, right on the lip of the shoreline, the mansion had been breached.

And the chaos began.

24

— · —

JAX

You could hear a pin drop.

My heart slowed, my vision sharpened. Every part of me was coiled and ready to spring where I was crouched beneath the stairs on the second landing. The waiting part was always hard. I wasn't a fan of edging, and here I was, constantly on the fucking edge.

"They're in," Zola whispered, so softly that it could've been a caress beside me. Another stretch of unnerving silence followed. The mansion was built to contain, to keep quiet. The windows were soundproof, potentially bulletproof, though we'd had no way to test that theory. They were also an illusion, a pretend freedom, looking out but never in, holding my reflection and keeping me on display.

Exhibition, my mind supplied. The ghost of me stared back.

"Okay, we have movement." Zola paused, watching intently from the control room. *"The girls are secured."*

My chest loosened slightly. At least that part went off without a hitch.

"They've noticed the power off," Zola said sharply. *"They're headed to the fuse box now. Get ready."*

In my head, I saw it unfold—the men approaching the basement, wrenching open the wine rack, triggering the wire connected to the dye packs. There would be a sharp snapping sound right before they were hit with the neon dye, marking them as glowing targets in the dark.

And then Callum and Nate would strike.

I braced myself for the sound. I shut my eyes like that would make it come quicker. I wrenched them back open at the first gunshot, the sound muted and far away. Too fucking far. It was a testament to my messed-up head that I wanted to run toward gunfire and not away from it.

I dug my nails hard into my neck, into the brand behind my ear, until it anchored me.

Over the years, we'd learned and accepted our strengths and weaknesses. I was a good shot, but not as good as Callum and Nate. Ryle was our runner, our hyperactive rabbit capable of slipping behind enemy lines. Madoc was a calculated sniper who liked to play with his prey.

My gut swooped when I heard Callum's voice: *"Two down. One escaped. Comin' your way, Alpha."*

I wrenched up my mask, becoming the cold-blooded assassin in the shadows. Pounding footsteps came up the stairs, a flash of neon pink splattered across a broad chest. My finger curled on the trigger. My mark was panicking, startled like a racehorse, boots heavy on the wood.

When he came to the second landing, his ankle snagged on the barbed wire, causing him to topple over with a startled grunt. I sprang forward, and he sensed me in the dark, already scrambling for his gun.

Too late.

I shot him in the chest, right in the splatter of neon pink. *Bullseye.* He gasped wetly, fingers clenching on the trigger. His gun fired, sporadically, aimlessly, shattering something behind me. I rushed him, stepping hard on his arm until it cracked. He cried again, the sound like gurgling paint. The whites of his eyes flashed up at me as I leveled the gun at his head and fired.

"Alpha?"

"Clear," I grunted out, my voice hoarse, my mask hot and sticky on my face.

"The alarm's been raised," Zola said, trying to maintain her calm. *"Ginger, Scooby—go in, go left. Hurry, or you'll be caught in the open."*

"Roger."

I knelt and searched my dead mark. His gun was semi-automatic; his gear was low-quality—not a valuable asset, then. With a sneer, I fingered around his bleeding skull, finding the small radio device in his leaking left ear. Carefully, I wiped it clean on my chest and slotted it into my other ear.

My brain scrambled at the immediate flood of foreign voices and shouted commands. The two frequencies—my crew and the enemy—disoriented me so much that I had to take a step back and find my equilibrium. The loudest, most pressing noise won out.

"...girls...ambush, si! Come, come quickly!"

"...shoot on sight!..."

"¡Sí, girls! Shoot them!"

My heart stopped. Then, a pulse of pure, animalistic rage took over.

Ripping out the foreign bud from my ear, I clenched my weapon and sprinted down to the basement. Sensing my urgency, or perhaps tracking my movement on the monitors, Zola snapped: *"Alpha? What's happening?"*

"They're taking out the girls."

Zola sucked in a sharp breath. *"Shit."* Fingers clacked on keys. *"That's why they changed course—shit, shit. Scooby, Ginger, pull back. Find the girls. Alpha—"*

"Coming." I pushed myself harder, taking the stairs four at a time, slipping on blood and dye and whatever else was left behind in the ambush.

The basement looked like an alien threw up all over it—splatters of pink and green neon dye all over the walls and ceiling, bodies sprawled like chunks on the floor. I didn't stop, launching over the corpses and lunging down the dark tunnel, relying on memory alone.

The sound of rapid gunfire echoed around me. Callum was breathing heavily in my ear—Nate was suspiciously silent. *Not them, not them, not them.*

Snarling, I swung around the corner, my gun raised. But it was too dark—bodies moved intermittently against the flashing backdrop of gunfire, indistinguishable. Dangerous. I growled in frustration, the sound tearing from my throat.

Fuck.

Pain lanced through my forearm as metal pinged beside me, a bullet ricocheting. I needed cover. Shoving my shoulder into the nearest door, fingers slippery on the latch, I wrenched it open and stepped inside. There was a tiny startled sound. I spun, finding a shivering form on the bed.

My anger, momentarily dulled by the chaos, became fucking nuclear.

"It's okay," I said gruffly, not moving, trying not to spook. I knew I looked like a nightmare—masked, bloody, eyes wild and hungry beneath my sweat-slick hair. The girl made no other sound, trained to be quiet.

I took a deep breath, tasting iron. I was going to murder these fuckers.

When I spoke, my voice was flat and controlled. "Crows, find cover. Nova, turn on the lights."

Zola launched into action. *"Roger, Alpha. Sunshine is headed to the fuse box."*

Five heartbeats later, the lights blinked on unceremoniously, a muted yellow like rot that filled the cell around me. I purposely didn't look at the girl, keeping my eyes trained on the door.

The gunfire ceased abruptly. Marks were exposed in the open. I called for Callum and Nate, and they responded in tired chirps.

Alive, alive, alive.

There was no time for relief.

I dug into my pocket and pulled out the palm-sized metallic egg. Visibility was both a blessing and a curse. My mind crunched over the numbers—six hostiles, two dead in the basement, one upstairs, three remaining.

"One left," Callum corrected me, half-imbedded in my thoughts, tuned with the same battle instincts. *"Bastard's locked himself in a cell. He'll take the hostage."*

My jaw clenched. "Which one?"

I followed Callum's instructions down the tunnel, veering right. When I saw them—Nate, leaned against the gritty wall, face ashen and blood spattered, Callum standing firm on his feet—my chest seized up like a heart attack. Both of them jolted when they saw me, their eyes raking over my body with the same clinical relief.

Without speaking, I lifted the device in my hand.

Callum nodded, then pointed down at my left thigh. Crowbar.

I handed it to him, then risked a peek into the room through the tiny window. My lip hitched into a snarl. The man was huge, easily Callum's stature, and was facing the door, holding the frightened girl in front of him like a shield. His gun was pressed to her temple, his hand unsteady. When our eyes locked, he bared his teeth in challenge.

The violence in me surged, fire meeting fire. I stepped back and nodded to Callum. He hooked the crowbar beneath the latch, then waited, biceps tensed in preparation. Nate pressed to the left side, so he wasn't in the direct firing line. I took the right side, covering the bases, my thumb clipping the tiny pin in the device in my hand.

We needed to be quick. No margin for errors.

Counting together, we matched our breaths, our blinks, our fucking souls. On the third blink, Callum wrenched downwards and kicked the door open, and I tossed the device across the floor where it burst with a deafening bang.

A blinding flash, then smoke, smothered the room in a thick curtain. Nate and I moved in as one unit, guns raised. Our mark was easy to find—big, stooped, covering his eyes with a howl. The girl was on the floor, unmoving. Callum lifted her easily and tossed her over his huge shoulder, exiting the room in three strides.

There was a gunshot, a scramble, and for a heart-stopping moment, I thought Nate spasmed, as if hit. He recovered a second later, lifting his gun and shooting twice at the bastard.

I added a third to his lower half, and finally, *finally*, he went down with a groaning gurgle. The smoke was suffocating, pawing at my senses. I reached for Nate at the same time he reached for me, gloves slapping flesh. We guided each other out of the room.

I slammed the door behind me, containing the smoke. Then I flipped around and shoved Nate against it, my hands patting him down, searching him fervently.

"I'm good, Ja—Alpha. I'm good."

"Shut up." My hand brushed his hip, and he stiffened, hissing. Giving him a flat look, I peeled aside his vest.

Blood oozed from a bullet wound on his hip, just below his belt.

For a second, I just stared at it, mind blanking.

"It's just a flesh wound," Nate insisted, grimacing. "Doesn't even hurt."

"That's not a good thing." My voice was small. Fuck. I swallowed around the bile, the lurch of anguish already trying to take over.

I had to fix it.

"Scooby is hit."

There was a sharp, wretched silence. Then Zola's voice cracked: *"What?"*

"We need a med kit—"

"I told you, I'm fine—"

I slapped his cheek, softer than I normally would. "I said shut up. Sunshine, bring the med kit to the war room. We're going up."

Callum stepped forward, the girl now conscious, and latched onto his arm like a nervous passenger. She had big, round eyes and short, reddish hair that I hoped was natural, not blood-soaked. "The girls," Callum reminded me gently.

"Open the doors but keep them here until we take the beach."

"Roger." Callum didn't move right away, his eyes lingering on Nate behind me. For a second, his face cracked, furious and devastated and vengeful, before he reined it in. With a brisk nod, Callum turned to the girl at his side.

"Let us free the others now, lassie. Come on."

The girl blinked up at him, then stubbornly shook her head. *"Schwester."*

"Eh, what now?"

"Meine Schwester." She tugged on Callum insistently. At our blank looks, she exhaled in frustration and carefully formed her words. "My...sister...is...boat."

"She was in the boat?" Callum translated slowly.

But the girl shook her head again. She pointed down the far end of the tunnel, toward the east entrance. "Still. *Still.*"

"*Still* in the boat?"

The girl nodded.

Footsteps pounded around the corner, revealing Zola, her face stricken as she rushed to Nate's side. Nate batted her away half-heartedly, but he was starting to sag.

I locked eyes with Callum, a terrible fizzling under-standing between us. I pressed a bloody finger to my ear.

"Sparrow. Come in."

No response.

My tongue lashed over my dry lips, doom tart in my mouth. "Princess? Talk to me."

Radio silence.

Zola turned to me with glistening eyes. "They're out of range."

And we were out of time.

25

OLIVIA

A s much as I loathed to admit it, Madoc was good at what he did. Even if what he did was commit cold-blooded murder and taunt pretty girls like me for kicks.

I watched him from my new post in the tree as he stood behind the dunes, his gun silenced and steady. He shot the first man when he stepped too close to Madoc's hiding spot. The man went down silently, blood splattering, then oozing between his eyes. The sight was somehow less disturbing in night vision, as if I were far removed from its reality.

Madoc zipped forward and dragged the body by its feet behind the dune, out of sight. Then he searched the body, quickly and efficiently.

"Stealing his candy?" My mouth spoke before my brain, my voice weaker than it should be.

Madoc didn't look up at me, but I felt his glare all the same.

Movement caught my eye, another man beelining directly toward Madoc. "Incoming," I said, twisting my lens. "He's seen the tracks, Sparrow—what are you doing?"

Instead of hiding, as I expected, Madoc popped up like a whack-a-mole, giving the man a half-second of shock before he raised his gun. Madoc used that split second to shoot him between the eyes. His accuracy was impressive, even if it made my stomach roll uncomfortably.

Two down, six to go.

"That was risky," I said, my body running hot, my thighs sweating where they straddled the branch.

"Shut up."

I did.

Watching Madoc drag the second body was oddly calming, which I knew was my brain's weird way of coping. Protecting itself. I'd never seen someone die before, and now I'd seen two in the last few minutes. They were piling up in my subconscious, tucked in the corner like skeletons in the attic.

My gaze snapped to the boat, where voices began to shout and gesture. "Sparrow."

"I know." There was no fear in his voice, just flat determination. I understood why Jax relied on him so

much—the world could end, and Madoc would still be as solid, as immovable, reliable.

Safe.

I shook my head at the thought. Ridiculous. Madoc was clearly an unfeeling killer, remorseless and cold.

Callum's voice crackled deep and startling in my ear. *"Two down. One escaped. Comin' your way, Alpha."*

My lungs seized. The communication signal was poor so far from the mansion, but the odd snippet still got through. I told myself to tune it out, focus only on Madoc. I ignored the needling concern that pressed on my edges—the image of Jax, bloodied and shot, sprawled like those corpses at Madoc's feet—and shoved them away with the rest of my unwelcome ghosts.

I exhaled when Jax's voice broke through a few minutes later: *"Clear."*

I watched the boat, tracking the disorder of the armed men as they started to suspect something was amiss. They no longer approached the treeline, and I knew that was a bad sign. Madoc crouched low again, his breathing steady in my ears, so I matched it with my own.

It was us against them. Despite my vehement dislike of Madoc, I didn't want him to die. He needed me, even though he'd hate to admit it, and being needed felt good.

I was powerless in so many other ways, in so many things, but not in this.

Clearing my throat, keeping my voice low and soothing, I gave Madoc my eyes. "They're nervous. Hovering near the boat. One of them is pointing toward the mansion—they're probably clued in to the ambush."

Madoc didn't speak, didn't give me any acknowledgment. However, when I shot a glance at him, his face was turned down, as if listening intently.

"One of them is turning to the boat. There must be...must be someone else in there, someone I can't see. They're talking." I narrowed my lens, trying to see into the cabin of the yacht. "Ma—Sparrow, what's the plan? We're outnumbered."

I didn't expect Madoc to reply—I was merely voicing my concerns aloud, just in case he needed to consider them. But Madoc surprised me by answering in a clipped voice: *"We need to draw them out."*

"Okay. Sure. Cool. What did you have in mind?"

Madoc paused, then said: *"You."*

I blinked down at him blankly. "Me?"

"Pretty girls are distracting."

I ignored the rush of warmth that gave me. Coming from Madoc, it was probably intended as an insult.

"You can cry and play victim. Or you can scream. Choose one. Draw them out."

I shifted on the branch and stared at the armed men, the monsters on the shoreline. "And if they shoot me on sight?"

"Bad luck for you."

I huffed in annoyance. "And what are you going to do while I'm bleeding out on the beach?"

"I'm going to make them pay."

Not exactly the most comforting plan.

I wondered if Madoc saw value in my life—enough that he would actually regret it if I died—but I decided not to prod too hard at that thought. Carefully, I climbed down the tree, awkward and clunky with all my gear. On the ground, I dumped my backpack and goggles, hesitating for a moment before I removed my tactical vest. I knew Jax would hate what I was about to do.

He's not here, my mind said, sounding oddly enough like Madoc. *Focus on here.*

"Okay," I said, voice dry but steady. "I'm ready. I'll start screaming."

I took two steps out from the treeline, sinking into the soft sand. I purposely didn't look over at Madoc, who was invisible to my straining eyes, and paused, testing my throat. When I was confident I wouldn't shred my vocal cords, I unleashed a high, ringing scream before stumbling out into plain view.

Immediately, men's voices pitched over toward me, demanding and full of threats. A light flashed over me, and I winced, raising my hands pitifully. With a gentle squeeze, I unleashed the welling tears that tracked down my cheeks.

Boots pounded across the sand. I allowed my shoulders to slump, despite the tension in my frame, the instinctive urge to clamp up and hide. Run. *Madoc is right there,* I told myself firmly as they descended on me. *He probably won't let them hurt you.*

"Who the fuck are you?" The voice was rough and heavily accented. A hand gripped my arm hard enough to bruise and shook me. "Got away, huh? Thought you'd make a break for it? *Das pena.*"

Hot rank breath washed over my face. "Please," I begged softly. "Let me go."

"Agh, pathetic." A second hand gripped my ponytail and yanked it back so hard I saw sparks. Multiple faces leered at me from above.

"This one pretty," another voice piped in, and fingers brushed against my side, probing. My stomach lurched sickeningly. "Bring her to the boat, si? With the others?"

There was a beat, and I saw a flicker in the corner of my eye, near the dunes. Madoc.

"Wait!" I exploded, and the movement stopped; the men paused, startled at my outburst. "Yes," I said in a raspy, desperate voice. I hoped, *prayed*, Madoc was listening. "Yes, please, take me to the boat."

Let them take me, I pleaded to myself. I knew it was unlikely Madoc would receive my message, but as I was marched down to the water, there was no sign of him.

Not until his voice ghosted in my ear: *"Idiot."*

I bit back a miserable smile.

Madoc needed my eyes, and we needed to know how many were in the boat. They'd mentioned others—Other men? Other girls? I knew it was stupid and reckless, and probably going to end with a bullet in my brain. But I was too far in it now. Everything that had happened—the tunnels, the secrets, *Jax*—it all led to this moment.

I was herded across the narrow dock and onto the yacht. The hands were unyielding, calloused, and punishing as they thrust me downwards, my sneakers fumbling over the stairs. The yacht was absurdly decadent, with fine-fingered chandeliers and warm gold accents, shiny hardwood floors that squeaked beneath me. I was forced down a short hallway, passing three closed doors, to the last door at the end. The men didn't bother knocking and shoved me inside like a stray animal thrown into a cage.

The room was dimly lit, the bulbs covered in grime, just like the tunnels. It took a few seconds for my eyes to adjust—for the panic to recede enough for my brain to switch back online. When it did, I stared numbly at the space in front of me, the upturned faces, the haunted eyes, the careful stillness. The room was bare except for the single bed in the middle, which was pointedly untouched. The girls sat on the floor around it, hugging their knees.

Fear, sweat, and unwashed bodies tainted the air. I nearly choked on it. With my back against the door, I used the pressure to ground myself. The girls didn't react except for their empty, lifeless stares.

"*Talk to me.*" Madoc's voice was blunt but breathless, as if he were running. I wondered if he was already on the yacht.

I barely moved my lips. "More girls in the cabin. Four of them."

"*Men?*"

"I don't know. I passed three closed doors, so there could be more inside."

"*Windows?*"

I blinked, frowning. "What?"

"*Can you get them out?*" Madoc bit out in frustration. "*Windows? Air vents?*"

I looked around, taking in the dry, windowless room no bigger than the bathroom in my dorm. "No." The word was laced with despair.

"I'm coming."

Distantly, I heard the sound of more gunshots, but it was like we were underwater. The girls didn't even flinch. They were so still, so quiet, even their blinking looked co-ordinated. I tried to summon up some words of comfort, but my throat felt raw. I settled for an overly big smile that hurt my cheeks. When all they did was stare at me, I gave up and listened for Madoc.

A loud thump at my back made us all jolt.

I instantly recoiled as the door opened behind me. Long, sinister shadows stretched across the floor.

"No one move."

The words—the *voice*—hit me like a physical blow to my chest. I was tucked behind the door, unseen by the intrud-er, but it didn't matter. My body reacted, disconnecting so quickly that I felt like I was floating, up, up, and away.

Shock, my brain supplied helpfully, right before it went silent.

The new intruder stepped into the room, dressed in all black, clutching a gun with thin, quivering fingers. Her hair, once a warm blonde, was lifeless and greasy, balled up in a messy bun with strands stuck to her neck. Her skin was sallow and bruised, her frame so bony that it jutted beneath her too-big clothes.

When she turned, sensing the unfamiliar presence in the room, our eyes locked—grey blue, lifeless, hazy.

Gone.

Her name stuttered out from my lips. "M-Molly?"

26

OLIVIA

Molly stared at me like I was a ghost.

Her mouth parted in shock, eyes still too distant, too unfamiliar. It was like seeing each other across a vast landscape, hopeful yet uncertain, and too far away. I worried that if I blinked wrong, she'd disappear.

Was I hallucinating?

Had I finally cracked?

My hands twitched at my sides, desperate to reach out and touch her. To feel her realness. Her living warmth. Except she didn't look warm. She was shivering, the gun clinking in her hands. Despite it, she looked steady, feet braced, shoulders tight, like she'd trained herself to overcome her fear.

She looked like a soldier. War-weary, refugee-eyed, and terribly resigned.

Then she frowned, her brows pinching in foggy confusion, and the landscape between us widened, tearing us further apart. She shook her head once, not in acknowledgment but a sharp, firm denial.

"Move," she said curtly. Her voice was ragged now, like she hadn't spoken in a long time. There was no sign of remorse on her gaunt face.

I didn't move.

"Molly," I said her name like a prayer, a plea. Memories flooded my brain like a broken dam—Molly chasing me when I stole her hairbrush, Molly teaching me how to use an eyelash clamp without flinching, Molly forcing me to drink green tea when I was sick, even though the taste made me feel sicker. *Molly, Molly, Molly.*

She'd always been a nurturer, a born helicopter parent, even as a kid.

That same neurotic know-it-all lifted her gun and pointed it directly at my face. I stared back at her in shock.

"I said move."

I couldn't feel my legs, but they moved on command, away from the wall and toward the bed. All the while, Molly tracked me, gun trembling but deadly. Her fingers looked like pure bone where they gripped the trigger.

"Mol—"

"Shut up."

This couldn't be happening.

I was dreaming. Or maybe I was dead.

Maybe I'd fallen out of the tree and onto my head, and as punishment, I was trapped in a coma-deep nightmare.

At the same time, my heart was bursting with such profound joy that I could hardly stand it. *I found her.*

Molly was alive.

All this time.

"You're not here," Molly said, and motioned the gun downwards in a clear sit order. The bed was hard and spring-sharp beneath me. My hands curled on the mattress, gripping it for dear life.

"Who are you?" she demanded.

"Who—it's me! Olivia."

Her jaw flexed, so sharp, so hollow. Uncertainty flickered over her haunted face. "No," she said quietly.

"Yes."

"No." Firmer now, resolved, she curled her finger around the trigger. I slammed my eyes shut.

I'm dreaming.

When she shoots me, I'll wake up.

No shot came. Carefully, I cracked open one eye. Molly hadn't moved. A small, confused frown marred her face. It was the tiniest opening, the barest of hope.

"It's really me," I said, forcing myself not to gasp with each panicky word. "It's Olivia. I promise. I've been looking for you, Molls."

The gun wavered, not dropping but hesitating.

Her eyes flickered over me and away, a restless, jumpy tick. Then she became distant, staring at the far wall like she was caught in a memory. Judging by her sudden wince, it wasn't a fond one.

"Someone else is here." It wasn't a question, just a quiet observation.

I nodded and answered anyway. "That's Sparrow. He's with me. He will help you."

"Help me?" Her head cocked, as if the very notion of help was foreign. Her eyes flared briefly. "Olivia."

I leaped to my feet. "Yes," I sobbed. "It's me."

She recoiled slightly, clutching the gun tighter. "No," she whispered again. "No, you can't be here. T-They promised. They said..." Her face shuddered, haunted eyes swimming with tears.

I moved automatically, stepping around the gun and wrapping my arms tight around her. She was so small, so fucking tiny, that my arms overlapped on her bony back. The gun jutted uncomfortably against my ribs. I didn't care. For a whole blissful second, we held each other, rocking slightly, soothing and sweet and stable.

Then we heard footsteps.

Molly's reaction was whip-fast and instinctive. As if a trance had been broken. She stiffened in my arms, then lashed out, shoving me back with surprising force. I lost my footing and just barely managed to grip the bed before I hit the floor. Around me, the girls whimpered.

The gun was raised and pointed, and the Molly I knew was gone again, replaced by the ugly enforcer. Real fear shot through my bloodstream.

"Get up." Gone was any recognition, any softness from her voice.

The girls obeyed quietly, rising and waiting like dutiful ghouls. I was slower. Molly jutted the gun at me. "Come here."

Approaching her a second time was not as easy. I eyed her warily, the space between us, the things unsaid, the horrors that had twisted her into jagged edges. I was crying, real tears that burned like acid down my face. Molly glanced at me coolly, with only the tiniest wobble in her chin, before she used the gun to herd me out of the room.

"What about the others?" I asked her. The gun stabbed my spine in response. I zipped my fat mouth and marched dutifully down the narrow corridor, past the doors, up the stairs that led to the main deck.

The smell of blood and grime hit me at once, and behind me, Molly blanched. The deck was shiny with blood, so fresh that it looked like an oil spill under the moonlight. Signs of a struggle were evident—stray bullet casings, upturned chairs, what looked like a shattered dinner plate. The beach was empty and dark in front of us, no sign of the men. Or Madoc.

"Sparrow?" I murmured into my earpiece.

There was the faintest crackle in my ear, a purposeful exhale. My shoulders dipped in relief.

He hadn't left me.

A shadow flickered in my periphery, and I turned, before realizing my mistake. Molly whipped around, gun cocked, and caught the shadow as it climbed over the side railing.

"Wait," I shouted to Molly, but she didn't listen.

Madoc was straddling the railing, but paused, his viper-like eyes narrowing on us, reevaluating. He was dripping wet, dark hair plastered to his face. His eyes held mine, not a question but a warning.

And then Molly fired.

It happened in slow motion, like watching a bad replay. I saw the moment the bullet hit Madoc, the way his body recoiled, the way his gloved hands tightened, then loosened on the railing. He didn't fall so much as slip away. There was a sharp, pointed silence, and then a quiet splash.

My knees gave out from under me.

"No," I whispered in horror. It played again in my head—his shoulders, his hands, his silent fall—and I went numb, totally numb. I didn't feel the blood soaking beneath my bare legs. I didn't hear the sound that wrenched out of me, didn't understand why Molly was looking down at me like I was a wounded animal.

I'm sorry, Jax. I'm so fucking sorry.

Cold metal brushed my temple, jolting me from the murky nothingness. I lifted my head and stared up at the demon wearing my sister's skin.

"There is no saving me," Molly said hollowly.

And her finger curled back over the trigger.

27

—— • ——

JAX

Something was wrong.

It was more than a feeling, more than a constant sense of foreboding. It was like missing a step and free-falling, like gravity itself had turned on me and I was scrambling to keep upright.

Nate was shot.

Madoc and Olivia had gone silent.

There was blood on my hands and salt on my tongue and in my eyes. Everything was burning.

"Hold him still," Ryle hissed in frustration as he battled a delirious Nate spread out on the dining room table. I moved on autopilot, pinning his torso down, cupping his head in the crook of my arm. His eyes found mine feverishly, wild and white, like the man I'd killed earlier.

Was this my karma?

He needs you.

Right.

I forced myself back to the present. My hands softened on Nate's jaw, finding his pulse hammering erratically beneath it. "Hey, you're good. You hear me?" My voice was rough as shit. Not exactly the most comforting sound.

Even so, Nate's body softened.

Zola hovered at his other side, holding his hand and trying not to cry. She was losing the battle. Meanwhile, Callum and Ryle were patching him up as best they could with what they had on hand. The bullet had punctured muscle and bone, but nothing vital. It was the shock and infection that worried us, plus whatever else the idiot had been funneling into his body lately.

"I better have a cool scar," Nate said weakly.

Zola smacked his chest. "You fucker."

"Ow," he whined, reaching up with his free hand to nurse his pec. "I'm wounded here. Be nice to me."

"I hate you," Zola said, her voice breaking. Nate fell silent, watching her. The rest of us pointedly ignored the tension between them, the wordless grief of nearly losing each other.

The silence in my ears was deafening.

Ryle appeared in front of me. "Your turn."

I shoved him away with a scowl. "I'm fine."

"Nope. We're not doing that anymore." Ryle glared at me. The expression was so odd on his usually grinning face that I found myself wanting to smile. The weak imitation made Ryle glare harder. "Just accept my mother-henning, asshole. It won't kill you."

So I gave him my arm and watched him clean and bandage the wound with too much aggression. Still, I didn't complain, and once we were all in reasonable condition (i.e., not bleeding out on the nice hardwood floors), it was time to bounce.

Rounding up the girls was easy. They were lifeless, puppets pulled on strings, obedient in a way that made my heart hurt. It was the sheer number of them that proved challenging. Callum did a head count, and the first girl we'd rescued continued to howl and plead for her sister still on the boat.

Madoc can handle it.

The assurance did nothing to soothe the pit of snakes in my belly.

Moving such a large group through the mansion and back into the rainforest was slow going. Ryle and I carried Nate between us, pausing often to adjust him or check his condition. He was pale but still a whiny bitch, so I knew he wasn't both boots in the grave yet.

Time was continuing to rush away from us. I crunched the numbers in my head. Five hours until our boat returns. Then two hours across the sea to the mainland. We'd take the girls, hand them over to the authorities. Then we'd run.

The question was: Where the hell did we go?

It made sense to lie low for a while. Even though we'd secured the painting, Dr. Z wouldn't be thrilled when word got out that Salvadore had been exposed. He'd immediately look at us, and the Compound was the first place he'd search. Thankfully, I'd had the foresight to start stashing away large wads of cash just in case things went awry. I had a few reliable contacts who could give us new identities. We'd have to split up for a while, change our appearances, set up new lives somewhere far off the grid.

Even then, it was unlikely any of us would make it to the end of the year. Dr. Z didn't keep heroes, and if this job proved anything, it was that he was a damn spiteful bastard.

As if hearing my thoughts, Ryle glanced over at me in the dark. "I hear Haiti is nice this time of year."

Nate groaned. "No more islands."

"Agreed." I stumbled over a thick bramble. My ankle rolled, and pain lanced up my calf. "No more fucking islands."

The girls moved in a single file in front of us, Zola leading at the front, Callum's thick silhouette guiding from the rear.

"Okay, well. Alaska is also nice."

"Too cold, dude," Nate whined.

"But *puffins*."

"I'm not freezing my balls off for some bootleg penguins."

"I bet Madoc would love it," Ryle said, and I felt them both glance at me slyly. I very deliberately didn't look back at them. "All that nature and open air. I mean, we'd lose him once the local wolf pack adopted him."

"We could always make fur coats from the sick ones," Nate piled on.

"You're a fucking monster."

The two of them devolved into arguing, the sound soothing and familiar. I breathed properly for what felt like the first time in days.

The relief was short-lived.

There was a vibration in my back pocket. I stumbled again, catching myself, the two of them laughing at me. I wasn't laughing. I could feel the shape of it, the implication weighing heavily on my every step. There was a lump in my throat that I couldn't swallow down. It had been there for hours, choking me with unspoken grief.

I saw the opportunity in the dip ahead, between the trees. Pretending to stumble on my rolled ankle, I hissed and bent down, relying on Ryle to hold Nate steady.

"Jesus, you good, man?" Nate asked. "You sneak a few beers while my back was turned or what?"

The knife slipped out of my boot and into my palm. "Let's rest up ahead for a minute."

"You sure? What about Callum and Zola?"

Callum, my stoic giant, didn't falter, didn't look back, already knowing what I was about to do.

"He'll reach the beach and protect the girls. We won't be long." My voice was steady. My pulse was not. We came to the dip and carefully lowered Nate to a nearby rock, where he sagged in on himself. While Ryle fussed, I stalked a quick path around the clearing, mentally gearing up.

Then I stopped, took a beat. "Ryle?" I called.

"Yeah?" He wandered over.

As soon as he was within my reach, I shoved him hard against the tree and pinned my knife to his throat.

"*What the fuck?*" Nate started to rise, wincing, but I snapped at him over my shoulder.

"Stay out of it."

Ryle went completely slack against me, completely unresistant. His wide eyes swam over my face, confused and hurt and too fucking convincing.

Had I really been so blind this whole time?

"Tell me everything," I growled at him. "Who are you working for?"

"What!?" His voice was a squeak. "You, Jax. Only you." His hand came up, his fingers sweaty and nervous as they wrapped around my wrist. He didn't try to pull the knife away. "What's going on?"

"You tell me."

"I don't know, I swear."

"Jax." Nate's voice was tinged with unease. "What did you find?"

I didn't loosen my grip. The knife was sharp, beads of blood already welling around the tip. I could see his pulse hammering beneath his skin. "You have five seconds," I warned him. "You will tell me everything. Starting with the burner phone."

Ryle's eyes bugged. "What burner phone?"

With my free hand, I pulled out the cursed device from my pocket. Ryle gawked at it, not in panic but in stark disbelief, like I was presenting him with a dead fish. "This yours?"

"No," he said, face furrowing in confusion. "No, Jax. I swear."

I pressed the button on the side, illuminating his pale face. His eyes whizzed over the message thread.

14:01: is the package secured?

14:03: ?

"Funny," I said humorlessly as he blanched under my knife. "Can you guess what the passcode was?"

"Jax, plea—"

"It was the same combination to the safe."

Ryle was shaking. Sweat dripped down his temples, catching fragments of moonlight where it siphoned through the overhead canopy. I looked at him, and for a moment all I saw was my kid brother—the same kid who rescued old cats and injured birds, who made us watch Christmas movies all year round, who insisted on eating at the dining table like a real family because he'd never had one, because that was all he'd ever wanted.

Family.

My chest tightened. I blamed myself as much as him. I should've seen it earlier—I should've protected him from whatever manipulative influence had got to him. Ryle was impressionable. He was eager to please, more eager to prove himself.

He'd betrayed me, but in a way, I'd betrayed him.

I sucked in a brutal breath, my throat working around the grisly lump. "Five," I warned.

Ryle just stared at me.

"Four."

He stared and stared, and then his eyes filled with tears and his mouth opened, but there was no sound.

"Three."

"Where," he choked, then wet his lips. "Where did you find it, Jax?"

"Your backpack."

Ryle shuddered, like that was the last thing he wanted to hear. He looked down, tears clinging to his lashes. "I swapped out my pack before we left the motel," he said in a quiet, wounded voice. "I carried the tech instead."

I stared at him, processing that. "Then who carried your pack?"

Something clicked behind me.

My spine stiffened before my brain made the connection between the sound and the immediate danger. Slowly, I loosened my grip on the knife and turned, keeping it slotted in my palm. With each second that went by, a new crack opened, the foundations of everything I knew becoming unreliable beneath me.

Nate didn't smile as he leveled the gun at me.

There was no hint of amusement or warmth on his face as he aimed it. My heart splintered, and I moved on autopilot, taking a purposeful step in front of a wide-eyed Ryle. The knife weighed like an anvil in my hand. But the betrayal sat heavier.

"Why?" I gritted out. Salt bled onto my tongue. I'd bitten something, or maybe I was coming undone at the seams, unraveling like a frayed crash test dummy.

Not him, my mind pleaded.

Nate's arm shook. His face was pale and anguished. "Fuck," he moaned. "Fuck, fuck."

"It's not—it wasn't supposed to be like this," he said in a rush, the gun quivering at my face. "I didn't know about the girls, Jax. I didn't know about the goddamn tunnels, what they were..." He swallowed thickly. "I didn't know."

I said nothing.

Behind me, Ryle pressed a hand to my back, a subtle reassurance. My protective instincts roared. "Put the gun down, Scooby." I didn't recognize my own voice.

Nate blanched and jerked the gun downwards. "I'm not going to shoot you. I would never—I'm just wigging out."

I'd seen him wigged out before. I'd seen him high and miserable and obnoxious. But I'd never seen him like this.

Never so broken.

Without a gun at my face, the words came easier. "What did you know?"

"I knew about the safe," he said, looking down, avoiding my eye. "I swear, it wasn't—it wasn't planned or anything. Not the way you think."

"You don't want to know what I think."

He flinched. His eyes darted up, dark and haunted. I thought Ryle had been the weakest link, but I was wrong. It was him.

"One of Dr. Z's men contacted me after the last job," Nate said quietly, defeated. "He told me that Dr. Z was unhappy, that he was looking to eliminate us. If I didn't—if we didn't deliver—he would make the call. Unless I did what he wanted."

My jaw clenched. "What did he want?"

"He wanted me to destroy whatever was in the safe."

Ryle ghosted up beside me. "You mean that weird book?"

"Yeah," Nate whispered. "You can guess why."

It took a minute, and then it clicked. My fists clenched, raw knuckles stinging. "He's in the book, isn't he?"

Slowly, Nate nodded.

"This was never about the painting," I said in a hoarse voice. "This whole job has been a goddamn ruse from the beginning."

My mind flashed to Olivia, the giant question mark that surrounded her. The coward in me wanted to remain oblivious. I didn't want to know.

Unlocking my jaw, I grunted out: "Was Olivia in on it?"

Nate made a face, and my fucking heart lurched into hyperspace, before he shook his head. "No. She's just a weird coincidence. She was never supposed to be here."

Madoc didn't believe in coincidences. Neither did I.

"I'm sorry," Nate said, sniffing. "I'm so fucking sorry, Jax."

I'd heard enough pointless apologies to last a lifetime. "Is this why you've been using?"

Nate nodded, forehead scrunching. "I don't know how to live with myself," he croaked. "It was just easier to numb everything, to stop feeling for a while." He shifted, staring down again. "I never wanted to betray you, Jax, I swear. Any of you. I just—he didn't give me a choice."

A harsh exhale left me. "You're a fucking idiot."

He looked up glumly. "I know."

I stepped forward, ignoring the gun, and reached for his collar, giving him a rough shake. His teeth clicked, and he winced. "Why, in all fuck, didn't you tell me?" I growled at him.

His eyes widened. "I couldn't."

"Jesus." I scrubbed the back of my hand over my face. The constant surge and dip of adrenaline was making me woozy.

"I'm sorry," Nate said again.

"Shut the fuck up."

He slumped against me, looking resigned to whatever punishment I inflicted on him. For a second, I considered it. The prick more than deserved it. But he wouldn't fight back, and the idea of breaking him while he stood there, already broken, made me hesitate.

That didn't mean I wasn't going to murder the fucker later.

I shoved him hard, and he stumbled back awkwardly, clutching his side. The gun dropped to the ground between us. Quickly, Ryle dipped around and scooped it up.

I inhaled sharply. "You're out," I said.

Nate went rigid. "What?"

"You heard me."

"Jax, please—"

"The second we return to the mainland, you're on your own."

Nate's knees buckled, and he went down, hunching over on himself. His face contorted in agony. "Just shoot me," he spat. "I'm nothing without the crew. I've got no one, Jax. You know that. Please, *please*."

"You had a choice." My voice cracked, but I forced the words out. "You could've told me the truth. We could've handled it together. You chose wrong." The lump in my throat swelled, choking me. "You don't betray family."

"Jax." He moaned my name like a hymn.

"Good luck, Nathanial." He flinched at the use of his full name, which felt just as wrong and tacky on my tongue. "I never want to see you again."

And then, because I needed some outlet, some way to ease the rupturing in my body, I smashed my fist into his face. He went down easily, crumpled on the dirt. Ryle made a pained noise but didn't move, remaining loyal by my side. I needed that. Now more than ever.

We stared down at our lost brother for a long moment.

When I moved, it was like wading through wet cement. My body resisted, but my mind was quiet. I walked out of the clearing and didn't look back.

28

— · —

OLIVIA

Molly didn't shoot me.

She didn't let me go, either, despite my broken pleas, my begging for her to snap out of it. To wake up. I remained kneeling for so long that my legs pricked with needles and a deep ache settled in my hips.

The beach was a graveyard, the boat a forgotten battlefield. Every time the water lapped softly at the sides, I jolted, hoping it was Madoc.

If anyone could rise up from the dead, it was him.

The radio silence in my ear was just as devastating. Where was Jax? Was he hurt? Was he also dead?

Molly shifted, alerting me to a new threat. I looked up and squinted blearily across the beach. A lone dark figure emerged from the treeline and raced toward us. It wasn't a man I recognized, and by the time he pounded across the dock, I knew I was in trouble.

He came to a wet, skidding halt in front of us, panting and cursing. He snapped something at Molly in a language I didn't recognize. She responded in a dead voice as she jutted the gun at my temple.

The man was bleeding from his nose and a deep gash on his chin. There was a wild, fervent desperation to him, an unhinged panic that poured out around us. He gestured to the beach, then back at the cabin of the yacht.

Molly said drolly: "No. All dead."

The man scowled, then spat on the deck in front of me. "Useless," he said thickly. "Ah, it's over. We leave now." He pointed a finger at me. "Kill this one."

Molly hesitated, her voice taking on a stronger edge. "Where is Marco?"

The man bared his teeth. "Dead."

"And Luis?"

The man flapped his hand dismissively, an answer in itself. His impatience was palpable.

"They're all dead," Molly said softly, as if absorbing the words, considering them in full. "It's just us now."

The man started to curse, then paused and looked at Molly as if seeing her for the first time, clocking whatever expression accompanied the awe in her tone. Apprehension settled over him. He stepped back, wary.

Molly took a quiet breath, so quiet that I knew only I'd heard it. Then she lifted the gun from my head and shot the man at point-blank range.

Unlike Madoc, it wasn't a clean shot. It was messy and loud. The man jerked as the bullet struck him. He staggered and clutched his chest, but he didn't fall.

I scrambled to my feet. "Shoot him again!"

Molly did.

Once.

Twice.

Three times, and then the gun clicked empty. The man crumbled downwards, face ashen, chest hitching wetly. Molly stepped forward and kicked him swiftly in the head. He died a slow, gurgling death at our feet.

Mind numb, I turned to the sea.

I didn't realize I had moved until I was leaning fully over the railing. The wind whipped at my hair, and the cold bit at my face. I searched the water frantically, jumping at shadows. I knew it was a long shot. I knew Madoc was probably dead.

Something slapped hard beneath me, and I jumped—

—A pale hand gripped the bottom railing below me.

I didn't think. I just jumped overboard, into the frigid waters below. The air was punched from my lungs. I came up gasping, lips stinging, hair plastered over my eyes. Something brushed my ankle, and I recoiled with a yelp.

Now what, genius?

My eyes zeroed in on the dark figure clinging to the boat. I padded over noisily, like my life depended on it.

Like *his* life depended on it.

Madoc was in bad shape. He was still conscious but barely, his hand on the railing, clinging to the last of his strength. Or at least I thought so, until his eyes fluttered open, and even in the near-darkness, the glaring green was potent.

"You're alive," I said breathlessly as I bobbed in front of him.

He didn't speak, but for once I knew it wasn't by choice. He was ice cold to touch, his lip trembling as he fought the shock.

"She shot you," I rambled nervously. Relief thumped through me. "I saw it. She—"

"Shut up."

My mouth clicked shut before it started to chatter. The cold sank into my bones, different from the shock. I stared at Madoc, and he stared back as the water slapped between us, blood-tinged and salty. Then he adjusted his grip, and his mouth hitched up into a familiar snarl.

"H-hurry up."

My hands fumbled over him, finding his waist and hooking into the material of his vest. His head turned away, like he couldn't stomach the sight of me.

"Can you swim at all?" I asked him, struggling. He wasn't exactly small.

"Yes." His teeth flashed.

"Then why haven't you?"

His silence was pointed.

His body collided with mine under the water, all hard muscle and bone. My frustration mounted when he refused to let go of the railing. "Will you swallow your humongous man pride already?" I snapped at him. I was losing feeling in everything, and not in a good way. "I will let you drown."

His eyes narrowed. "Big sis still up there?"

I grimaced and nodded.

He stared at me for a moment. Then he sighed and loosened his grip before grabbing my shoulder. I sank immediately under the additional weight before my legs remembered how to be legs and kicked us back to the surface. It was awkward and clunky—our chins knocked together, and Madoc growled when my hand slipped low on his back. "Watch it."

"You could help me!"

"My left arm is numb," he growled in my ear. "I can't move it."

Shit. That meant the bullet had lodged somewhere vital.

Somehow, miraculously, I managed to drag us to the shore in one piece. Madoc didn't struggle but his breath grew short and choppy near my ear, and I knew he was in pain.

When my knees hit the ocean floor, his weight became crushing for a moment before he lifted himself up and staggered the remaining distance to the sand. He clutched his limp arm to his chest.

I struggled after him, pausing only long enough to gag at the sickly pulse in my stomach. There was nothing left to purge, but my body didn't care. It wanted to remove the gross feelings, the swirling relief, betrayal, and *a man dying at my feet.*

Sandy boots appeared in my line of vision. I looked up at Madoc, who returned my stare coldly. His skin was tinged green under the moonlight. He didn't express any gratitude, but he was there—he was always there. Behind the door, in the shadows, in the wardrobe. How could one person be so constant and so unreliable at the same time?

"Are you okay?" I wheezed up at him.

"Are you?" His tone dripped with scorn. It was rather touching.

"I don't know." That was the truth.

"What you did was stupid."

"Oh yeah? Which part?"

"Exactly." Madoc glanced away, toward the water. The breeze moved his wet-stiff hair, revealing the striking portrait of his face. Even wounded and bleeding, he was beautiful. Vulnerability lurked beneath his skin, bruises that mottled his jawline, deepened the crescents under his eyes. He looked tired and angry and beautiful.

And he was hurt.

My heart slammed into my chest. The urge to comfort him was overwhelming. Luckily, I wasn't a total idiot, or I would've acted on it and probably lost my fingers.

Then there was movement behind me, and just like that, his face snapped shut, returned to familiar territory. He stepped in front of me, ripping a gun from somewhere near his boot. He aimed it at the dock where a listless Molly stood, watching us with an unreadable expression. Her gun was gone, her hands dangling uselessly at her sides.

I grabbed Madoc's wrist. "No."

"She hurt you."

"She didn't—"

"She did." His tone was cold, final.

Something about his words jarred with me. It wasn't *she shot me*. It was *she hurt you*. Like Molly's actions against me far outweighed what she'd done to him.

"She's not herself," I said, trying to be soft, coming across desperate. "She's dissociated. Traumatized. They hooked her on something."

Madoc's brow dipped, and there was a flash like understanding on his face. But he didn't lower the gun.

"She needs time," I said, hoping it was true. "Time to recover and heal. Her mind is all messed up." I shot her a quick look, wincing. I still felt her phantom gun pressed to my temple. "She's a victim here, too."

"Some people can't be redeemed."

"Can you?"

His eyes flickered to me. I gazed back at him evenly. "How many people have you killed?"

"Twelve," he said, not even needing to think about it. At my incredulous look, he snarled: "I never said I wanted redemption."

"Molly deserves a chance, even if you don't." I lifted my chin, ignoring the tremor in it. "I won't let you kill her. You'll be my one before she becomes your thirteen."

Madoc considered that for a moment before he lowered the gun with a scoff. "Pathetic." Apparently, that was his limit because he wrenched himself away from me and moved up the shore. His gait was awkward, hindered by his injury. I watched him go, my energy flagging. I wanted to bury myself in the sand like a sullen crab.

And then a deep voice crackled in my ear.

"*...princess?*"

29

JAX

There was a hole in my chest. It was deep and jagged-edged, carved out by Nate's betrayal and expanding every minute of silence that followed. I felt like I was shouting into a void. There was nothing. No hope. No fucking light at the end of all this.

"Princess?" My voice had reached new levels of pathetic.

Beside me, Ryle sniffled. He hadn't spoken since we left Nate behind. I waited for it—waited for the guilt, the regret, the cussing me out—but it seemed our resident optimist had lost his spark. Him and me both.

I wanted to sleep. More than anything, I wanted to get so blindingly, *ridiculously* drunk that I couldn't tell my ass up from my boots.

"Alpha?"

Olivia's voice floated into my ear. I stopped in my tracks, relief chasing away the exhaustion.

My girl was alive.

"Thank fuck. Are you alright?"

"Yeah?" But it sounded like a question. I frowned at the dark trees ahead, as if I could see her face if I squinted hard enough. *"I see Ca—Ginger coming down now. Um, I found Molly."*

Ryle staggered in shock beside me. I echoed the sentiment. "Is she...?"

"She's...alive." Again, it sounded uncertain. I didn't like the hesitation in her voice. Something had happened.

"Sparrow is hurt."

My blood turned to ice.

I took off at a sprint, no longer caring about being quiet. When I burst out from the treeline, slipping recklessly across the dunes, I found the bodies. Piled next to each other like a mass grave. I recognized Madoc's handiwork, the cleanness of his kills, the almost ritualistic placement of them.

My eyes scanned the beach, finding too much movement—Callum and the girls, a lone figure on the dock, another one near the shoreline. I found Madoc a bit further along, separated from the rest. I chewed up the distance between us, ignoring the pain in my ankle, the dull throb in my chest.

Remembering myself too late, I pumped the brakes, kicking sand up at him. He gave me an unimpressed look as he dusted himself off. His left arm was tucked tight and awkward against his side.

"What happened?"

He stared at me. It wasn't his usual needling stare—it was deeper, like he was searching in every crevice, looking for something that he needed. I would give it to him. *Tell me and it's yours.*

When the distance between us still felt unbearable, I reached for him. "Can I just...?"

He nodded tersely.

I stepped forward and dragged my hands over him, starting at his face, his jaw, down his neck, and across his shoulders. He jolted suddenly, a hiss escaping his lips. There was wetness on my fingers, and when I withdrew them, they were dripping with blood.

"Jesus, fuck, Madoc."

"I'll live."

The hole in my chest widened, threatening to swallow the rest of me. My hands clutched at him, no longer searching but just holding on. "Put pressure on it, you dumb fuck."

Madoc rolled his eyes. He searched my face, mouth pinching. "Sentimental idiot."

My cheeks warmed.

Knowing what I needed but couldn't ask for, Madoc tipped forward. His forehead knocked into mine, our cheeks brushing, and his warm breath tickled my chin. We didn't embrace often, or ever, really. Tactile as the rest of them were, Madoc wasn't a fan of physical touch. He put up with me.

Sentimental idiot was right.

"Nate," I exhaled into his temple. "He fucked up."

Madoc stiffened and pulled back, and I already regretted opening my mouth. His eyes were hard and laser-bright. "What'd he do now?"

I swallowed bitterly and told him everything. I expected his anger, but Madoc surprised me by becoming weirdly distant, like he was reflecting on something.

"What is it?" I asked.

His lip quirked up on one side. "Funny."

I gaped at him. "You hit your head as well?"

"Molly."

"What?"

"She shot me."

I reeled at that. "The fuck?"

"Your little girlfriend saved my life," Madoc said, giving a half shrug and then wincing when it jostled his shoulder. "Apparently, some of us are redeemable."

"Not him," I said, unwilling to let go of my anger, my last thread of sanity. "I can't forgive that shit. He could've got us killed."

"He has one functioning brain cell. He thought he was saving us."

I frowned at him, waiting for the punchline. "Since when are you the forgiving type?"

He gave me a flat look in return. "I'm not in the mood for your sulking."

"I don't sulk." My voice sounded sulky, and I coughed harshly to clear it.

"You'll forgive him eventually."

"Not fucking likely." I shoved him in outrage, remembering too late his injury. "Shit. Sorry."

Groaning at myself, I reached into my pocket and pulled out my cigarettes. It barely touched my mouth before Madoc stole it. We shared it between us, silent and bleeding. I tracked the beach with foggy eyes and found my target. For a moment, nothing else mattered but her.

I didn't like how she made me feel, or the fact that she made me feel anything at all. Jesus, I'd known her less than a fucking day. I've had one-night stands that have lasted longer. It definitely wasn't long enough to justify the sheer possessiveness that roared in my chest. I wanted to grab her and shake her and trap her and keep her.

The little priss was never allowed to leave my sight again.

"You're thinking too hard."

I finished our cigarette and nursed it in my hand until it cooled. "First time for everything." Then I tucked the butt into my back pocket with the rest of them.

Madoc arched his brow curiously at the action.

"I've been saving them," I admitted to him quietly. "I know you care about the birds and shit."

He gave no reply, so I slanted him a careful look. My gut twisted at his intense gaze, like he was trying to needle under my skin. "Why?" he demanded coldly.

I sighed and looked up at the stars. "Because I'm a sentimental idiot."

And I love you, you giant asshole.

Madoc hissed a furious sound. I knew if he wasn't injured, he would've punched me for it. Instead, I simply turned and stared at him, trying not to succumb to my overwhelming love aggression. *Don't squeeze him. He's injured.*

Madoc wrenched himself away. "Fuckhead." He flicked his good hand toward the others. "Go bug the drama queen."

"Which one?"

Madoc rolled his eyes. He was still too pale for my liking, but I knew my fussing would go down like a spoonful of razorblades.

"Get Callum to patch you up properly," I said, wasting my air. Madoc would do only what Madoc wanted to do.

With a weary sigh, I walked away, my boots sinking heavily into the sand. My headache was back, the band tightening around my skull. I took a quick inventory: Zola had the painting, Callum and Ryle had the girls. I checked my watch. The boat would arrive in less than three hours.

Talk about a long working day.

My gaze stalled on the pale blonde sitting on the dock. Even from a distance, their similarities were shocking. Molly was taller, but her face was heart-shaped like Olivia's, her nose slightly upturned. They had the same frown.

Before I could react, steps pounded toward me, and a body flung itself against my chest.

"Don't," Olivia said, her voice muffled in the fabric of my t-shirt. I lifted her up and crushed her against me. Her legs locked automatically around my waist.

She inhaled deeply, as if memorizing my scent. I knew I probably smelled like a cheap whorehouse, and the little priss wrinkled her nose in confirmation.

"You stink," she said.

"Nobody told you to sniff me."

Apparently, it wasn't bad enough to stop her from doing it again, her nose sliding along my collarbone. I patted her down, looking for injuries. My hands swatted at her ass, and she giggled breathlessly.

"You alright, princess?"

She shrugged against me. "I have no idea." She pulled back and tried to wriggle out of my grip. I smirked and held her tighter, pinning her against me.

"This has been the longest day of my life," she said quietly. "I keep thinking the whole world has moved on and we've been stuck here in purgatory."

I knew the feeling. "Most jobs feel like this."

"Bet they don't end like this."

I glanced around at the broken girls and dead bodies. No, it wasn't usually like this, but the heaviness was familiar. We'd made it through another job, pulled off another impossible heist. Hell, we were even a few million richer, not that it mattered anymore. The painting could go to hell with its former owner.

I looked at Olivia, finding the stars in her tired eyes, the collapsing galaxies. "I found Molly," she said, like she couldn't believe it. But there was no relief in her voice—just a deep exhaustion that I felt just as profoundly.

Fuck, I wanted to sleep.

Without warning, I dropped down onto the sand, causing her to yelp as she scrambled into my lap. I adjusted her easily, slotting her against my side. She shivered, clinging to my warmth.

Around me, my crew orbited and dropped one by one. Even Nate, who I couldn't look at, not without grinding my teeth and wanting to drown the fucker. But Callum was near him, making sure he didn't expire prematurely from his injuries. I appreciated that more than I should.

My burning eyes stared unseeingly up at the night sky. Olivia shifted beside me, her head resting on my chest. There was a tiny smile on her face that made my heart blip. I could tell from the way her smile widened that she'd heard it.

"What are you thinking about?" she asked slyly, leaning up on her elbow. I drank in her face, my hunger stirring.

"Kissing you," I lied. Well, mostly. I wanted to kiss her as much as I wanted her to straddle my lap and ride me into a coma. We'd run out of time, and I genuinely grieved the loss of never having her like that. It was a crime not to know whether she was just as ballsy in bed, just as demanding and bratty.

My exhaustion vanished at once, replaced by a sharp throb of want.

Olivia hummed, her eyes narrowing like she didn't believe me. Then the little minx licked her lips, making them glisten in the moonlight. "Trauma porn," she said with a rueful grin. "I think I'm becoming a masochist."

"Not unless you *want* me to hurt you."

She said nothing, and my mouth went dry at the very pointed silence. Jesus fuck.

Olivia chuffed in amusement. "Now you're the one who swallowed his tongue."

"Maybe," I said, reaching up to grab her chin, framing that wicked mouth. "Help me find it?"

She didn't move quickly enough, and I was too impatient, so I swooped up and kissed her.

My head went silent, and this time, I welcomed it.

30

OLIVIA

I woke up feeling like a great big bag of dirt.

My head throbbed, my back ached, and there was sand in places, *all* the places. I groaned and opened my eyes. The pale mauve sky of dawn stared back at me.

How the hell was I still alive?

The events of the last twelve hours flashed through my head like a masochistic highlight reel. The boat, the air vent, the war rooms, the sex dungeon—god, the tunnels. A bitter taste flooded my mouth. *Molly.*

Panic zipped through me like an alarm. I sat upright, clutching my head, looking around frantically. A shaky exhale left me when I spotted her. She was still on the dock, standing like a sentinel. We'd never found the keys to the yacht, but part of me had still worried she'd find a way to disappear again.

She didn't feel real yet.

Our reunion hadn't gone anything like I imagined it. I knew it was stupid of me to hope she'd be the same person, like the last two years hadn't happened, and she was still that annoying, uptight, know-it-all older sister. But the Molly I knew was still missing, and I didn't know what to do with that.

An arm tightened around my waist.

Startled, I looked down. Jax was still asleep, his face tense even in dreams, but he held onto me. His hair was mussed and full of sand. Bruises littered his skin, including the ones I'd given him.

His split lip was mine. I did that.

I wondered what it said about me that I liked it.

Cringing at myself, I lifted his arm and tried to extract myself cleanly. Of course, he fought me, even unconscious. His arm tightened again, so tight that it felt like a boa constrictor was circling my waist.

"Jax!" I hissed.

His eyes snapped open.

He blinked once, registered my face. His arm didn't loosen—if anything, it tightened even more, so I felt my ribs begin to creak. "What?" he grumbled, voice thick with sleep.

"It's dawn," I wheezed, tugging at his arm.

"Five more minutes."

"Jax!" I let out a strangled giggle. His mouth quirked at the sound, and he opened his eyes fully. For a whole beautiful second, he looked peaceful and sleep-dumb, like we'd just spent the night frolicking on the beach and not taking down an international trafficking ring.

Then I heard the unmistakable sound of chopper blades.

Instantly, his face hardened, and the violence returned to his eyes. He snapped upright and squinted over the ocean. A white helicopter was approaching to land.

"Fuck."

He was on his feet and moving in the next second. I brushed off the sand and stood, ignoring the dull pang in my spine. The crew moved like trained soldiers, hiding the girls, finding the weapons, preparing for war.

Jax returned to my side just as the chopper landed and the door slid open. Sand whipped around us like a tornado, momentarily obscuring our vision. Jax grabbed my arm and shoved me behind him. My feet moved dumbly, my throat tight with fear.

Someone else put a gun in my hand.

I almost dropped it. Fingers squeezed my wrist, hard enough to bruise. A grinning skull with rose petals stared up at me like an omen.

"I don't—" I started.

Madoc shushed me and squeezed my wrist again. His touch was searing, even though his hand was ice-cold. There was no time to second-guess myself. The crows stood in a single line in front of me, the first line of defense. Between their bodies, I saw four huge men approach, armed to the teeth. They were bigger and more intimidating than the men from the boat. These were the *real* enforcers—the clean-up crew.

The gun was heavy and awkward in my hand.

I'd never shot anything before. Never even held a gun. But I was the queen of faking it, so I curled my fingers around it and pretended like I wasn't shaking like a leaf.

A flash of white caught my attention.

Between the four men walked a fifth man in a blinding white suit. A large silver cross glinted on his chest. I froze, my eyes widening into saucers. There was no mistaking him dressed like that.

A familiar voice floated over... "Olivia? Darling?"

The relief nearly floored me. *"Preacher."* I moved forward, trying to wedge myself between Jax and Callum. Neither of them budged, and Jax shot me a warning look.

Preacher was here.

Tears burned my eyes. It wasn't another wave of traffickers. It wasn't Salvadore. We weren't about to be gunned down and tossed into the sea.

Or so I thought.

"Who the fuck are you?" Jax demanded as soon as Preacher stopped. Jax raised his gun and pointed it directly at Preacher. The four huge men on either side of him responded in kind—guns pointed, tensions ran high.

My heart lurched. "Jax, no!"

Jax ignored me.

To his credit, Preacher didn't look perturbed by the crew of guns. He was a hard man to crack, his kindness and empathy so deep-rooted that I feared for him. I knew Jax could kill him. Just like I knew the men on either side of Preacher would retaliate if he did.

"No need for alarm," Preacher said, his voice warm and British. It wrapped around me like a blanket. It was the same voice he used to deliver sermons and console grieving widows. "I come in peace."

Jax didn't budge. He jerked his chin at the four huge men. "Peace has some pretty big guns."

Preacher smiled and lifted his hand. At once, the four men lowered their weapons. Jax and his crew didn't follow suit. Preacher gave him a considering look. "It's good to finally meet you, Jackson."

Jax stiffened in front of me. His eyes touched mine briefly.

"I didn't—" I started, then stopped. The lie felt tacky on my tongue.

Preacher spared me. "Olivia didn't betray your confidence. I've known about you for a while, Jackson—"

"Jax," he corrected coldly.

Preacher nodded. "I'm afraid we're running out of time. You don't know me, but I know you." His eyes lifted over the crew. "All of you."

"What do you want?" Callum asked, his voice deep and dangerous.

"To make you an offer," Preacher said simply. My heart sank at the determined twinkle in his eye. I knew Preacher had an agenda—I'd known it the moment I told him that Jax and his crew were on the island. But Preacher kept his cards close to his chest, and an awful, nervous feeling niggled at my mind.

Had I made a mistake?

A cold chuckle made me stiffen.

I looked over at Madoc, who, apart from his clutched arm, showed no sign of pain. His posture was loose and relaxed, as if we were discussing the stock market. Not bartering with loaded guns.

"He wants the painting," Madoc said, sounding amused, of all things. *Of course he is. Madoc is crazy.* He was wrong, though.

He had to be.

A jolt of pure shock went through me at Preacher's crinkled smile. "There is that infamous brain I've heard so much about. Very astute, Madoc. Yes, I will take the painting. It was stolen from the Vatican a good decade or so ago. It should be returned to its rightful place."

Madoc didn't react to the use of his name. But a tremor of disbelief traveled down the line. Jax barked a bitter laugh. "Right, godfucker. You'll just throw away a cool hundred million for the greater good."

"You laugh," Preacher observed with a patient smile, "but you risked that and more to save these girls."

"We're not saints," Jax said.

"No, you're not," Preacher agreed. "One good deed does not absolve a lifetime of sins. That is where I can help you."

"Save your breath," Jax said, his grin savage and dangerous. "We're not in the market for salvation, *father*. Hell looks pretty good from up here."

Preacher's smile dropped. He suddenly looked burdened, as if he were about to deliver bad news. The gun slipped in my sweaty palm.

"I'm afraid you might not have a choice," Preacher said gravely. He gestured to the man on his immediate left. Guns lifted in warning, but the man didn't raise his gun.

He pulled out a cellphone.

He tossed it at Jax, who caught it mid-air and glanced at the screen. "The fuck is this?"

"Your new contract," Preacher said. The huge men on either side of him bristled. A flash of something like excitement crossed their faces. The sinking feeling in my stomach worsened. *What the hell is going on?*

Whatever Jax saw on the cellphone made his shoulders drop. He lowered the gun, and his jaw flexed. "Fifty million," he said bitterly.

Preacher nodded. "Each."

Callum reached over and plucked the phone out of Jax's hand. I saw a glimpse of numbers and familiar profiles on the screen before Callum tossed the phone onto the sand between them.

I stepped forward, my voice strangled. "What's going on?"

Jax turned to me. His face was devastating—hard, distant, *cold*. I searched his eyes, hoping to see something, a glimpse of the man who woke up beneath me.

But it was Preacher who spoke. "Your employer, Dr. Z, is not a forgiving man. The contracts went live an hour ago. They are waiting to meet you on the mainland."

My brain churned. I still didn't understand.

Jax's teeth flashed. He didn't look at me as he explained: "Our boss has put a hit on each of us. Fifty million a pop. Every crew in his syndicate will be hunting us down."

"The Vipers," Ryle whispered, shuddering.

Preacher's mouth pressed into a grim line. "They're already on their way, child. Which is why we must act quickly. We don't have time to negotiate."

Jax laughed again, the sound cruel and hoarse. "How convenient for you," he spat.

"I will protect you," Preacher said. "If you work for me."

Madoc was nodding away, like that was exactly what he'd expected.

"There it is," Jax mocked sharply. "The fucking punchline. What do you want from us?"

"I am not delusional, Jackson," Preacher said. His voice deepened, as if delivering a sermon to a large, eager crowd. "I know what you are—what you have all done. You are sinners on a path to damnation. I am offering you a different path, one that serves a greater good, even if it require certain...extreme measures."

Zola scoffed. "You want vigilantes?"

"I want prophets," Preacher corrected her softly. "You all stand at a crossroads. One path leads to certain death. Another to rebirth. Choose wisely."

"Or else what?" Jax asked. His smile was not kind. "You'll kill us here?"

Preacher waited a beat, then said: "Yes."

My body lurched into action before my brain caught up. "No, wait!"

Suddenly, I found myself standing between the guns, like a total moron. Jax reached out to snatch me back, his face pale, lip lifted furiously.

"Get the fuck back over here," he growled.

I didn't move.

I *did* flinch when Preacher's hand landed softly on my shoulder. It was probably intended for comfort—instead, it felt awfully like a claim.

Look at what you did now, Molly said in my head. My eyes flashed over to the real thing. She hadn't moved from the dock, not even an inch. But she was a stark reminder of everything Preacher had done for me. He was the only one who'd believed in me—who'd given me everything I needed to find the island and Molly.

But there was also Jax.

Violent, infuriating, impossible *Jax.*

Jax, who looked about two seconds away from a full-on coronary, his gaze pinned to where Preacher was touching me. "She's not part of the deal," Jax said, each word forced out through clenched teeth. "You can't have her."

Preacher, either oblivious or secretly having a death wish, squeezed my shoulder deliberately and said: "Olivia is already one of mine."

Jax's gun arm started to shake. Beside him, Madoc smiled dangerously, a slow, terrifying slip into unhinged bloodlust.

A shiver wracked down my spine.

"What will it be, Jackson?" Preacher said.

"Go fuck yourself."

Jax lifted his gun. The men on either side of Preacher reacted instantly. My eyes slammed shut, waiting for a ringing gunshot. Preacher's hand tightened on my shoulder. He didn't try to move me out of the firing line. A tiny, hurt voice whispered: *you are his shield.*

When I opened my eyes, Jax was watching me over his gun. "He's got you fooled, princess," he said quietly. I hung every word. "He's a mob boss, just like our boss. He takes advantage of desperate people."

"No, Jax, it's not like that."

Right?

Jax smiled. It looked final.

Preacher shifted behind me. "Time to choose, Jackson. Join us, and I will protect you. Give you a chance to redeem yourselves. Or I will kill you here and remove the corruption from the world."

Jax's eyes didn't change. His smile didn't waver. His arm shook, then steadied. "Move, Olivia."

I shook my head tearfully. "Jax, *please*." The gun was too heavy in my hand. I wanted to drop it. Instead, I clutched it tighter.

From the corner of my eye, I saw Madoc's smile widen. "Choose."

His finger twitched on the trigger.

EPILOGUE

The island screamed.

It was a hoarse, wretched sound. It was also fitting—nature thrived, and nature died. The predator found the prey, and the screams joined the bird song.

Perfect, the man thought.

He stood at the window, looking out over the island's rainforest. Whiskey, smoke, and death surrounded him. Good whiskey, he noted. The kind that belonged in an unhallowed place like this.

Behind him, the captive screamed again as another strip of flesh was removed from his body. The man's surgeon was quiet, mechanical. A tray of instruments sat on the coffee table, some bloodied, some untouched. His gekai liked to take his time.

The phone buzzed in his pocket.

He answered the call, his reflection in the window darkening. "Yes?"

A nervous voice replied: *"No bodies, sir."*

His eyes narrowed.

Silence made the caller nervous. *"We've searched the beach—the blood was fresh. Multiple hits."*

But no bodies.

Nothing confirmed.

The sound of a drill filled the room. Another scream, bone splintering.

But the man lost patience with it. He hung up and spun on his heel, drawing a blade from his pocket. The broken man gasped wetly in fear. He was in pieces—arranged and reassembled like a work of art.

He sliced his blade across the man's throat.

"Goodbye, Salvadore," The Viper whispered.

He had bodies to find.

And a new hunt to begin.

THE STORY CONTINUES

I know, I know. I'm terrible.

Who do I think I am leaving you on a cliffhanger like *that?* Well, rest assured, you beautiful human, the story is not over.

THE CROWMARKED SERIES

Heist In Paradise

Mile High Heist (August 31 2026)

FIND ME

If this book made you smile, gasp, or stay up *way* too late, share the love and leave us a review.

Goodreads: Elliot Ray
Instagram: @elliotrayofficial
Email: elliotray.author@gmail.com

www.ingramcontent.com/pod-product-compliance
Lightning Source LLC
Chambersburg PA
CBHW021229060726

47590CB00005B/1691